W9-AQA-397

Another Helen

Books by Lane Kauffmann

Another Helen
An Honorable Estate
Waldo
A Lesser Lion
Six Weeks in March
The Perfectionist

Another Helen

A novel by Lane Kauffmann

And, like another Helen, fir'd another Troy.
Dryden

J. B. Lippincott Company
Philadelphia and New York

First Edition

Library of Congress Catalog Card Number: 68-14131
Printed in the United States of America

For Fox and Dijour

PART ONE

The Return from Ilium

1.

The noise in Monte Carlo, during the annual running of the Grand Prix de Monaco, is appalling. The fierce roar of the little racing cars and the constant chopping of the autogiro overhead echo back and forth among the old houses and the hideous new skyscrapers, rumble across the yacht-crowded harbor, even climb the spectator-clad hill to rattle the windows of the sugar-candy palace above.

On this particular May afternoon a few years ago the noise was even worse than usual, for the crowd was contributing its share with rare enthusiasm. As a rule the race is spectacular, if only because of the lovely and sophisticated setting, but not very thrilling as a spectator sport. The course through the streets of the city is too winding to permit of high speeds. Accidents are rarely serious and almost never fatal. Once in a decade a driver will misjudge the chicane and go flying off the road to splash gloriously and harmlessly into the harbor, but even this is nothing you can rely on. It is a drivers' race, a race of technique rather than speed, a race for the cognoscenti who gloat over the subtleties of things like split-second downshifting. Most of the audience—which decorates the hillside below the palace or peers from balconies along the route, which perches uncomfortably and expensively on the makeshift grandstands or wanders about in disrespect of the signs saying *Prière de Respecter les Fleurs,* which can see only one small portion of the race from any chosen spot—most of the audience watch the cars hurtle past and have difficulty keeping track of who is ahead.

There were few who cared, that cloudless Sunday. The professionals were leading, of course. No matter whether it was Brabham or Clark or Surtees out in front, the professionals were going about their coolly efficient job of winning—and only the officials and the cognoscenti noticed. There was a race within a race, and the crowd was caught up in the duel between two of the most colorful amateur sportsmen of Europe. And to add to the fun, here so close to the Franco-Italian border, one of the men was French and the other Italian.

When Pierre de Saint-Euverte's silver-gray Lotus battled into third place before the race was a few laps old, thousands of French hearts responded and a great roar went up—paying no heed to the fact that the race still had two hours and a half to go. And a lap or so later when Pierre took the St. Dévote Corner a shade too wide, and Vincenzo Borsarelli's dead-black Ferrari snaked through on the inside and went snarling up the hill towards the Casino a few feet in the lead, the Italian contingent which had come along the coast road from Genoa or over the mountains from Turin tried to make up in volume what it lacked in numbers.

There was plenty to cheer about.

Never more than a few yards apart, the two cars went streaking around the circuit, flashing past at ninety-second intervals, sometimes the silver car in the lead and sometimes the black. The cognoscenti might complain that they were playing tag with danger and spoiling the race for the *real* drivers, but the crowd loved it, and showed its partisan fervor not merely by cheering. Some of the bitterness of the rivalry between two men known to dislike one another personally spread out into the audience. Amiable French voices speculated whether Vincenzo's entourage of willing wenches had allowed him enough sleep last night to finish out the hundred laps of the race. Equally amiable Italian voices discussed the doom that awaited a dilettante who had stumbled into a man's sport for a change.

For the most part this dialogue was conducted good-humoredly, even hilariously, although one spectator (from Naples, it was presumed) became so inflamed that he was whisked away between two gaily uniformed Monegasque policemen before he could do himself some injury with a broken wine bottle.

At that point Vincenzo Borsarelli was trailing by an inch or two.

Of the two men he was the more flamboyant, the more newsworthy, if only because of his eclectic taste in blondes and his fondness for knocking down any man who smiled overlong at one of them. Heir to an ice cream fortune, he had been racing for years—less for the thrill of it, some said, than for the glamour it brought him, the appeal to girls. Stocky, swarthy, almost bald, almost ugly except when he smiled, Borsarelli was never seen without two or three buxom blonde youngsters clinging to his arms. The turnover was rapid, but the supply seemed endless. A pair of them was decorating his pit at the moment, getting in the way of the waiting mechanics, playing at time-keeper, posing prettily. Baby-soft cheeks and shiny-moist lips, noble breasts and firm buttocks and legs that went on forever. Either one of them would have stripped down without hesitation for a Playboy gatefold.

Pierre Dagobert, le marquis de Saint-Euverte, was a very different sort of man, reserved, quietly proud. The publicity that followed him was unsought, unwanted; product of his family's position, his remarkable good looks, and his feats of daredevilry. It was said that he had never failed at anything except breaking his neck, despite years of trying. An Olympic skier in his youth, with several gold medals to his credit, he still spent his winters hunting out the most impossible slopes. Above Kitzbühel they point out a headlong descent which no one else has brought off without checking. He had come back with hair-raising photographs from an

African safari, had climbed a number of the uglier Alpine faces, had appeared with credit (under a nom de guerre) in several of the provincial Spanish bull rings. But it was only in the past couple of years that he had turned his attention to motorcar racing.

Much too recently to be appearing in a Grand Prix, according to Vincenzo Borsarelli, who had given interviews pointing out that *he,* Borsarelli, had earned his way into the big time by his successes in Formula III and sports car races—and hinting openly that Saint-Euverte must have arrived in some less scrupulous fashion.

Saint-Euverte gave no interviews, but somehow the columnists were able to report his comment: that he quite understood Vincenzo's anxiety: it being one thing to lose to people you could snub and another to be beaten by a social superior.

By the twentieth lap one of the "socially inferior" professionals had taken over third place, but the dogfight between the two amateurs went on unheeding. In the space of ten minutes the lead in their private race changed hands four times. The sporting members of the audience were laying bets as to which car would be ahead the next time the pair roared into view. The reminiscently inclined were boring their neighbors with tales of the famous duel between von Brauchitsch and Caracciola back in 1937. The classicists continued to deplore the introduction of personal hostility into a good clean race, and prophesied trouble for someone before the afternoon was over.

This hostility was comparatively new. Once Pierre and Vincenzo had been friends of a sort. Never close, because their adventures in those days had lain in different directions. But between exploits they were both a part of that idle, moneyed society along the Mediterranean coast: they would meet at the cocktail parties of Cannes or Portofino, be guests together on the same Greek yacht. Though contrasting in character they had got along well together, forming a sort of defensive alliance as two of the most eligible bachelors of their little world.

Overnight, some four or five years back, this camaraderie had changed to animosity, waspish on Vincenzo's part and contemptuous on Pierre's. No one was certain of the cause of this change, but it was assumed that somewhere at the center of the quarrel was Saint-Euverte's exquisite American mistress, Eleanor Davenport, who was now sitting alone at the corner table on the terrace of the Hôtel de Paris, sipping a citron pressé and watching the race with bemused eyes.

No prancing about in the pits for Eleanor. That was not at all her style, nor did she approve, or so the rumor went, of Pierre's new craving for speed and yet more speed. Yet if she disapproved, if she was apprehensive for her lover's safety, no trace of this was visible to the onlooker—and there were many onlookers, both open and surreptitious, for Eleanor's beauty was of that extraordinary delicate intensity that makes mere loveliness seem vapid. It was a beauty which transcended fashion and laughed at age itself: for she had to be several years older than Pierre, boasting of having back in her own country a son of college age. It was simple beauty—startling, almost shocking in its perfection. And while such perfection often gives a feeling of coldness, that this was untrue of Eleanor could be seen when some friend paused by her table to chat for a moment: she would look up with an expression of such ironic, impish warmth you were reminded that some poetaster along the Coast had apostrophized her as "a goddess with a girl's heart."

In the normal course of things Vincenzo Borsarelli would covet any goddess who came within range, and Vincenzo's covetousness was flawed by a profound belief that all any woman asked of life was the chance to go to bed with Vincenzo. He had never had to work very hard for his little trollops, and his approach was not noted for either subtlety or patience. After a drink too many he could be grossly direct. He had met Eleanor Davenport for the first time at a party at Cap d'Antibes after he had been away a year in South America, and perhaps he had not appreciated the strength of her attachment to Pierre. Or perhaps he had, and found the challenge irresistible. Certainly Vincenzo had been tight that evening, and certainly it was during the course of that party that the friendship between the two men collapsed. And the next day Vincenzo was adding to international amity by remarking, to anyone who would listen, that no doubt poor Pierre felt safer with a woman old enough to be his mother.

Thenceforward the feud had flourished, egged on by those columnists who spice their paragraphs by inventing fresh insults of their own when genuine ones aren't forthcoming frequently enough. Even sixty years ago the two men might have dissipated their spleen harmlessly on some dueling ground, to the great relief of hostesses who preferred not to take sides. In these more civilized days their rancor had simmered on until it could express itself far more dangerously on the streets of Monte Carlo.

On the terrace of the Hôtel de Paris, out of Eleanor Davenport's earshot, they were giving odds of two to one against either car completing the race—but this crowd had to be reckoned as sophisticated rather than knowledgeable. And through this crowd Tony Taylor-Yeovil, plumply elegant in several shades of yellow, elbowed his way until he could slip into the chair opposite Eleanor, dabbing at his forehead with a silk handkerchief.

"We can't possibly stay till the end, my pet." he complained apologetically. "The traffic afterwards is going to be too beastly, it always is, and I promised Boo we'd get to Cécile's before the gin gives out. Will you be at Pauline's this evening, do you think?"

"I have no idea," Eleanor said.

"Yes, I expect that will depend on whether Pierre is feeling manic or depressive," Tony said. "Perhaps Vincenzo's car will pack up; quite a few of the others already have. I don't think there are a dozen left."

They fell silent as a couple of the survivors came charging up the hill. The corner they overlooked was not a bad one, but every so often in the past some driver had failed to appreciate it and gone smacking into the side wall of the baroque Casino—trying, as the phrase went, to enter without paying.

"You really should try to get to Pauline's," resumed Tony, raising his fluting voice against the receding racket. "Monique will be there. It may be the last time we'll see her for a while."

"Where is Monique off to?"

"She and Gino have had a battle."

Eleanor smiled at Tony's transparency: he loved to tantalize, unpeeling his gossip a fragment at a time like a stripteaser waiting to be coaxed for the next disclosure. "Gino and Monique have lived in a battle for as long as I've known them," she said. "It makes the nightly reconciliations so much more exciting."

"This was the ultimate battle," said Tony.

"It's been three or four months since the last ultimate battle. That seems about right."

"Not the usual excuse for one or the other of them to go on the tiles for a weekend. This was apocalyptic. Apparently the studio is an utter shambles, with half Gino's autumn show slashed to ribbons. But what's so enchanting is that Monique has decided suddenly to go back to her husband. When I say suddenly I mean on tomorrow's train. Can you imagine André's expression when she walks in on him?"

"I've never met André," Eleanor said. "He's in Paris, isn't he?"

"That's right. He's at home where all good husbands ought to be: looking after the offspring." Tony's round face was guileless; he cultivated a mask of cherubic innocence for these little entertainments of his malice. He would have hugged himself in delight, bringing this nugget of gossip specifically to Eleanor Davenport, for she too had a husband at home looking after her offspring, a husband who had incomprehensibly never divorced her, thereby marring the American image on the Côte d'Azur where divorce was believed to be the national American pastime.

If Eleanor was discomfited she gave no sign of it. "Good for Monique," she said. "I never thought the life down here agreed with her."

Doe-eyed, Tony gave another twist to the knife. "My pet, she hasn't been home in five or six years," he said, describing Eleanor's own position precisely. "Think of the shock to the poor man!"

"As I said, Monique has an erotic weakness for reconciliations," Eleanor replied placidly. "I'm sure she'll make the most of that one, too."

Several times this tête-à-tête had been interrupted by the cars as they charged through the curve, accelerating just for a second and then shifting down for the right-angle turn that took them along the length of the ornate, copper-green-roofed Casino before dropping to the hairpin turns of the *virage de la Gare*. Defeated but unchagrined, Tony stood up, still beaming blandly, just as Saint-Euverte's silver Lotus swung past them, followed only an instant later by the black Ferrari. "It's going to be hell to get Boo away from here before we know how it comes out," Tony remarked. "He's bet every penny he could borrow on this little do; unless Pierre wins the poor boy won't be able to touch a card until next month. Well, my pet, jusqu'à ce soir, j'espère." He waggled his plump fingers in farewell and squirmed back through the crowd, leaving Eleanor to her lonely contemplation of the race.

By now the cars were well spread out over the course. The three leaders had remained bunched together for a while, never more than a second apart. A few hundred yards behind them came a green car which was actually a couple of laps off the pace but still hanging in there grimly, for this race took such a toll of the machines that finishing at all could sometimes mean points towards the championship. Then a gap, and then the private duel between Saint-Euverte and Borsarelli —but Pierre had held the lead for some dozen laps now and even seemed to be increasing it inch by inch with each circuit of the track. After another gap came the other five cars still in the race, strung out like beads on a chain, led by another of the blood-red team Ferraris that seemed to snarl even more ferociously than the other motors.

And in that order the cars flashed into sight and disappeared again for lap after lap, until the procession came to seem monotonous. Whatever changes there were were insignificant: perhaps the green car was falling back a little farther and the red Ferrari creeping up a bit, but one could not be sure. The cars were as fixed as the horses on a circling merry-go-round, and there was no reason why they could not stay that way for the remainder of the afternoon.

Once again the autogiro swung overhead, signaling the arrival of the first car, and the leaders swept by, one, two, three, and then—nothing. When the mind has become habituated to a rhythm, any interruption is an outrage: the subdivided seconds stretch into minutes waiting for the next tick of the mental metronome. So to the watchers on the terrace it seemed a small eternity before the next car appeared, and that was the red Ferrari that led the rear guard.

The green car and Pierre's and Vincenzo's had all vanished from the race. A hum of speculation swept the terrace, the more optimistic voices talking of pit stops. But a pit stop should take only some fraction of a minute, and when the leaders sped by again and yet again, with no sign of the missing cars, it was clear that something had gone wrong.

Eleanor Davenport sat where she was, perhaps a trifle paler, lighting a cigarette from the stub of her last. What else could she do? The track stretched from one end of Monte Carlo to the other. There was no sensible place for her to go, and—on this afternoon when the barricades could force you through a detour of half a mile to change your vantage point by a hundred yards—no sensible way to get there. She had to wait for word to come to her.

It came in the shape of a bronzed young man with some sort of official ribband on his sleeve, who loped up the walk on the Casino side of the road. He glanced back over his shoulder, then hurdled the metal barrier and darted across the street, to the anguish of the policeman at the corner. Apparently the young man had spotted Eleanor at her place by the railing, for he wasted no time going to the steps but bounded on top of the nearest bale of straw protecting the façade of the Hôtel de Paris. From there he delivered his message to Eleanor, bending over the railing. She straightened and turned; the watchful crowd parted for her; and still expressionless, still heartbreakingly beautiful, she disappeared.

With her departure, the buzz of speculation rose. Then rumor came, then the first fragmentary, contradictory details, and then—in that mysterious way bad news has of arriving—the full story was there on the terrace.

Far below them the green car had come thundering out of the tunnel, the driver instinctively pressing down on the accelerator in his relief at being out of that enclosed inferno of noise with a straightaway ahead. And like many a driver before him he misjudged the deadly wiggle of the chicane. The green car skidded into the wooden roadblock, scattering fragments flying in all directions, spun and smashed to a stop, half blocking the track.

By this time close on his tail, Pierre had had only a choice of crashes and only a heartbeat to make the choice. He swerved smartly, into the barrier of straw bales, and slammed to a halt, shaken but unharmed.

Directly behind him, Vincenzo had faced the same dilemma with an extra fraction of a second in which to react. Braking hard, he had tried to swerve in the other direction, hoping even to squeeze through unscratched, but a front wheel struck a portion of the broken roadblock; the car leapt and twisted off onto quite the wrong path, climbed up the back of the silver Lotus and burst into flames there, with Pierre trapped in the center of the fiery sandwich. Vincenzo scrambled from his car, and with the immense strength and courage which no man could deny him, wrested the burning Ferrari over onto its side before being driven off by the intensity of the heat. But it was too late anyway.

The driver of the green car was untouched. It always happens that way.

Vincenzo had been rushed to the hospital, badly burned about the arms and face, but in no danger.

And Pierre Dagobert de Saint-Euverte had become the second man to be killed in the history of the Grand Prix de Monaco.

So there it was: one man's death by a freakish accident in a world which has its quota of daily deliberate slaughter. A few headlines and photographs for the newspapers which pander to the appetite for other people's misadventures. A story which would quickly be forgotten by all but a small circle of friends—and that circle was not one to waste much emotion on lamentations. Pierre left no surviving parents, no widow, no sorrowing children. It was a small tragedy, really, as tragedies go. There was nothing grand or heroic about it, much less Homeric. Nothing to make one liken it to the grand calamities of history, such as—for example—the downfall of the fabled city of Troy.

Yet the comparison was made, nonetheless, and only a few weeks later.

2.

"Offhand, I don't see the resemblance," said Ken's uncle, Alan Briggs, peering into the bowl of his pipe for enlightenment and finding it empty.

"When Troy fell—" began Ken Davenport, and was cut off sharply.

"Now just a minute!" said his uncle, patiently reshuffling the papers on his desk until the tobacco pouch appeared. "You've thrown this at me, and I'll work it out for myself. I don't want to upset your opinions of businessmen, but I'm neither illiterate nor unimaginative; in fact I've been peddling my imagination for twenty-five years and not done too badly. So let's see. You've cast your mother in the rôle of Helen of Troy, that much is obvious."

"I'd say she cast herself in the rôle," Ken said bitterly.

"Eleanor is a remarkably beautiful woman," Alan Briggs said. "I'll even go so far as to admit she's even more beautiful than her sister. That's quite an admission for an uxorious husband to make, and you needn't repeat it to your Aunt Cathy. But Eleanor is in a class by herself, no argument. If ships were so easily set in motion nowadays I daresay her face could launch a thousand of them, so that part is all right. But I can't seem to remember what became of Helen after Troy fell."

"King Menelaus went looking for her, sword in hand," Ken said. "Some of the stories say that when she saw him coming she bared her breast for the thrust."

"The analogy already begins to fall apart," Alan said. "I

can't picture your father stalking about the French countryside brandishing a sword. Nor Eleanor being so exhibitionistic."

Ken shook his head, refusing to be put off by this typical flippancy from one of his elders. "The whole point is that Menelaus didn't kill her. He changed his mind. All those wasted years, the elopement with Paris, none of that seemed to matter. He just brought her back home again. And if they'd had telegrams in Menelaus's day, *that* is exactly the sort of cable he'd have sent ahead of him!" Ken declared, pointing dramatically at his uncle's desk. The gesture was somewhat spoiled since in the course of reshuffling the yellow sheet had vanished under one of the folders.

"'Your mother and I arrive next Friday,'" he quoted angrily. "What kind of news is that to burst on you half an hour before a Philosophy exam? Dear God in Heaven! How did he expect me to react? 'Your mother and I arrive next Friday.' Prepare for rejoicing! Hang up the streamers! Unfreeze the fatted calf!"

"You're tangling up your legends," Alan said.

"I got a C when I was figuring on a B-plus at least. There'd been no warning. He phoned me at college before he flew over, Uncle Alan. Said he felt it was his duty to make sure she was all right, provided for, after that gigolo got killed. That made sense of a sort. Frankly, I figured maybe they'd get the details of a divorce straightened out, at last. But *this!* Who could have expected it? Why did he *do* it, Uncle Alan?"

The irony of it was that this banal, adolescent wail (which humiliated Ken as soon as it escaped his lips) got him a more considered reply than when he had been speaking seriously.

"George's doings are really George's concern, even if you happen to feel the most important person involved," Alan said. "I'll confess I was surprised by the speed with which he reacted to the newspaper report of that fellow's death. George went off as if he'd just been waiting for that cue. But I'm not so surprised to hear he's bringing Eleanor back with him. That part of it seems quite natural in a way. Even inevitable."

"But she ran away with another man," Ken protested. "Six years ago!"

"Yes, even so. I think your father never stopped being in love with Eleanor, which was why your little plot to remarry him never got off the ground—and you needn't make faces as though love was a monopoly of the young. You're smarter than that. But I can appreciate your sense of shock, Ken. Six years ago, was it?—you were fourteen, almost fifteen. Still just a boy. And now you're what passes for a man and suddenly, out of the blue, you're going to have your mother back again. Yes, I can well imagine how you—"

One of the phones on Alan's desk rang, preventing Ken from blurting out exactly what he did feel, assuming he could have found the words for it.

"Sure, Mary, put him on," Alan said into the receiver, leaning back in his swivel chair, puffing at his pipe. When he spoke again his voice had altered from the natural tone he used with Mary to one that was at once sterner and more jovial. "What's the problem, Bob? . . . Yes, of course he is, but have you ever come across a client who wasn't?"

It was the shoptalk of Watson-Briggs, Advertising, and Ken wasn't interested.

He had had the greatest difficulty sorting out his feelings about his mother, despite hours of unconstructive brooding since his father's cable had arrived. Part of the trouble was that Ken's part in the story (the most important part, from his point of view) had been such a muddled one, because back at the beginning everybody had lied to him so successfully and for so long. He had been off at prep school at the time of his mother's departure, preoccupied by school affairs and more than willing to accept the explanations given for her absence. Even after his return home for the summer holidays the explanations continued, explanations that implied his mother's homecoming in some near future, without ever specifying a date. At times he had missed his mother, fiercely and resentfully, but at that stage the behavior of adults had still seemed arbitrary, inscrutable and not especially interesting, and he had never thought to question what he had been told.

Besides, there had been compensations. For a while the house had the atmosphere of a somewhat disreputable picnic. Grandmother had been no help at all, Dad didn't seem to know one end of a frying pan from the other, and the various cleaning women who came and went had done little more than keep total squalor at bay. Life had had something of the flavor of camping out—at least until Martha had started coming in daily, had taken charge of them all, and desserts were better than they had ever been. And Dad had made a special effort that summer, taken unexpected days off from the office for little fishing trips, and then an earlier vacation than usual which they had spent together in Maine; a wonderful, unforgettable fortnight.

Part of the shock later, after Ken found out, was recognizing the conspiracy of deceit which had surrounded him. Just about everybody in the exclusive little suburban community of Bradley's Bluff must have known the truth. Dad might go on shoring up his structure of explanations, but Mom's sister, Aunt Cathy Briggs, could never keep a secret for more than ten minutes. Everybody must have known, yet nobody so much as hinted at the knowledge. It wasn't until most of the way through the summer, when Ken had goaded some girl past the limit of endurance, that he got a glimpse of the truth. All she said was "Your mother's run off to Europe with some man," and this was so close to Dad's version (George Davenport had conjured up an aged relative dying lingeringly abroad) that at the moment he had dismissed the words as typical of a girl's inability to get things straight.

But there was a horrid, knowing taunt about the tone of her voice which went on echoing in Ken's mind, nagging at him with the suggestion that there might be something discreditable about his mother's absence. First he fought against the disloyalty of the thought; finally, almost masochistically, he had badgered and blackmailed his closest friends until he could piece together the story from fragments of conversations they had overheard.

Ken's closeness to his father dated from that terrifying evening when he had confronted him with the truth and called him a liar to his face. It was an act of considerable courage. George Davenport was a large and burly man who had once played left tackle for his college football team, and still (he was fifty then) kept himself in reasonably good condition. Although the gentlest, most civilized of men, he had an air of latent brutality about him (probably merely the effect of a nose which had been broken some half-dozen times) that kept people apprehensive of the explosion of temper which never came, but which never could be excluded as a possibility.

"In a sense you're right, of course," George Davenport conceded. "But I haven't really been lying *to* anybody. I've been lying *for* Eleanor."

"Is that supposed to mean something?" Ken demanded, bristling with righteous indignation.

"All along I've taken it for granted that your mother would be coming back soon," replied his father. "I still do. And when she comes, she has to be able to slip back into her life here in Bradley's Bluff without too much embarrassment for everybody concerned. From what you say, I gather nobody really believes my stories, but even that doesn't matter. When the time comes they can damn well pretend to have believed them, and that makes life simpler than having a scandal flapping about in the open where people feel they have to be shocked by it."

"I don't understand any of that," Ken said. He understood simply that he had been betrayed on either hand. His mother had deserted him and his father had told lies about that desertion. And he needed to strike out at the betrayer he could reach. "You lied to me. She's my mother, and I had a right to know."

"You knew she was gone," said his father. "I don't see your right to details that are none of your concern."

"She's my mother," Ken repeated.

"Yes, it's terrible the way we all put people into utilitarian pigeonholes," said his father. "We think of Mr. Smith as 'our plumber' and forget that he's also a father and a husband and a homeowner and a pillar of the Methodist church and a devoted worker for the Boy Scouts—and every one of those capacities is more vital to him than repairing our leaky radiators."

"I don't see—"

"Just a moment," George Davenport said with a hint of anger. "Of course Eleanor is your mother. But that isn't *all* she is, not by a long sight. She is also my wife. She is also your Aunt Cathy's sister. And she is also an exceptionally beautiful young woman. Look, son, your mother is just nineteen years older than you are; that makes her thirty-four. Which may strike you as late middle age, but it isn't, believe me."

"She hadn't any right to go off like that!" Ken cried.

"What you mean is that you're hurt because she went," said George Davenport. "Naturally you are. I'm hurt myself. Has that occurred to you?"

"Yes, of course," Ken lied, "but—"

"But that didn't seem as consequential as your own misery, and no doubt you're right. It's a shattering thing to lose one's mother. But your *hurt* isn't affected in the slightest by the circumstances of her leaving. Mine may be, but that's strictly my own affair. Your loss isn't altered by whether she went to France or California, or whether she went in the company of a handsome young man or an elderly lady. All that matters is that she's gone, and you'll just have to take that like a man. Are you the least bit happier for having discovered what you regard as the truth?"

"I don't suppose I am," Ken acknowledged.

"Then let's have no more nonsense about my lying to you," rejoined his father. "Truth is a precious substance for scientists and doctors; the rest of us are generally better off with a few illusions."

"I still say she didn't have any right to go off like that," Ken said sulkily, feeling that he was being outargued in some sneaky, adult fashion.

"Suppose she'd died," said his father. "Would you have sat there complaining that she didn't have any right to die?"

"That's not the same thing at all," Ken protested. "You can't do anything about being dead."

"Be grateful for something and stick to the thought that one of these days she'll be coming back," said George Davenport. "It's time you realized that relationships don't come with guarantees of any kind. People mean well, but life plays funny tricks. Friendships dry up, marriages fall apart. We have children with every intention of bringing them up as best we can: it's an implicit promise, but sometimes we drop dead before we can keep the promise, and sometimes something comes along that seems even more important than the promise. Let's do your mother the credit of believing that she had a difficult choice to make, and made the one that seemed right to her at the time. And we'll swallow our disappointment like a couple of gentlemen, eh?"

On that evening, what had most struck Ken about this conversation was that for the first time his father had spoken to him not as to a child, not even as to a son, but simply as to another person, and certainly their relationship had shifted to a different, closer, more man-to-man footing as of that date. But when he had thought about the conversation later on, and he had thought of it frequently, he had gradually come to recognize the remarkable sagacity and tolerance—the magnanimity!—which his father had shown. Not a word of criticism or blame for the faithless wife, just a wonderful, dispassionate understanding. How many people would have been capable of such generosity? Ken felt that he had never properly valued his father before, and as his opinion of his father grew he had found room in his private resentment to despise the woman who could have deserted this saintly man.

Yet the following summer, when it seemed unreasonable to hope any longer that his mother might be coming back, and Ken had tried to speak of his disillusion (thinking he could thus indicate his new admiration for his father), he had been cut off sharply before he could properly get started.

"There are times when it's smart to keep your mouth shut, son," said George Davenport. "I'll give you a common example. Say a friend is unhappy because his marriage is cracking up. It's natural to want to cheer him up, and before you know it you're agreeing the wife is a selfish, no-good tramp who never understood him, and he'll be much better off without her. But the next week they fall back into each other's arms and *you're* the bastard who said all those nasty things about the woman he loves."

"I wasn't going to say anything nasty," Ken had protested.

"Possibly not, but where you were heading you couldn't have said anything complimentary about your mother, and she's still your mother even if she's not here. Somehow the things we think are never as real as the things we say aloud, and once something is spoken there's no graceful way of taking it back. Circumstances change, and we're left with the echo of words we blurted in another mood. We all have to live with the fools we've made of ourselves from time to time, but some opportunities for foolishness are more easily avoided than others. I think this is one of the avoidable ones."

So Ken had had to find other ways of expressing his appreciation of his father, and his feelings about his mother, unspoken, had fluctuated wildly over the years. There had been resentment, secret moments of tearful yearning, periods of black hatred, more sophisticated intervals of cynical contempt, and even a grudging admiration for someone who had done something glamorous. This last was the result of knowing, his freshman year at college, a French boy who proved (after subtle interrogation) to have an awed knowledge of Saint-Euverte—forcing Ken to realize that his mother was not leading the life of squalid degradation he had hoped for. None of these sentiments ever appeared in any of the occasional letters he exchanged with his mother. She would write amusing descriptions of cities she had visited, and ask for news of him and snapshots. He would reply courteously, itemizing his activities; his letters were grim exercises in English prose composition, with the emotional content of a book report on *The Life of Charles Darwin.*

If in time he outgrew his view of his father as an out-and-out saint, his respect for his father's tolerance and good sense deepened as Ken himself matured. George Davenport was a fine and sophisticated man albeit a businessman (Ken's admiration was for the more dedicated callings, such as baseball, the exploration of space, and teaching), and he was not a happy man. This last understanding was a product of the increasing closeness between the two men, for George Davenport gave no sign of unhappiness. To the world at large, even to his own mother, he showed his usual calm, good-natured reserve. But Ken could sense that Eleanor's departure had left an aching void in his father's life—a void which his father, incomprehensibly, showed no sign of trying to refill, either because he found a perverse pleasure in hugging his misery to himself or because he was trapped in some psychological inertia.

Eventually Ken had grown impatient with this state of affairs and decided it was his duty to jog his father out of this lethargy. This had not seemed a formidable task, since there was a handy Eleanor-substitute waiting in the person of Laura Sydrock. Mrs. Sydrock was a handsome woman, a widow, and she and Ken's father had been close, comfortable friends for years. Here surely, considering that these were people in their sober years, were the makings of a satisfactory marriage. Ken had set out to promote the match—subtly, so as not to appear interfering.

He had shown an intelligent interest in the divorce laws of the state. He had found occasions to hint how pleasant it would be to have a woman around the house again—and it was only very casually, by way of illustration, that Laura Sydrock's name entered these conversations as someone who arranged flowers beautifully or baked her own bread. Last year he had exaggerated a bad summer cold into something bordering on pneumonia, giving Mrs. Sydrock reason to stop by more frequently, bringing baskets of fruit and books of crossword puzzles for the invalid. A generous woman, Mrs. Sydrock, considerate and motherly. . . .

It hadn't been easy to determine how this campaign was faring. There had been some hopeful omens—or at least some episodes which Ken's imagination had interpreted as hopeful. Enough so that he could regard his father's morbid flight to France as perhaps the beginning of the end: with luck his father would return cured of his procrastination, ready to embark on a new and happier life.

The cable, then, had come as a double shock to Ken, overturning his expectations and throwing his emotions into a state of complete chaos.

What was he to think of his father now? Was this some

new manifestation of saintliness, or a weak, unmanly sentimentality? And the problem of respect for his father was the least of Ken's worries.

How was he to react to Eleanor? The mother who had been the joy of his childhood had become the villainess of his adolescence and then the stranger of his manhood. On what footing could he meet her now? When he had needed her most he had had to learn, painfully, to live without her; now that he had achieved indifference she was going to saunter back into his life, no doubt expecting to be treated as a mother. It was an intolerable situation, especially coming in the middle of exam time, and more especially since any attempt to think sensibly about the matter merely led him into recapitulating all the phases he had lived through; so in his mind the tearful little-boy-lost warred with the bitter brooding stripling, and their more cynical senior was too confused himself to still these voices from his past.

At such a time, when his academic career and perhaps his whole future life depended on his keeping a clear head, he simply could not afford this internal turmoil. He had needed an escape, and he had found it in discovering the numerous parallels between his mother's career and that of Helen of Troy—she, too, having left a child behind her when she ran off to foreign parts with her lover. Instead of gnawing over his mother's misdeeds in odd moments he could track down Helen's through the various reference works in the library. Instead of gloomily picturing the reunion with his mother he could divert himself on the train from college with a hilarious novel called *The Private Life of Helen of Troy,* the only trouble here being that the author had perversely insisted on treating Helen as the heroine of his work. But Ken's personal dilemmas had been sublimated into the materials of legend, his grievances kept at bay by a grander tragedy. No need to puzzle out a flesh-and-blood George Davenport while there was King Menelaus to contemplate; no need to think of his mother except as Helen of Troy, whose conduct had been answerable to a different set of gods. There were no anxieties in playing onlooker to a mythological melodrama.

And the resemblances between the two situations were truly remarkable, a fact which Ken tried to impress upon his uncle as soon as Alan Briggs had finished on the telephone.

"It's not just what's happening now," Ken said. "Mother ran away exactly the way Helen did."

"What?" said Alan, clearly not having yet returned from the inconsequences of advertising.

"You remember when Mother left," Ken said patiently.

"Better than you do," replied his uncle. "You were off at school at the time."

"Saint-Euverte was staying as a guest in our home."

"That was an unfortunate happenstance," said Alan, "and it wasn't exactly a social visit." The Saint-Euverte family had a considerable holding in American investments, and when Pierre became titular head of the family he had come to get some firsthand acquaintance with the firm that handled these investments: Underwood, Murch and Glossop. As chance would have it, Glossop was recovering from a heart attack, Murch was away on business, and Underwood had just been arrested for indecent exposure on the corner of Wall Street and Broad. The task of entertaining the foreign client and eradicating any unfavorable impression he might have formed of the firm had fallen upon the most senior of the junior partners, George Davenport. No doubt it had seemed like a smart idea to invite Saint-Euverte to his home.

"I don't know how social it was when princes went visiting," Ken said, "but that was how Paris met Helen. Paris was a guest in Menelaus's palace, or whatever the King of Sparta lived in. And when Menelaus had his back turned one day, Paris and Helen eloped."

"Between that trip and the time she returned there was the small matter of the Trojan War," Alan pointed out.

Ken dismissed the Trojan War with a wave of the hand. "All that meant to Helen was that her lover was killed. And now Saint-Euverte has been killed. And Menelaus is bringing Helen home all over again."

"All right," said his uncle. "You've introduced an epic quality into our life in Bradley's Bluff which I'd not noticed before. That's all to the good, I suppose. But I'm still waiting for you to get to the point."

"The point?" said Ken.

"I'm sure there is one." His uncle stood up, stretching, and tilted the blind so he could look down on the segment of Madison Avenue below. He was lean and tall above average, bald, with small features and large, bushy, grey eyebrows and a look of competitive cleverness. "You stop in on your way home from college, and I'm not complaining," he said, relighting his pipe. "It's not a busy afternoon, and I'll be delighted to have your company on the train ride home. But I'm sure you had some better reason for coming than to entertain me with this nonsense about Helen of Troy."

"In a way," Ken admitted, hurt by the word "nonsense" and resentful that he wasn't allowed to lead up to things in his own way. "Did you read that cable?"

"Not really. I assumed it was much the same as the one we got."

From among the disorder Ken retrieved the yellow form. " 'Your mother and I arrive next Friday,' " he read aloud. " 'Have Martha plan accordingly. Break news tactfully to your grandmother.' "

"I'm with you, finally," said Alan. "You don't feel your tact is equal to the occasion."

"What good will tact do?" Ken demanded. "How do you set off dynamite tactfully?"

"The news will be a shock to the old lady. I can see why your father didn't want to cable her directly."

"I can't," said Ken.

"Suppose it came when she was alone in the house. We know what she thinks of your mother. The shock might give her a heart attack."

"Grandmother would never have a heart attack unless there were witnesses to be impressed by it."

"That may pass for wit in collegiate circles," Alan said. "Nowadays a little respect for your elders is all the more impressive for being unfashionable."

"It's the truth!" Ken protested. "When the world offends her she has palpitations, when one of *us* offend her she takes to her bed with ominous pains in her chest. She has everybody terrified of that weak heart except her doctor, and he says she'll outlive all of us."

"Be as that may, the news will be a shock to Mrs. Davenport. She's said some pretty harsh things since Eleanor left, and that's only natural. Any mother will take her son's part when his wife walks out on him."

"Grandmother was saying harsh things long before that," Ken said. "She always hated Mother."

"Well, Eleanor wasn't the only woman on earth with mother-in-law problems."

"Do most mothers-in-law call up the F.B.I. to denounce their daughters-in-law as Communist agents?"

Alan chuckled reminiscently. "Mrs. Davenport is a character," he conceded, "and I don't altogether blame you for being terrified of her. Look, I'll tell you what. We'll be traveling out together—where's your luggage, by the way?"

"I only brought one suitcase with me. It's outside in Mary's office."

"All right. I'd be dropping you off at your house anyway. If you like, I'll come in and see you through the crisis. That's precisely what you were counting on, of course."

"You think it's going to be a lark, don't you?" Ken said darkly.

"I enjoy Mrs. Davenport," his uncle admitted.

"That's because you don't live with her."

"Possibly. She has a wicked tongue and a flair for language we could use here in this office. She's amusing."

"She takes in most people," Ken said. "You all look at that frail little old white-haired lady and take it for granted that she must be sweet and gentle. Her wicked tongue is just amusing. It never occurs to you that she means exactly what she says. It never occurs to you that behind those large round china-blue eyes lives the soul of Lady Macbeth."

"A liberal-arts education has given you a distinguished ancestry," said Alan. "Your grandmother is Lady Macbeth, your father is King of Sparta, and your mother is Helen of Troy."

"I'm terribly amusing too, aren't I?" said Ken angrily.

"No, just a trifle tiresome at times," replied his uncle, turning from the window and smiling affectionately at Ken. "I don't doubt that you find your family something of a trial; most young people do. Yet despite the unconventional recent family history, you have a very decent pair of parents, you really do. And you owe them at least the respect of treating them as real people."

"I'd like some respect myself," Ken said. "I'm tired of being excess baggage—not wanted on this particular voyage. I'm remembered when they need me for some reason, like breaking the news to Grandmother. Betweentimes they never give me a thought."

3.

"If I feel any anxiety it's about the meeting with Ken," Eleanor remarked after a long silence during which she had been gazing down on the featureless Atlantic drifting by far beneath them.

"Yes, I would imagine so," said George Davenport, relieved to meet a comprehensible emotion for a change. Many of Eleanor's attitudes he found bewildering, but there was no surprise in a mother's apprehensions about her reunion with a child she had abandoned years before.

"Twenty is a cruel age for these family upheavals, especially for boys," she said thoughtfully. "They've lost the insulations of childhood and they've had no practice as grown men. Their poise is so precarious and they are so belligerently terrified of losing it."

Inwardly, George groaned. Stupid of him: he should have known that Eleanor would see no awkwardness in her own position, and would be concerned only about whether Ken would prove equal to the occasion.

"And American young people on the whole can be an embarrassing lot," Eleanor went on. "Not so bad as the English: at twenty *they* are still trying to decide whether puberty was a good idea. But the American youngsters are bad enough. We've seen them every summer by the hundreds; they seem to believe that growing up is an act of heroic defiance which the rest of us ought to admire."

"I think you're going to be pleasantly surprised," George said. "Ken isn't like that at all. In most ways he's mature for his years. A little overearnest, perhaps, but there's no lack of poise."

"Then you've done a splendid job with him, George—or was there a girl to help? Does he have a girl? Seriously, I mean."

"Very, very seriously. Hasn't he been writing you?"

"Oh, pages!—once a month like clockwork. About books, the professors he dislikes, and something amusing that happened to his roommate. Who's the girl? Anyone I know?"

"Jessie Sydrock. Laura's daughter."

"I remember her mostly as scraped knees and a mouthful of braces, but I'll keep that memory to myself," Eleanor said. "Is she nice? If he's really serious I hope she doesn't take after her mother except in looks: Laura's passion for good works and civic duties never left much energy for her home life."

George smiled, grateful for these moments when Eleanor seemed to be looking forward instead of looking back. "Gently, dear," he said. "You are speaking of the woman who was selected to be my second wife."

"Who did the selecting? Your mother?"

"Hardly. You've forgotten, she hasn't a good word to say for any woman since Mary Baker Eddy. As a matter of fact, it was Ken."

"That seems a little impertinent of him."

"He tries to look after me," George said. "I believe he's decided I'm one of Nature's victims."

"Because I walked out on you?"

"That, of course. And because I never had the gumption, as he saw it, to get a divorce."

"Someday you'll have to explain that to me," Eleanor said. "I kept urging you to divorce me. I can see that if a man is in no hurry to remarry there's a certain convenient safety in having a wife in the distant background, but that doesn't seem to go with the rest of your character."

He stared in wonderment at his wife's lovely profile silhouetted against the milky blue of the airplane window; Eleanor was serene and relaxed, apparently quite untroubled by traveling at several miles a minute towards a situation rife with tensions, perplexities and embarrassments. "I will never get used to the way you take everything in stride," he said. "Because your heart is pure there's nothing to worry about. Do I need to warn you that Ken feels that you've treated him very badly?"

"Naturally he does, and he's absolutely right," Eleanor said. "I treated him abominably: I hurt him, and I knew at the time I was hurting him, and there's no point in pretending otherwise. But in the same fashion I've been hurting people all my life."

"You're exaggerating," he said. "You're not as hard as you pretend."

"I'm not hard at all!" she said indignantly. "I'm as tender and emotional and sentimental as any woman can afford to be."

"Then—"

"But I'm a realist," Eleanor interrupted. "There are people who try to make everybody happy all the time, and the only ones who succeed at it are the better class of prostitutes. The rest of us have to make decisions, and the important decisions often reduce to choosing among the people we're going to hurt. When I went to college I broke my mother's heart because she thought my looks would be ruined by all that studying. When I quit college to get engaged I broke my father's heart because he knew I'd be a nitwit all my life. When I got engaged to you two other men threatened suicide and a third pledged himself to lifelong celibacy. And if I'd broken our engagement to make one of them happy, you would have been miserable. At that point, anyway."

"There are those who would argue that adults have to

look out for themselves," George said, "but that a child deserves special consideration."

"I would be the first to argue that way myself," Eleanor replied.

"I believe you," said George. "I'm not sure everybody would."

"A child is both a joy and a responsibility," she said, "and I'm very proud of my record as a mother—as far as it went. If you think back you'll find that for fifteen years there was never a moment when Ken needed me that I wasn't right there. But a healthy boy of fifteen isn't a child except when he's unusually upset. For the most part his mother is a convenience and an exasperation: a housekeeper who claims the right to lay down the law—and who gets impatient with his fledgling experiments with manhood. It's quite likely that Ken was far better off left to your masculine understanding."

"That's a point of view," George said. "You mustn't expect Ken to agree with it."

"I don't expect to discuss the matter at all."

"Then you're bound to be disappointed. Ken is discreet within limits, but I don't think your reappearance after six years will pass without remark."

"That's not what I meant," Eleanor said. "Of course we'll have a great deal of talk about, and I intend to be as honest with him as I can."

"In certain respects you haven't changed at all," George observed with fond amusement.

"If he's curious about why I left, I'll tell him as much as I think he can understand. If he's curious about why I came back, I'll leave that part of the explanation to you."

"Fair enough. I've had some practice in accounting for your travels."

"But I will *not* have my son sitting in moral judgment on my behavior," Eleanor declared firmly. "At least not until he's had a few firsthand encounters with morality and time to acquire his own judgment."

"Both you and Ken have some surprises in store," George said.

The stewardess came by, distributing the forms which had to be readied for passage through Customs. Eleanor glared with the little frown which he had come to recognize as impatience with anything which didn't accord with her new-found notions of what was "civilized." "Everybody says that our *douaniers* are the beastliest in all the world," she said, hunting through her purse for a pen. "With all my luggage, there's bound to be trouble."

"Oh, I shouldn't think so," said George, aware of the emptiness of this reassurance from one who was re-entering his country for the first time. "I certainly hope not." But this was a new source of worry: a possible obstacle in the homeward path he had done his very best to smooth. It had become a superstition with him these past few days, the feeling that if he could just get the two of them home without any intervening awkwardness, then everything would be all right. There was little sense or logic in this feeling; obviously home would be bristling with complications. But these would be complications he could understand, in a familiar setting. The familiarity of the setting made all the difference; he would be able to cope again, he would be on his own ground. In France he had quickly found himself out of his depth, on the edge of situations he could not comprehend, while transactions which might be important to him were conducted in a language he could not follow. Since he could not come to grips with this world, it had seemed unreal, intangible, and vaguely threatening. He had lumbered through a darkening fog of ambiguity, clinging to the thought that once back on his own territory this fog would begin to lift.

Yet when he had set out on this trip to France, a few weeks before, everything had promised to be so simple.

From the airport in Nice he had been driven to the Ruhl Hotel, where kindly people speaking English as well as he did confirmed his reservations, settled him in a comfortable room, and volunteered to assist with his touristic pleasures. Although this was his first time in a foreign land, George had not the faintest interest in sight-seeing; he had come on a mission, and wanted only to get on with it as quickly as possible. He explained his wishes at the desk, was installed in a taxi, directions were given to the driver, and they set off for Cagnes-sur-Mer.

With a respect for French logic left over from his school-days, George assumed that a village addressed as Cagnes-sur-Mer would lie at the water's edge, and was contented as long as their road skirted the sea. But just as the road signs were announcing Cagnes the driver turned inland, went further inland, and finally began climbing a house-encrusted hill. George was convinced there had been some mistake and would have expostulated except that the driver spoke not a word of English; perhaps it was here that George's feeling of helplessness began. They stopped in a little square at the very summit of the hill. The driver got out and jabbered with one of the loungers, presumably making inquiries. Then, beckoning, he led George on foot through a tangle of narrow, cobbled alleys, and down a long flight of stone steps. Halfway down he stopped, pointing at an unprepossessing green door. George knocked without confidence. A girl opened the door, listened to him blankly for a moment, then shrugged and led the way to a large room, unexpectedly light and airy, where Eleanor was working at a massive desk covered with papers.

She looked up, and he saw that she was as beautiful as

ever. She smiled happily at the sight of him, and came to him as easily and naturally as if they had been together the day before yesterday. "At the back of my mind I think I knew you'd turn up," she said, kissing him. "You're still quite the sweetest person I've ever known. And you've put on weight."

"There's been no one to stop me from nibbling," he said, admiring her. And then: "Isn't it time you came home, Eleanor?"

The phrasing of this invitation, which seemed to him highly tactful, preserving both their dignities, was as far as George had rehearsed their meeting. He hadn't the sort of overactive imagination that tries to anticipate these critical moments, inventing vivid emotional scenes down to the last harrowing detail, creating lengthy passages of dialogue, brilliant in their eloquence but destined to remain unspoken. He had simply prepared a question in the belief that a question was bound to elicit an answer of some kind. He had not exactly pictured Eleanor falling on his chest with gratitude; neither had he seen her patting him on the cheek and showing him to the door. Yet he had vaguely expected something along the lines of one such reaction or the other. His suggestion, which was as reasonable as could be expected from any man and as delicately put, would have to be accepted or turned down. And then he would know where he stood.

"I've been too busy to think about the future," Eleanor said. "You have no idea what a muddle it's been, and all the worse, in a way, because everybody is being terribly decent about it. Pierre left me this house and a couple of other properties he bought along the coast as investments, and the family takes this in stride, but of course they expect all Pierre's records and stuff, and it turns out that he wasn't nearly as businesslike as he should have been. It will be awful if they think I'm holding something back, but I've still not found half the papers they want. It's a blessing you've come! I've not even turned up the correspondence with Underwood, Murch and Glossop. Here, you try."

So instead of a response to his invitation George found himself with a drawer full of bulging envelopes, and nothing to do but sit down and search for the familiar yet humiliating documentary evidence that his firm had gone right on looking after his wife's lover's American securities.

After a while he saw that perhaps it had been foolish to expect any immediate response; this had been too much to hope for. He knew his own mind simply because he had never changed. He still loved Eleanor. Knowing her as no other man possibly could, he had no doubt she was still fond of him and missed her son; he was confident that if she wanted to come back then time and tolerance would set the marriage working again. But until his arrival Eleanor could not really have been thinking in these terms. Even if she knew in her heart that this was the right answer, she would need some time to become accustomed to the idea. So George telephoned his office that evening and settled down to wait patiently, meanwhile offering such assistance as he could, commuting daily from the hotel, courting his wife with the gentle insistence of his presence.

It would have helped (his own feelings, at least) if he had been able to cut masterfully through the complications which beset Eleanor; instead, much of the time he had been little more than a hindrance. There were meetings with lawyers, notaries, and other men of business whose functions George but dimly understood, and those meetings were conducted in high-speed French—at which Eleanor, naturally yet surprisingly, had become proficient. George understood nothing, and afterwards when she told him the gist of what had gone on the advice he offered usually proved to conflict with French law or French custom. He got little from these sessions but the knowledge that Saint-Euverte had done him the final disservice of leaving Eleanor an independent woman: if she chose she could go right on living in the house in Cagnes-sur-Mer, supported by the income from her other properties.

And he got a glimpse of what such a life would be, as friends of Eleanor's and Saint-Euverte's came drifting in and out of the house: charming and attractive people, exquisitely dressed, seemingly always on the move from one party to another. They might accomplish nothing but keeping boredom at bay, but at least they did that much with great energy and style. Proud of his puritan conscience, George saw no appeal in a lifelong holiday, but he could appreciate that others might. If Eleanor had seemed to be irresistibly attracted by this life, he would have found this disappointing but understandable. What baffled him utterly was the gradual realization that she was thinking less of the pleasures of staying than of the privations of returning.

This weird feeling of Eleanor's that he was inviting her back to some sort of second-rate existence appeared first in casual, passing comments on trivial differences between the two countries. She was driving them through the back streets of Nice to an appointment one day when a child darted out from between two cars directly in front of them. As he braced for the impact George had a fleeting vision of a couple of foreigners being torn to pieces by a mob of frenzied French mothers. But Eleanor stopped the little Renault just in time, leaned out to give the child a scolding, and drove on unruffled, remarking only that it had been a lucky thing for the child that they hadn't been driving an American car.

Next evening they were dining in a little restaurant; the meal was good, but George had eaten just as well hundreds of times in New York. They had reached the point where the waiter had left them with a great platter of assorted cheeses. George waved them aside but Eleanor would not accept that; she chose one carefully, spread some on a crust of bread, and insisted that he try it. He admitted it was delicious if you cared for cheese, which he didn't especially. "It's a taste that grows on you," she said. "And there's something appealing, symbolically, about finishing a meal with the very same foods we were eating a couple of thousand years ago. Bread and cheese and wine. Don't you feel it? But look at us back home. We haven't any wines to go with the cheeses we haven't got to put on the bread which hasn't been edible for a generation or more."

George held his peace, but a few days later he could hold it no longer. A neighbor stopped by with her children at the house in Cagnes-sur-Mer (by this time George had discovered that Eleanor knew many more people than the idle rich circle he had first met). After the woman left Eleanor went into raptures about the children. Had he ever seen anything so beautifully behaved in all his life? And Mme. Vettard was of peasant stock, she had gone up in the world by marrying the postman, yet her children were so poised, so polite, so this and so that and above all—the implication was there in every second word—so far superior to all American children, however carefully brought up.

"This is the first time I've known what they meant by 'going native,'" George burst out. "You've reached the point where you see a host of virtues in a couple of kids too terrified to be natural."

"They weren't terrified, George!" Eleanor protested.

"Well, they weren't natural, either, sitting there like a couple of trained seals. You've got yourself seeing only one side of things, and from a topsy-turvy point of view. The kids at home may not have such beautiful manners but they have a damn sight more personality. The bread here may be all you say, but I haven't had a good piece of beef or a decent cup of coffee since I arrived. And our cars may be a bit overgrown but they're more comfortable and they get you where you're going just as often."

"Dear me, I'm sorry if I've been sounding like a silly expatriate," Eleanor said. "You notice these things when you think of going back. The other day you asked if it wasn't time for me to come home, but it hadn't occurred to you that I've come to think of this as my home."

"It isn't, all the same," said George bluntly. "You may have learned to rattle away in the language, but you'd never be anything but a displaced American."

"Is that so frightening? When our forefathers went to America they were all displaced, too, and preferred it that way."

"Because they found a better way of life," George pointed out.

"Perhaps I've done the same," said Eleanor.

"Don't be ridiculous," George said impatiently. "Bradley's Bluff isn't exactly the backside of Alaska. The houses are well heated and they'll be putting in electricity any day now."

"It's not easy to explain, George," she said seriously. "I'm not talking now of the superficial things. They don't really matter. But there's an atmosphere you don't begin to appreciate until you've lived here for a few years. In a lot of ways this *is* a more civilized country, less violent, more grown up. I don't say that's a reason for staying. But it makes you aware of what you'd be missing if you left."

This was the low point of George's hopes, for he felt that he had run out of arguments. He had known from the beginning there was no romantic way to woo a woman who had lived with him for better than a decade and a half; she knew his attractions and defects better than he knew them himself; he could do little more than offer himself with his affection still intact and leave the decision to her. In the same fashion, there was no sensible way to extol the charms of the country where she had lived most of her life; either she recognized their appeal or she didn't. He felt utterly helpless. His fate was being decided in some manner which he could neither understand nor influence, and he feared the worst.

And then, just when he was at his most discouraged, things took a turn for the better, although he hadn't the least idea why. One evening Eleanor seemed especially pleased with him, gayer, even (unless he was deluding himself) slightly flirtatious. And the next day it was implicit that she was coming back with him. It took George some time to recognize this, for nothing was stated openly. Eleanor's verbs simply shifted from the conditional to the future: where before she had said "It would be sort of fun to—" now she was saying "Won't it be nice to—" And to remove all doubt, the agent was instructed to find a tenant for the house in Cagnes-sur-Mer.

Eleanor was coming back with him—and only a boor would have insisted that the obvious be put into words. And such a boor would no doubt have been punished with equally clear language to the effect that her return carried with it no guarantees and no promises. Eleanor was honest, she would come back with an open mind, but she was not burning any bridges behind her. The house in Cagnes-sur-Mer was to be rented for the summer season only; in October she would have to decide whether to let the place on a longer lease, if she didn't want it for herself.

With this circumspection George was obliged to be content; in fact, much as he would have preferred a surehearted enthusiasm, he had to respect her good sense since she *was* unsure. A more foolish woman would have acted more impulsively, but George was not one to admire folly merely because it suited his wishes. Eleanor had her reservations about coming back; well and good, but she was giving him the chance to prove those reservations ill-founded. He was confident that he could do it, and therefore more than grateful to get the chance. The affair with Saint-Euverte could be regarded as a wayward detour in Eleanor's life; there had been more reasons for that detour than the Frenchman's attractiveness, but those reasons were now as dead as Saint-Euverte himself; the incident was closed. George felt sure that if he could just get his wife home again things would fall into their proper perspective, the doubts that flourished in this foreign air would wither away. At the back of his mind he knew there were storms ahead. His mother would not be delighted by Eleanor's return. Eleanor's sister's marriage was in trouble. He could not be sure that Martha would consent to stay on as their housekeeper. Above all was the large question mark of how Ken was going to react. But none of these mattered, he was convinced. In spite of them all, Eleanor would recognize where she really belonged. With him and with her son. At home.

Glad to have something he could grasp at last, George threw himself into the task of making their trip home as easy as possible. He was a spendthrift about telephone calls to New York and tips to everyone in sight. He made plane reservations and then changed them when a client could ensure him more deferential treatment on another airline. With the help of people at the hotel he arranged for the shipping of effects of Eleanor's which couldn't go in her luggage. He saw to it that they would be met at the airport by a hired limousine which would whisk them in comfort out to Bradley's Bluff.

He was positive he had foreseen and forestalled every hitch that could arise—a state of mind which the gods find diverting.

4.

"Good afternoon, Mrs. Briggs."

"Afternoon, Martha. It's too quiet for me to suppose that my sister and her husband have arrived yet."

"You're way early. The airplane's due in about now, but we don't expect them for another couple of hours. Maybe longer."

"I might as well wait, anyhow," said Cathy Briggs, passing inspection on herself in the hall mirror. "Is Ken around?"

"Down in the basement, tinkering. Mrs. Davenport is in bed."

"Not ill, I hope."

"I don't really think so." Martha's round face glinted with suppressed amusement. "She was all right till about half an hour ago. Then she looked at her watch and said she was going to bed and expected to stay there till they carried her out in her coffin."

"My sister doesn't seem able to cross the ocean in either direction without upsetting somebody," Cathy said. "There will be a few others in Bradley's Bluff disappointed by her return."

"Not among the menfolk," said Martha drily. "They'll swarm like bees."

Cathy stared and then nodded. "I forget," she said. "Because you started coming steadily after Eleanor left, I forget you'd known her before."

"My, yes," said Martha. "Until the accident, Joseph and I catered just about every party the George Davenports gave.

I never got much help out of Joseph at those parties, either; he just wanted to stand around looking at Mrs. George. I can recall the first time you were here: that must have been when you got engaged to Mr. Briggs. Joseph gawked and said 'Lordy, there's *two* of them!' and that afternoon I made *all* the cocktails."

"How is Joseph?" Cathy asked politely. She scarcely remembered him, and she hated hearing about invalids, but it was the sort of courtesy you forced upon yourself nowadays to show you were no part of the color nonsense.

"Always the same," said Martha. "It's no life for anybody, lying in bed all the time. Mrs. Davenport will find that out after a few days."

"I'd better pay my respects to the old lady," said Cathy. "Bring me a bourbon on the rocks when you have a moment, would you?"

She went through the dining room, for the layout of the ground floor was such that only here had it been possible to add on a bedroom and bath, a few years back, when Mrs. Davenport decided that stairs were too much for her heart. Cathy knocked at the open door and went in, saying, "I hear the excitement's got you down."

Mrs. Davenport laid aside on the mauve coverlet a murder mystery with a particularly lurid cover. "The vultures gather," she said in her sad, sweet grandmotherly voice. "No, I am the one member of this household who is not excited. I can regard the antics of my son's infatuation with the calm resignation of approaching death."

"Lucky Eleanor," said Cathy as she sat down, "coming back to a deathbed scene that will stretch over the next twenty years."

"I sincerely trust it won't. Are you planning to smoke in here?"

"It appears that you do."

"But I never inhale. I only smoke to clear the taste of wormwood and gall from my mouth. Other people's cigarettes make me cough."

"I'll sit nearer the door," said Cathy, pushing her chair back a few inches. "The truth is, indignation puts color in your cheeks. You look better than I've seen you in ages."

"It was good of you to come by early to pay compliments to an old woman. I suppose that's a sign the handsome Mr. Fred Palmer is unusually busy this afternoon."

"How is it that people who never set foot out of doors manage to collect more gossip than anybody? But I had several reasons for coming. First of all, Alan and I have been worrying about Ken."

"So has Ken," said Mrs. Davenport. "If George had to bring that woman back with him, he'd have been kinder to his son to do it unexpectedly. Of course, my heart would never have withstood the shock, but that's not of the least consequence to anyone."

"Ken's a sensitive young man," said Cathy. "Because he's healthy and athletic we tend to forget how sensitive he is. And he was only a boy when Eleanor went off."

"I have never forgiven George for making me support his falsehoods that first summer," said Mrs. Davenport. "I kept telling him it would do no good to put off the day of reckoning, but he threatened to cancel my account at the lending library if I disobeyed him. The Davenports are stubborn men."

"Ken is more imaginative than his father, more high-strung. In that respect he takes after our family."

"If he takes after his mother," Mrs. Davenport said genially, "he will deserve to be strung as high as possible."

"How is he reacting to the prospect of his mother's arrival?" Cathy asked.

"That varies from one moment to the next. He is trying

on poses to find out which one suits his temperament best. The haughty indifference isn't entirely convincing. The languid, girls-will-be-girls cynicism is rather better and has a certain juvenile charm. My favorite is the charitable, long-suffering forgiveness; he makes you feel that at any moment he will ask you to join in an uplifting hymn."

"He must feel horribly insecure," said Cathy.

"It would be remarkable if he didn't," said Mrs. Davenport. "No one but a mother can find anything lovable in a fifteen-year-old boy, and if your own mother prefers to be on another continent that cannot add to your self-confidence. It is wonderful that Ken has turned out as well as he has—I give George full credit. Eleanor is returning just in time to undo all the good work."

"I daresay George felt that Ken was suffering from a lack in the house of anything resembling a woman's influence."

Martha came in, bringing Cathy's bourbon, and Mrs. Davenport looked on this display of hospitality with a resentful eye.

"You might have inquired if I wanted anything, Martha," she remarked.

"At this time in the afternoon?" Martha said in surprise. "You never do."

"This is hardly a normal afternoon," replied Mrs. Davenport. "It isn't every day that the good fairy of the Davenport household reappears. My needs are medicinal."

"You want some of that blue tonic the doctor left?" Martha asked.

"Something stronger," said Mrs. Davenport. "I tried to take my pulse a while ago, just before Mrs. Briggs looked in, and it seemed to have stopped altogether. Perhaps matters have improved by now, but I think I'd like an old-fashioned. A large one."

"Coming up, Mrs. Davenport," said Martha.

"I wish there was something we could *do* for Ken," Cathy said. "It's all wrong to let him brood and brood until things get out of all proportion."

"Perhaps you might help him with a problem that's been bothering him," said Mrs. Davenport. "He can't seem to settle on a method of addressing his mother that isn't either too familiar or too impolite. When your sister left he was calling her Mom, but this doesn't accord with his new dignity or his present sentiments. Ma, Mother, Mummy, Mater, Mrs. Davenport, Eleanor and Hey You are all lacking in one respect or another. He needs advice."

"I thought he had taken to referring to her as Helen of Troy," Cathy said.

"Naturally I reprimanded him for comparing his mother to a Greek strumpet," said Mrs. Davenport. "So far as I know there is no Greek blood in your family."

5.

Eleanor's luggage, spread out for Customs inspection, must have contained much that was innocent, yet it seemed overflowing with just those articles which Customs frowned upon. Flagons of perfume and handmade shoes, fur wraps and fancy handbags and dresses that looked, even to George's inexperienced eyes, fresh from the salons of *haute couture*. What most unnerved George was the sight of a great deal of costly-looking jewelry he had never seen before. What unnerved Eleanor was the sight of her open suitcases.

"There's no point to this," she told the Inspector. "I've been living abroad for the past six years; my permanent address is Cagnes-sur-Mer, Alpes-Maritimes, France: it's on my passport. I'm a nonresident of this country, so my personal belongings come in without duty—I checked that at the consulate in Nice."

"Is all your stuff here, lady?" asked the blue-uniformed officer, "or is there more coming?"

"Four crates are being shipped," George said.

"Four crates. I don't suppose you know which line? Thank you. Are you related to this lady?"

"Uh, yes. I'm her husband."

"And your place of residence?"

"Fourteen Elmwood Drive, Bradley's Bl—"

"We've been separated for years and years," Eleanor put in hurriedly.

"I see. Was that a legal separation?"

"Comme je l'ai dit, les plus grands salauds du monde," said Eleanor.

"I didn't catch that," said the Inspector.

"She said no, it wasn't legalized," said George.

"Then I'm sorry, lady. Where your husband lives is your place of residence."

"That's barbarous," announced Eleanor. "The suffragists must be spinning in their graves."

"Maybe so, but it's the law of the land. I'm afraid I'll have to treat you just like a returning tourist."

"After six years!"

"A nice long vacation," said the Inspector. "I wouldn't mind a vacation like that myself. Do you happen to have the receipts for this jewelry?"

"Those were gifts," Eleanor said. "Do you usually have receipts for the gifts you get?"

"Nobody's ever given me a ruby necklace," said the Inspector regretfully. "I guess we'll have to get the appraiser over."

Eleanor turned to George. "I kept telling you to get a divorce," she pointed out. "I think you would have found an uncontested divorce a good deal less expensive than this is going to be."

It wasn't just a question of the expense, as they quickly found out. If he'd had his way, George would have left the luggage there to be sent after them with a bill for the duties owed; he would have paid the bill cheerfully if only their homeward trip could have been completed without exasperation and delay. But even if such a plan were feasible, Eleanor would never hear of it. Her European friends had so filled her with stories of the wickedness of U.S. Customs that she clearly believed that if she turned her back for an instant her most precious possessions would vanish into the pockets of these blue-uniformed gentlemen—who were, in all truth, as decent and helpful as they could possibly be. Some sort of superior officer involved himself with their problem, promptly became one of Eleanor's admirers and showed the most avuncular sympathy with her position. Far from wielding the law in all its severity, the officials seemed eager to find every excuse for waiving the duty, or at least keeping it to a minimum. Nevertheless it took time to inspect all the dutiable articles and discover the legal loopholes through which many of them could be squeezed, and several hours had passed (and considerable damage been done to George's bank balance) before they were permitted to continue on to the waiting limousine.

Eleanor had never relented. She retained her serene good temper throughout, but she emerged from the building with the air, faint but unmistakable, of a gentlewoman who has inadvertently passed through a street full of rowdy and catcalling young hoodlums. "That was absolutely, disgraceful," she remarked.

"A very small price for the pleasure of having you back," George said.

"Your gallantry is more than I deserve. I feel stupid; I should have expected this, enough people have warned me. At very least I could have left the jewelry for Claude to bring in with him next time. He travels on a diplomatic passport, and they never open anything."

"That wouldn't be legal," George objected.

"If I'd been your mistress instead of your wife they couldn't have charged us a penny," Eleanor replied. "I hope you noticed that, George. If you'd picked up one of the divorcées living over there and brought her back with you, she could have sailed through unquestioned with every jewel in Cartier's: she'd have been a proper nonresident. Your mistake was in bringing back your own wife instead of somebody else's.

What you paid was a tax on morality. If the government is trying to undermine the American family, we should do all we can to defy them."

"It becomes our duty to avoid duties, in fact," said George, smiling. "Very neat, my love. I hope I never see the day when you find yourself in the wrong."

In the limousine (after the driver had been reconciled to his waiting by promise of a generous tip) they purred towards Bradley's Bluff in a silence that was companionable without being entirely easy. George could sense that Eleanor was still seething inwardly at what she regarded as an outrage, and he was at a loss to distract her, return her thoughts to the delights of homecoming. Fortunately the route they were taking skirted New York completely, so she would not be obliged to remark on how much dirtier, uglier and more congested the metropolis had become during her absence, but this was small comfort. The problem was to get her thinking ahead to life in the house on Elmwood Drive with something like anticipation, but most of the conversational paths in that direction were beset with pitfalls. There was certainly no advantage to be gained by reminding her of his mother. The subject of Ken, whose present state of mind was quite unimaginable, seemed best left alone. He relied upon Eleanor to deal with any awkwardness there; she had a knack for pointing up the absurdity of exaggerated emotions, a rare talent for imposing her serenity on other people. On the other hand she had not been—prior to her life abroad, at any rate—a gregarious person; they had many acquaintances in Bradley's Bluff, but few close friends; to speak of the small doings of the Hendersons or the Updykes might merely recall just those aspects of suburban living which she had come to think of as boring. It was difficult.

He rolled down his window slightly; the ventilation of the limousine had not been designed for French cigarettes.

If he was to end this silence, lure Eleanor into thinking ahead a little, it would have to be with talk of Eleanor's sister and her husband, Cathy and Alan Briggs. There were drawbacks to this topic, too, but at least they didn't reflect on the house on Elmwood Drive—for whatever that was worth. Cathy was Eleanor's younger sister by nearly seven years and Eleanor's sororal feelings were strongly tinged with the maternal; she could be fiercely protective, and might not take kindly to the news that Cathy had been behaving, to put it mildly, indiscreetly. If this should be news. Regrettably he had no idea how frequently the sisters had been corresponding; it was not impossible that Eleanor was better informed than he.

"I've been seeing quite a bit of Alan and Cathy," he said, hoping that Eleanor's response to this might give him a cue.

"Yes, you were saying something about that the other evening," she replied. "We got sidetracked. No, I remember. Vincenzo Borsarelli was just out of the hospital and stopped by to pay his condolences. He was quite put out to find you there."

"Why was that?"

"Probably because he has rather simple ideas on how to console a grieving woman. But we mustn't let him distract us again. How is Cathy?"

"Oh, fine, the last I saw of her," he said vaguely. "You may be as up to date as I. She must write you."

"As a correspondent, Cathy fills up the blank spaces on a Christmas card with promises to write oftener in the coming year. Before she has a chance to keep that promise it's time for another Christmas card. Alan is the more faithful of the two of them."

"I would have thought he was too busy," George said. "The agency has been doing very well."

"Don't they say that it's the busy people who find time

to get things done? Three or four times a year I've had a long letter from him, very amusingly and wittily written: I've served as the outlet for his belief that he really should have been a writer. He's had great fun describing the social tug of war in Bradley's Bluff, and always managed to throw in a few sly asides about my foolishness in neglecting such a sterling husband."

"He's a loyal friend," George grunted in some embarrassment, not having guessed at the extent of that loyalty.

"And he's obviously grown very attached to you," said Eleanor. "When I left you weren't much closer than most brothers-in-law, so I concluded you'd been seeing rather more of one another than mornings on the train."

"A great deal more. Especially in the winters, when Ken is off at school. I've been going over there . . . oh, as much as two or three evenings a week."

"Leaving your poor mother all alone?" Eleanor asked with mild mockery.

"She has grown fond of television: it feeds her contempt for the human race. So I've been going out a fair bit, generally to the Briggs's. Sometimes there'll be someone else, and we play bridge. Usually it's just talk. I've become quite dependent on them—yet I've come to feel that we were wrong to talk them into buying a house in Bradley's Bluff."

"Really? How is that?" asked Eleanor. "Of course it hasn't turned out the way we all hoped it would: the babies never appeared. But that would have been true wherever they lived."

Cathy had continued working for a number of years after her marriage; she had been one of the highest-paid photographic models in the field, and her income had been an important factor in the household in the days when Watson-Briggs was still a struggling young agency, fighting to keep afloat in a pirate-infested sea. But Watson-Briggs had flourished beyond expectation, Cathy's natural laziness had asserted itself, and the doctors had agreed that the chances of her becoming pregnant would be increased if she didn't have to juggle both a home and a career. It was at this point that Eleanor and George had urged the advantages of buying a place in Bradley's Bluff, pointing out that when children did start appearing the Briggses certainly wouldn't want to live in the city, so the time to move was right then, while they were still unencumbered and before property values rose any higher. Some persuasion had been needed to get Alan over his horror of commuting, but then the old Merrivale house had come on the market at too good a price to be passed over. Alan and Cathy had become suburbanites just a year or so before Eleanor had found other parts of the globe more attractive.

"If a baby or two had arrived, it would have been all right," George said. "Our mistake was in taking those babies for granted."

"We aren't a fecund family," Eleanor said. "One child out of two sisters is poor going."

"And of course you thought it would be great fun to have Cathy in the neighborhood, but that proved to be a short-lived pleasure."

"I'll accept many reproaches, but not that one," Eleanor said. "Fond of Cathy as I am, I can't say I ever gave a thought to leaving her stranded among the two-car conveniences of Bradley's Bluff. What went wrong? Has Alan gone back to resenting the daily commute?"

"No," said George. "He's not fond of it, but he prefers it now to living in a rented apartment; he's surprised himself by becoming very house-proud. In the summer we're glutted with tomatoes from his garden, and in the winter he invents projects like rigging the place with loudspeakers from the hi-fi, so he can have Beethoven in the basement if he's so inclined."

"Then it must be that Cathy hasn't enough to keep her busy."

"That's it exactly. I think she's a city person at heart; the suburban activities seem to leave her cold. Laura Sydrock tried to get her interested in the hospital, but that didn't work out at all."

"No, she's had a thing about sick people ever since our mother died," Eleanor said. "I recall Alan's writing that she'd taken to playing a lot of golf. At the time I was surprised, since she'd never played anything more strenuous than a fast game of backgammon. Don't you remember how we used to laugh when she turned up in an ad looking as if she'd just been for a brisk canter with the hounds?"

"Golf can be a pleasant way of getting a couple of hours in the fresh air," said George. "It can also be a sign that time has become something which needs to be killed."

"She's always been high-strung, and now she's restless," Eleanor summed up. "And for you to be bothered about her restlessness, there has to be a man in the picture."

"His name is Fred Palmer," George said tersely.

"I don't seem to remember him."

"He's new. Old man Addison got to hankering for the Florida climate, and last year Fred Palmer bought him out. So he's The Agency now, our bastion against the unwelcome world outside—and a snake in the grass in our midst."

Although exclusive, Bradley's Bluff was a law-abiding community: there were no open covenants against Negroes, artists, Jews, writers or Catholics. Instead there was the Bradley's Bluff Insurance and Realty Company, locally known simply as The Agency. By gentlemen's agreement, all houses were sold through The Agency. They were never advertised for sale, so that any undesirable citizen who showed an interest in settling there could be told regretfully that there were no properties available, or likely to be in the near future—which was usually perfectly true, since the turnover was slow, and The Agency had to find most of its income in its wide assortment of insurance policies. Yet whenever a house did come up for sale The Agency was sure to produce (through its devious contacts with other real-estate agencies) a well-heeled purchaser who might prove to be dull company, whose wife might prove to drink too much, whose children might prove to be destructive young gangsters in the making, but whose ancestry, religion and choice of occupation were unexceptionable. Anyone passing The Agency's inspection was sure of acceptance at the Country Club on the first ballot.

On the whole, this arrangement suited everyone. In Addison's time nobody had noticed that Mr. Addison (firmly under the thumb of his Junoesque wife) was for most of the year just about the only able-bodied man, over school age and under the age of retirement, visible in Bradley's Bluff during working hours. Only an inflamed imagination could have seen Mr. Addison as a peril to the home. Fred Palmer was another story. He was youngish, a bachelor, ruggedly attractive with a touch of gray at the temples; he had the sort of easy charm which arouses the instant distrust of uncharming men. Gossips and young husbands began to picture workday Bradley's Bluff as a harem spread out for Mr. Palmer's selection.

"I assume you've met him," said Eleanor. "What's he like? I don't see Cathy more than flirting with the bluff and hearty type."

"He's not what you'd expect, that's just the trouble," George said. "He's a salesman, but not a hungry salesman. He seems to be quite well off. The story is that he made a real killing with some developments on Long Island, and that's it as far as he's concerned; he runs The Agency mostly as a way of keeping himself occupied. His real love is the theatre: during the season he's in the city two or three evenings a week keeping up with the new shows."

"You sound as if you rather like him."

"I haven't had a susceptible wife around to cloud my judgment. Yes, the few times I've met him I found him intelligent and likable. I could change my mind."

"If you've brought me back to be suspicious of me, it will never work," said Eleanor. "Have you any idea of how seriously Cathy's involved?"

"I know very little apart from the gossip I've picked up."

"And that comes filtering through your mother."

"Not entirely," said George. "As a rule Laura doesn't indulge in tittle-tattle, but knowing I'm so close to Alan she's let a few things drop. People are talking, no question. A week or so before I left there was some sort of confused incident on Saturday evening at the Country Club; I couldn't get it straight, the accounts varied so. Apparently Alan showed up late for the sole purpose of taking Cathy home. Maybe he knocked Mr. Palmer down. Maybe he merely offered to."

"Making the usual allowance for exaggeration," said Eleanor, "I imagine he said 'Good evening' to Mr. Palmer in a sarcastic tone of voice. Alan isn't the fist-waving sort. Has he said anything to you?"

"Of course not. He isn't that sort either."

"I didn't mean to impugn the myth of manly reticence. You're his closest friend, evidently. He might let an emotion peek out now and then."

"I'm also the husband of his wife's sister; it's a time when he could wish he'd chosen his closest friend elsewhere. Obviously something is troubling him deeply, but when I ask questions he just talks about the pressures of work. There's some truth to that, too. Watson-Briggs has been profiting from the theory that the smaller agencies can give more personal attention to their accounts. Alan has been as busy as an overworked beaver, and I don't suppose that has helped the situation at home."

"This has really been bothering you, George?" she asked gently.

"It's a damned good marriage," he replied.

"People were doubtless saying the same about us a week before I left. No matter how close you are, you only see just so much of a marriage; the rest is a private affair. Nevertheless, even knowing I'm sadly out of touch, I'm inclined to agree with you."

"It would be a pity to see things go wrong only because Cathy's feeling restless," George said. "Anyway, it's something you had to know about. And something for you to think about."

"I'll think about it, certainly," Eleanor agreed. "I don't see that there's much I can do. I'm scarcely in the best position for making a display of conventional disapproval."

"That would inhibit many women," George said. "I haven't noticed that you find your position uncomfortable, and in any case your disapproval would never be conventional."

"After six years there's no telling how close Cathy and I will still be," Eleanor observed thoughtfully. "I have the impression that affection between sisters needs frequent reinforcing if it isn't to crumble. That may not be true in our case, but I'll be wise to go cautiously at first and take nothing for granted." Her voice shifted gears, into bright unconcern. "But I can't believe that Cathy's is the only scandal I should be brought up to date on. Has Karen Updyke survived all these years without being poisoned?"

Thus encouraged (though he saw that Eleanor's main interest was to get away from a topic she found perturbing), he could chronicle the small cataclysms of life in Bradley's

Bluff, confining himself to those anecdotes which could be made to sound amusing. The drive passed quickly. All too soon familiar landmarks began to appear, warning that home was only another ten or fifteen minutes ahead. George continued to talk, sustained by the glibness of stories that moved in well-worn grooves, but a part of his mind had gone ahead to the moment of arrival, sending forward telepathic commands to his son to show the poise with which George had credited him. He was perfectly aware that his cable must have come as a great shock to Ken, but there had been no sensible alternative. A telephone call would have been too embarrassing to both of them. An airmail letter would have taken too long without adding anything material. The middle-aged emotions and considerations which had brought about Eleanor's return could be of no help to Ken, who had to deal on his own terms with the reappearance of a long-resented mother: no amount of preaching about how he ought to react would have the slightest effect on his reactions.

The cable, in fact, had served two useful functions. It had forced Ken to absorb the initial shock in solitude, where no impulsive, outraged blurt could do any harm, and it had given him the maximum of time in which to adjust to the new shape of reality. George was confident that he had taken the best possible course of action, yet this gave him no confidence in the outcome. His son, though good-natured, was introspective, intellectually inclined, and given to acting on principle; therefore his reactions were quite unpredictable. Ken might feel one way, while obedience to some high-minded, muddle-headed abstraction led him to act in another. He was entirely capable of deciding that loyalty to his father required him to treat his mother as a hostile intruder. There was simply no telling—and as always, when he had no control over a situation, George tended to fear the worst.

Eventually the driver slowed and pushed back the glass

panel to ask for more precise directions. As if on cue, Eleanor fished out her compact and studied her reflection in the mirror, making minute adjustments to her make-up—the first sign of nervousness she had shown, if, indeed, the ritual could be regarded in that light. Satisfied at last, she leaned back again and glanced about in placid curiosity. "The trees have grown a lot," she remarked. "That's the only difference I can notice."

The last turn brought them onto Elmwood Drive. The driver slowed to a crawl, peering at house numbers; then brought the car to a gentle stop and leapt out smartly to hurry around to open the door for them.

"Well, here we are," George said fatuously. Eleanor gave him a small reassuring smile.

They stepped out just in time to see the front door of the house fly open and Ken emerge in a remarkable gait, somewhere between a glide and a stumble, probably meant to be a saunter.

He cut directly across the lawn, towards them, smiling as he came. "Hello Dad, hello Mother," he called out. "Was it a pleasant flight?" The voice wasn't quite right either, missing by several degrees the intended effect of airy nonchalance, but George relaxed in relief, suddenly discovering how tensely he had been holding himself. At least there wasn't going to be a crisis here on the front lawn. Ken had come to some kind of terms with himself, he was trying to behave gracefully, and the emotional slack could be taken up in the hours and days ahead.

It was Eleanor's reaction that took him by surprise. For once her serenity was shaken. She was half in tears, half in laughter.

"My darling, darling boy!" she said in a choked voice as Ken approached. "But couldn't *somebody* have prepared me for the beard?"

PART TWO

The Spartan Youth

I.

When a grown man falls in love and finds some slight impediment to his romance he is apt to behave very badly. If the lady of his heart lives at an inconvenient distance, or has a husband who claims some of her attention, or follows a calling which makes meetings difficult, he storms and sulks and thinks in such immoderate terms as murder, suicide, or joining the Foreign Legion. No matter that the impediment can always be got around, that the next rendezvous is only postponed for a day or so. Enough that he wants her today and cannot see her until tomorrow; this is insupportable and leads, at the least, to the maudlin consumption of a great deal of alcohol.

Yet how much more dismally placed young lovers are, and how much more philosophically they bear it! Parted by the inexorable scissors of Autumn, he to his college and she to hers; sustained only by love letters scrawled between the demands of schoolwork; kept apart by the arbitrary caprice of relations (for naturally this will be the year when Aunt Grace whisks her down to Bermuda for the spring vacation)—they somehow endure all these deprivations with less fuss than their elders can make over the briefest frustration.

Even a few days' separation can be ample for a man to develop the most agonizing doubts of his lady's sincerity, constancy and even fidelity, yet young lovers have to meet again in June with all the uncertainty of whether last summer's deathless passion has survived the winter. Such reunions are best not held in private, where someone whose affections have wandered may be forced into being cruelly explicit; and best not held in public, either, where there would be witnesses to a humiliation. Ken Davenport and Jessie Sydrock met by arrangement on the side court at the Country Club, met with a brisk friendliness that informed all the world they were just there for a few sets of good, hard tennis.

"Hi," said Ken. If his heart turned over at the sight of his love, slender and tanned and very cute in her white shirt and short white shorts, he expressed this turmoil by asking, "You want to start on the shady side?"

"Spin the racket, you bum," said Jessie. "I'm not taking any handicaps this summer."

"You've got cocky, playing with other little girls," he retorted. "I'll soon attend to that."

As usual, from the very first they rallied with grim intensity, as though even the warm-up shots were part of a cut-throat competition. A casual onlooker might have thought that here was a rivalry so bitter that it carried to the brink of poor sportsmanship, for smashing a ball powerfully into the net or six feet past the base line would be rewarded with a cry of "Good shot!" whereas standing flatfooted and watching a ball sail into an unreachable corner was apt to elicit a jeering "Oh, nice try!" In the language of romance these ironic calls seemed scarcely adequate for conveying such delicate messages as "I love you! *I* haven't changed, have you?" yet they did the task as well as the most elegant innuendo. By midway through the first set Ken was happily, proudly sure of himself again. He had learned that everything was all right, that Jessie's love was as intact as his own and a long glorious summer of exploration lay ahead for the two of them.

He had also learned that her backhand had improved remarkably since last year, and she had perfected a maddening little drop shot which barely carried over the net and then expired with hardly any bounce at all. It was this shot that nearly cost him the first set and did cost him the second. His normal game was thrown off stride: instead of being able to drive from the base line, choosing his moment to come up to the net for the kill, he found himself all too frequently scrambling up to the net for no better purpose than losing a point. Tennis was not one of Ken's principal sports (he played soccer in the fall and was a middle-distance runner in the spring), but natural athleticism and his advantage in strength had always made it easy for him to beat Jessie in the past. He had given her various handicaps, and even then had been able to credit the sets she won to his magnanimity. Those days were done. He realized that her expression of love during the separation of the school year had been to turn herself into an opponent who could give him a real fight. The thought touched and elated him; he had an ecstatic vision of them playing together in the doubles tournament later in the summer; and he settled down to asserting his masculine supremacy. For the third set he played in closer, rushing the net at every opportunity, forcing Jessie to lob—still the weakest part of her game—and finally won with a series of exceptionally sharp services. They trotted off happily hand in hand to the showers, both satisfied by the outcome, and Ken with the knowledge that his own play had better improve before Jessie's lobbing became more accurate.

A little later they met again at one of the tables on the Club terrace, where they sat sipping collinses in murmurous contentment, watching—when they weren't looking at one another—the golfers waiting to tee off for the first hole. They were easy now. Not comfortable, exactly: the exchange of feeling was too intense for that. Confident, savoring their confidence. The tensions and deliriums of the long summer evenings were for another time, implicit but held in suspense. For the moment they were content to bask in the wash of a mutual emotion, content with the small sensualities of feet that brushed beneath the table and hands that met and clasped between the chairs.

They were disturbed by one of the older paunchy members of the Club, pausing in his stately progress from the parking area to the bar. "Morning, morning," he greeted them. "No, don't get up, Ken. They tell me your mother's back. Give her my regards, will you? Tell her . . . well, just give her my regards." He continued on his way.

"There will be a lot more of that," Jessie predicted. "You're practically a celebrity. All anyone's talking about is your mother's return."

"I don't like that," he said. "I can't see it's anybody's affair but our own."

"I guess it's a relief to talk about other people's affairs for a change," she said. "Especially when it's something glamorous."

"It isn't glamour they want, it's gossip. At times like this you wish you lived in the city, where people mind their own business."

"I wonder whether they really do. But I haven't heard any bitchiness, if that's what you have in mind. Everybody's talking about how remarkable it is that she doesn't seem to have changed a bit. Mrs. Plummer says it's witchcraft."

"If they mean her looks, I suppose they're right," he said. "For the rest, I wouldn't know. I've changed too much myself over the past six years."

"She must have been wildly excited at seeing you."

"Wildly?" he repeated. "I don't imagine she ever gets wildly excited. I mean, thank God she's not like Tony's mother, weeping over every little thing and clutching at you. Mother gets gay and bubbly and very funny."

"Funny!"

"Well, teasing," Ken said grinning. "Mostly at the expense of my beard."

"She doesn't like it," Jessie said accusingly.

"No, I'm used to that, and I don't find it amusing. Mother thinks it makes me look terribly young. She swore she'd have recognized me anywhere because I still look fifteen years old in masquerade. I don't think that's true at all, do you?"

"It isn't. You look very mature and handsome, and don't let her talk you into shaving it off."

"She's not like that. At least, I don't think she is."

"Still," said Jessie, "It sounds to me like a pretty crazy homecoming after six years, starting off teasing you about your beard."

"Oh, that stuff about my masquerade didn't come up till dinnertime, after things had calmed down a bit. But you're right in a way, all the same: it *was* a strange homecoming. Certainly not what I'd been expecting, anyway."

"What had you been expecting?"

"All sorts of things, most of them dramatic. I'd been brooding about it for days, naturally, and I thought I'd covered all the possibilities. Except the one which occurred. No drama, no awkwardness. She walked in without much more fuss than if she'd been away on a month's cruise."

"That seems a bit brazen," Jessie said with tentative indignation.

"Then I'm putting it badly," Ken replied. "Look, when she arrived you could tell she was excited to be back and excited at seeing me, sure. Right at first there were three or four times when she almost got teary, almost but not quite. Okay, plenty of mothers can work up that much steam after a week away in the Bahamas, but for Mother it was probably a big emotional scene. The point I'm trying to make is that after she'd been in the house for half an hour it was perfectly natural to have her there. And fun. Almost as if she'd never been away—and that's what I found so unexpected. She's a remarkable woman."

"I remember her as very beautiful and rather awesome, to a thirteen-year-old," Jessie said. "It will be fascinating to see her again from a grown-up point of view."

"She wants you over for dinner as soon as possible. You and Laura."

"Not for a few weeks, anyway. There's your Aunt Cathy."

A woman's foursome had joined the golfers waiting to tee off. Cathy Briggs spotted the two of them on the terrace and waved casually.

"She was there, too, for a little while," Ken said. "She'd been hanging around most of the afternoon, but when Mother and Dad finally showed up it was almost time for her to be getting home to start dinner. Just as well, too. Aunt Cathy was the one all set for a big scene, but she'd had three or four drinks by then."

"She always seems so cool and model-ish."

"Not yesterday. Tears all over the place: you'd have thought it was Aunt Cathy that Mother walked out on six years ago. Mother made her laugh by saying 'Here come all the emotions that wouldn't fit on the Christmas cards,' but even after that it was touch and go whether we could get her out before she broke down again. See how thin she is? It's happened so gradually I hadn't noticed, but of course Mother spotted it first thing. So of course she gets upset easily. Why can't you come for dinner?"

"Oh, I can come any time," Jessie said. "It's Mummy; I don't think she'll want to, not just yet. She's being extra busy and cheerful, which is a good sign she's pretty unhappy."

"Christ, yes, of course—oh, damn!" groaned Ken, flooded with a sudden sense of remorse that in the double turmoil of the past week—the anticipation of his mother's return, and of seeing Jessie again—he had never given even the most fleeting thought to the feelings of the woman he had regarded, until so recently, as his future stepmother. His remorse was all the more bitter because he had always argued strenuously against any suggestion that people his age were imbued with egoism, insisting that on the contrary they were far more sensitive than their elders, and here he had shown himself an absolute monster of thoughtlessness.

"And it's our fault, partly," Jessie added. "I mean, we did all we could to promote the thing."

"I know we did," he said. "We meant well, but we were wrong; it's as simple as that. You'll see what I mean when you see Dad. He's a different person. He doesn't carry on about it, but he's so pleased with himself that he practically shines."

"We were only wrong because that Frenchman got killed," Jessie said. "Except for that, your Mother would still be over there."

"I suppose that's right," Ken said, blinking a little at the realization that he had somehow lost track of this aspect of the matter.

"It's wonderful that it's worked out like this," Jessie put in quickly. "I really mean it, Ken! I think it's terrific that your father's so happy and you've got your own mother back, I really do. I couldn't be more pleased."

"But you're feeling sorry for Laura," he said. "Naturally you are. I am, myself."

"And I can't help thinking that some women have all the luck," Jessie said. "When my father died ten years ago there wasn't anybody else to pick up the pieces for Mummy. She's had a lonely time of it since, especially when I'm off at school. I know she was getting ideas of a different sort of life. So I don't think she'll feel like being bright and chatty at a dinner party with George and Eleanor for the next few weeks. That's all."

"Sure, I understand," said Ken, whose pity for Laura Sydrock (an abstract emotion, really) was already being submerged in the far more practical fear that Jessie could be finding reasons for resenting his mother, which would be a terrible nuisance. He was beginning to see that parents could create an infinity of complications for their children. "But you'll come, won't you?" he asked anxiously.

"All you have to do is whistle," Jessie said cheerfully. "I know that's the wrong answer. Taking me for granted will probably have a rotten effect on your character."

"Maybe tomorrow, I'll find out," he said. "You were right in what you said about seeing Mother from a grown-up point of view. When we're kids we never really see our parents as people: they're more like forces which have to be cajoled or placated or defied, you know? We're too busy reacting to them to notice that they are individuals. I can see now that when I thought I was remembering Mother I was really only remembering what she looked like and what I'd felt about her. I wasn't actually remembering *her,* if you understand what I mean."

"I'm beginning to," said Jessie.

"She's a very unusual woman," Ken said. "What strikes you right off is that she's completely relaxed and natural. She never acts. Nothing's artificial: this is how she is, take it or leave it. You'll have to admit most women would have been a bit unsure of themselves, coming back like that, but I don't think Mother knows how to be unsure. When she does something it becomes the right thing to do. And you have to admire that."

"I hope it's tomorrow," said Jessie. "It's best to know right from the start what the competition is up to."

However, although he might praise his mother to the skies to Jessie (to avert any stirrings of resentment), when Ken was by himself later on, driving home, his mind came back with a thump to the unattractive fact that his mother's presence was a direct consequence of Saint-Euverte's death. Far from a novelty, this had been one of the prime considerations back when he was trying to account for his father's earth-shaking cable. He had pictured his mother, bereft and penniless in a strange land, twining herself seductively about his father in a ruthless, cynical endeavor to keep a roof over her head. This view of things might not be flattering to either parent, but at least it got you past the objection that Saint-Euverte's death couldn't be regarded as the simple throwing of a switch, shunting his mother's affections back onto the orthodox rails.

It was all very well for Jessie to say that some women had all the luck, but there was precious little dignity in being the beneficiaries of such "luck"; it offended him to think that his mother was being tossed back into their household by a random spin of fate, not because she wanted to be there but because life's more inviting avenues had been closed to her.

And this had been his state of mind virtually until the moment his mother walked in the door. At the same time he had had to resolve the question of how he was to *behave* at his mother's homecoming. He had felt himself to be powerless: his parents were going to arrange their lives to suit themselves; and he saw that even a proper show of resentment coming from someone who was powerless could be misinterpreted as mere petulance. If he was going to be reconciled to his mother's return a bad-tempered start would leave embarrassing scars, and if he wasn't he ought to have the moral advantage of an initial display of good will. This was the logic of it, and logic had been reinforced by a strong undercurrent of longing to see his mother, and an even stronger dislike of making an ass of himself.

So he had strolled out to greet the limousine braced to an insouciant affability, and had brought it off rather nicely. He was proud of the way he had kissed his mother and shaken hands with his father and escorted them into the house—though the truth was that he had been too intent on the impression he was making to be aware of much else. The ticklish first moments had slipped by smoothly.

The trouble was that when the intensity of Ken's self-consciousness finally began to relax he had found himself already disarmed, like a castle bristling with defenses which had been silently and efficiently overrun during the night. His mother was a darling, which was another of the possibilities he had overlooked. She hadn't gone into great raptures over seeing him again (which would merely have been a reminder that the separation had been of her making alone), but had been delighted to find that he had grown into exactly the man she had hoped he would become. Instead of exclaiming over how much he had changed she had bantered very gently about his beard, as if it had been grown especially as a surprise for her. Somehow she had avoided every action which would have emphasized the novelty of having her there, and had made it seem so perfectly natural that she *should* be there that any question of how this had come to pass was lost in the shuffle. By the time Ken had modestly taken credit for the built-in bookcases which now lined one wall of his father's study, it had not been with any sense of showing off to a stranger but with pride in having contributed to the house which was also her house.

"What's so impressive is that they look as if they'd been there since the place was built," his mother had said. "Where does this come from, George? You could never put up a picture hook without hammering your thumb into the wall."

"There was a cabinet-making Davenport a few generations back."

"I might have known. When Ken won that spelling prize you dug up a Davenport who had helped Samuel Johnson with his dictionary."

"That was my father's story; I can't vouch for it."

"Whereas when he swindled the Henderson boy out of that

brand-new telescope we went hunting through my family tree for horse thieves and confidence men. It's a beautiful job, Ken, better than one could expect from most professionals nowadays, in this country. You'll have to defend yourself against the projects I'll undoubtedly dream up for you."

Not a trace of ruefulness or apology in her manner, scarcely an acknowledgement of her absence; just an assured settling in as if there weren't a problem in the world. That might all be very pleasing to his father, who presumably was content to have her back on any terms. But Ken was now inclined to feel that he had been hypnotized by this assurance, charmed all too easily for the good of his self-respect. He didn't mind: it had helped him past an awkward moment. Nonetheless the fact remained that his mother was there by the accident of Saint-Euverte's death, not of her own volition, and all her charm couldn't make the fact any more appetizing. Their lives had been rearranged by mere chance. They were heritors to one of Fortune's hand-me-downs—and Ken wasn't at all sure he liked the idea.

2.

"The point is, and we both know it," George Davenport said to Martha, "that you can replace me a damn sight more easily than I can replace you."

"There's no shortage of jobs," Martha agreed.

"We have to blame the generations that treated their help so badly that service became a misery to be avoided at all costs," George mused aloud. "Otherwise, how do you account for it? It must be a lot easier and more interesting to work in a pleasant household than to be chained to a typewriter in a stuffy office with a dozen other drudges."

"There's more than one way of looking at it," Martha said drily. "In an office, five o'clock comes and you put on your hat and go home. Even the nicest families take advantage sooner or later. 'My husband's boss is coming for dinner and you have to stay and help out, you can have all day Monday instead.' But maybe you were planning on the movies tonight and don't have any use for all day Monday."

"We've never done that to you, Martha!"

"No, you haven't, and that's a fact. I've enjoyed working here, Mr. George, don't mistake me. But there's bound to be some changes now. They've already started."

"They have?"

"Mrs. Davenport taking to her bed. How do you run a house when you have to stop every few hours to take in a tray or fetch it back? How can you clean a room when somebody's there complaining that the vacuum cleaner gives her the earache?"

"You know my mother by now, Martha. She's in one of her moods. It can't last more than another day or two."

"Maybe so, but I'm not so sure this time. And there's going to be more work anyway; it's always easier working for a man. If I feel like waxing downstairs I can let the upstairs go for a couple of days—men never notice a little dust. But Mrs. George will notice, that's her business. And I'll have to stop what I'm doing to go attend to something else."

"As against that, some of the work will be shared," George said, although suspecting this was a frail argument. "My wife loves to cook. Some things, anyhow."

"That won't be any help," Martha said implacably. "When I'm working in the kitchen I know what I'm doing and I can clean up as I go along. Get Mrs. George out there making one of those fancy French dishes and there'll be ten times as much cleaning up for me to do."

"I've taken it for granted there would be extra work," George said. "That's why I felt we should discuss a raise in your wages."

"It's not just the money," Martha said. "I'm not getting any younger, either."

"That's nonsense and you know it: ten years from now you'll still have more energy than any of us. I'm not going to appeal to your loyalty as an old family retainer, because you're nothing of the kind and you've no reason to feel loyal. But I *am* going to appeal to your good nature, Martha. I'm in a spot, and I'm counting on you to help me."

"How's that?"

"It's my wife. As nearly as I can make out she hasn't done a stroke of housework for the past six years."

"She hasn't been living in hotels," Martha said, puzzling it out curiously. "She had a house of her own, she told me so. What's she been doing with herself?"

"It's a very different life over there," said George vaguely, assuming that Martha's ideas of foreign domesticity were as hazy as his own. "Entirely different."

"Maybe the day in France doesn't have twenty-four hours," Martha said. "I don't get it. Look at Joseph, now. He's always been a reader, and I see he has the papers and plenty of books. Friends of his come in, and they play cards. He's got television. And he still gets fidgety with nothing to do but amuse himself, and he wasn't ever what I'd call a hard-working man."

"Don't ask me how they keep themselves busy, but it isn't with housekeeping," George said. "Servants are cheap over there and there isn't any shortage of them, at least among the people my wife has known. She's been leading what we'd think of as a rich woman's life."

"And you want that to keep going back here?"

"For a while, anyway, yes."

"Are you sure you're being real smart, Mr. George?"

"No, I'm not," he admitted. "Right at the moment I'm particularly aware of the dangers and drawbacks of leaving a woman with too much time on her hands. But that may depend on whether the woman is used to it or not, and my wife *is* used to it. I don't want the change to come as too much of a shock. I thought it would be better if she got used to things gradually."

"What's going to be gradual about it with me doing all the work?"

"There will be your days off, Martha. The house has to be kept running. She will get back into the habit of doing things."

"Plenty of families in the Bluff spend the weekends eating at the Country Club and let the breakfast dishes pile up until Monday."

"After six years of French restaurants my wife won't want to eat at the Club any more often than is absolutely necessary."

"Maybe you've got something there," Martha said with a grin—the first sign that she might be relenting. "My cousin Sarah who works there says she's downright ashamed of some of the food she has to serve up, but the people don't seem to notice."

"That's been attended to in the bar," said George. "Look, Martha, it's mainly the first few months I'm worried about, until she gets used to being back. Just so the contrast isn't too glaring, with the life there all fun and the life here nothing but work. If you could just see us through the summer I'd be terribly grateful. We can discuss it again in the autumn. By then perhaps she'll want to do most of it herself, with someone in to clean once or twice a week. Or if not, and you find it's too much for you, at least we'll have a chance of finding someone else. At this time of year there isn't a hope. Would you do that much for me, Martha?"

"Well, I'll tell you what, Mr. George," she said slowly, "I won't say yes, and I won't say no. I'll try it out for a couple of weeks and see how it goes." She shook her head in amusement. "But like I was saying, sooner or later even the nicest families take advantage of you."

3.

Unlike his father, Ken rehearsed scenes in advance. He couldn't help himself; it was the curse of an overactive imagination. Once committed to a situation he would live it through a dozen times before the actual moment, preparing the rôle he would play, planning the dialogue he would speak. Sometimes these rehearsals served him well, more often they left him singularly ill-prepared for what happened. A typical instance of the latter had occurred this past year at college, when he had written a particularly brilliant paper for his favorite professor and in due course the paper had been handed back with a filthy grade, barely passing, and a summons to see the professor in his office that afternoon. Ken was a good student and liked his work; he knew when he was spinning words to hide a shaky knowledge of a subject, and knew equally well when he was in good form. This paper had been one of his best, and had earned him his worst grade of the year. There could be only one explanation: as it happened he had taken a position which, although well reasoned, was in flat contradiction to the opinions of Professor Wentworth. Until this moment Professor Wentworth had seemed a large-minded, dedicated scholar; now he stood revealed as a petty classroom tyrant whose ideas had to be treated reverentially—and Ken had not had the least intention of knuckling under. Had he come to college to learn to use his own mind or to parrot back the views of other men? Over the course of hours he had constructed a savagely sarcastic defense of academic freedom and personal integrity, indifferent to whether he flunked the course or even got thrown out of the university. When he marched off to the appointment he had been ready for the scene in all its variations, including a couple of splendid ones in which Professor Wentworth was driven by remorseless logic to repent of his faults.

"Sit down, Davenport," Professor Wentworth had said briskly. "The last I heard you had some ambitions to become a teacher yourself. Is that still true?"

"Uh, yes," Ken had said, momentarily shaken, for this inquiry didn't appear in any of the conversations he had composed.

"You have some of the qualifications," Professor Wentworth had said, "and one serious temperamental defect: intellectual arrogance. I've noticed it in the classroom: when one of the other men commits a blunder, even if it's only a slip of the tongue, you are always the first to pounce. You show off at other people's expense."

"That may be," Ken had said, brandishing the offending paper. "Is this how I'm to be cured of my ways?"

"That grade was meant as an object lesson, yes," Professor Wentworth had admitted.

"I see!" Ken had sneered. "Am I being punished for my arrogance in class or my arrogance in disagreeing with your opinions of Henry VI?"

"I gave you a passing mark," Professor Wentworth had said, "because there was some originality to your defense of Henry VI. Unfortunately, you had been asked to discuss the policies of his grandfather, Henry IV. You muddled the Roman numerals. And that's where arrogance comes in, Davenport. Will you, I wonder, have the forebearance to give a passing mark to a student who has carelessly misread a question?"

The trouble with such episodes was not merely that they left him feeling two feet tall, not merely that they left him holding yards and yards of unused eloquence, but that they had no effect on the next time around except to make him flog his wits all the harder to be sure no possibility had been overlooked. Experience was a bum teacher. Once pointed on a course of action he was no whit less likely to start grinding out imaginary constructions of what was going to happen.

And it was all the worse when the course of action was one which he had inflicted on himself, for then he was burdened with all the additional possibilities that would arise if he changed his mind and decided to do nothing. The need to confront his mother, demand some accounting of her conduct, existed only in his own head. She seemed comfortable. His father was happy. (His grandmother was livid with outrage, but that would have been true even if his mother had somehow come home trailing clouds of moral glory.) There was no public demand for him to speak up; on the contrary, it would be easier for everybody if he held his peace, acquiesced in the status quo, went along with the tide.

Yet that way was cowardice and hypocrisy. It *was* unfair that his father's happiness should be based on a mischance. It *was* unjust that his mother's treachery should be glossed over with charm and silence. And above all, it was all wrong that the new relationship between Ken and his mother should be founded on deceit: in the long run this could only lead to distrust and disappointment for both of them.

Something had to be said, if only to clear the air.

Framing the conversation, however, wasn't easy. He wanted to maintain a tone of sophisticated objectivity. He would have liked to hold up his mother's actions for inspection impaled upon a pin of mordant wit, but even in his imagination his emotions kept getting in the way, and before he knew it he would be thundering away like a revivalist preacher denouncing scarlet women. And that would never do. Rather than fall into this trap he would have said nothing—but this, in turn, led him to picturing years of stilted dialogues while he and his mother went pussyfooting around the unmentionable subject of her six-year absence.

He was caught on this treadmill of the imagination when his mother discovered him and remarked on his brooding countenance: "You're looking out of sorts with the world."

"I'm feeling like the Spartan youth," he said; this was one of his prepared lines, but it didn't necessarily have to lead anywhere.

"The one with the fox gnawing at his vitals?" she asked, settling onto the other side of the sofa with more grace (he couldn't help noticing) than any girl he knew.

"No, not him," he said uncommunicatively, still uncertain how far he wanted to commit himself.

"Then you must be somewhere in the Helen of Troy story. She was from Sparta originally, wasn't she?"

"Someone's been making fun of me," he said sullenly.

"Not at all. I quite enjoy classical compliments, or at least I prefer them to being compared to that brainless movie star I'm supposed to look like. Did Helen have a son? I only have a hazy memory of a daughter."

"She got all the publicity, but there was a son too," Ken said. "His name was Megapenthes. Nobody paid him any attention."

"Then he must have had an uncommonly tranquil life for someone in a Greek legend. The main characters, as I recall, were usually occupied with mayhem and incest. Just how do you resemble this young man?"

"Our mothers come and go in an irregular way."

"Yes, I see," she said thoughtfully. "Then the comparison with Helen of Troy wasn't a compliment at all, was it? Your Uncle Alan made a remark in passing, and at the time I'm afraid I completely missed the point."

"The comparison wouldn't have been made of a homely woman."

"But it's not my looks that upset you," his mother said. "If we're going to discuss my sins I'd better have my cigarettes; there are some on the mantlepiece."

He stood up, resisting the impulse to flee, knowing he could not face his cowardice if he ran away from this opportunity. But he had no idea how to begin with someone who spoke of her sins so affectionately and cosily, as she might have said "my hats" or "my gloves," and not as anything she might be ashamed of. He threw out another of his prepared lines: "I know it's not my place to pass judgments."

"People generally say that just before passing a few, but you're quite right," she said. "I was sure you'd be intelligent enough to see that, though I don't understand what you mean by your 'place.'"

"I suppose I'm too young. And your son." He brought her pack of cigarettes and sat down again.

"It's not age or relationship that should stop us from passing judgments on other people, it's lack of enough information. And we never have enough."

"Some of us don't have any at all," he said.

"Ask me anything you like," she invited him affectionately. "I promise to answer as honestly as I possibly can."

Ken took a deep breath. "You wouldn't be here, would you, if Saint-Euverte were still alive?"

His mother lit a cigarette, frowning slightly. "That may be true," she said at last, "But I can't see that it's going to get us very far. It's a metaphysical proposition. It would be just as valid, and just as useful, for me to point out that if I hadn't met George *you* wouldn't be here."

"But you didn't really want to come back."

"What makes you say that?" she asked. "Of course I did! There were some very appealing reasons for staying, yet I came. So I must have wanted to come."

"Not until afterwards—after Saint-Euverte was killed. Before that you didn't want to come. Don't you see what I'm getting at?"

"Not very clearly," said his mother. "It sounds as if you want history rewritten for your personal benefit. I gather you would feel a great deal more comfortable if I'd grown tired of Pierre, thrown him over, and come back of my own accord. But his death prevented that from happening."

"Were you thinking of coming back?" Ken asked hopefully.

"Oh, dear," she said. "It's only a few seconds since I promised to be honest and already you're asking me to break that promise. And I shan't. No—I'd thought of it from time to time, but not just then. The day Pierre was killed I had no plans for coming home."

"So if he hadn't been, you'd still be there."

"I expect so. And that distresses you?"

"It makes it seem as if you're here under false pretences. As if you didn't really belong."

"Does it? I'm sorry for that. You know, the person entirely responsible for this muddle is your father."

"Dad!" he exclaimed indignantly.

"Oh, absolutely. It's all water under the bridge, so we mustn't hold him to blame, but it's all his fault. I kept urging him to get a divorce, but he never did."

"What difference could that have made?"

"Quite a bit in one way. Stop and think what the situation would have been. If I'd been divorced, the chances are Pierre and I would have married. I can't be certain of that, because the question never came up, but it seems probable. Not that this would have altered our lives in the slightest: there's no reason to doubt that Pierre would have been killed in the Grand Prix, just as he was. And what then? George would still have come rushing over to find out if I needed help, I think we can agree on that. A divorce wouldn't change *his* character or his generosity."

"Of course not," Ken said.

"Well, there we would have been on the romantic Côte d'Azur with exactly the same emotions at work, and all you have to imagine is a whirlwind courtship of a respectable widow. It's a perfectly ordinary story that way, isn't it?"

"I suppose it is," said Ken, dazed.

"So here I'd be sitting, just the same," said his mother, "but under those circumstances you wouldn't have been able to feel that I didn't belong, would you?"

"No, I guess not."

"Or that I was here under false pretences?"

"No."

"Yet the only difference is that George could never bring himself to go through a few legal formalities. And I really don't think you should let yourself be so upset by that. No doubt he had reasons that seemed good to him."

"Yes, well, but . . . I hadn't thought of it like that," he finished weakly, lightheaded from the sudden shift of perspective. He felt a great sense of relief, as if he had shed some great weight, even while suspecting that his mother had performed a sleight-of-tongue with the facts, and a flaw in her reasoning might become apparent later on. Yet he was bound to acknowledge that he would have found nothing odd in it if his parents had met and remarried after a more conventional separation, and to make a fuss about mere conventions was naive and stuffy. The shock was in learning that this was what he had been doing. "You really are outrageous," he told his mother, aware that this phrase, if spoken a few minutes back, would have been sharp and accusing, whereas now his tone was indulgent, almost admiring. "We were starting to discuss your sins, as you put it, and so far the only person at fault is Dad."

"Not even he," replied his mother. "He couldn't foresee

your reactions half a dozen years later. That's often the way with good intentions, isn't it?"

"It's a convenient philosophy you have there," Ken said. "If your intentions are good, then when people get hurt that's just an unpredictable by-product."

"You see half my point, anyway," she replied. "I've always believed that people can have very little understanding of the consequences of their actions, and I'm speaking of ordinary, decent people, not the few beastly ones. But quite as much suffering is caused by altruism and self-sacrifice as by simple selfishness."

"Even more convenient!" he jeered. "When you went off with Saint-Euverte you might have been doing us a world of good, for all you knew!"

"Is that as absurd as it sounds?" she asked. "Obviously I left because I'd fallen in love with Pierre, not as an act of philanthropy towards this household. My behavior was selfish, admittedly, but did that necessarily mean the results would be harmful? You were bound to be unhappy and embittered, and that was unfortunate. Instinctively we want our children to be happy. Even when we know that too much happiness makes for flabbiness of character we lack the will power to frustrate them on principle. But you weren't a child any longer, you were nearly fifteen, away at school most of the year, and more in need of your father's influence than mine. I made you a present of his undivided attention for six crucial years. Either despite your sufferings or because of them you have grown into an extremely appealing, well-balanced young man. Can you be absolutely sure you haven't profited by my absence?"

"There can't be an answer to a question like that."

"There's even less of one to the question of what might have happened if I'd stayed in residence as your mother. I could easily have made a fearful mess of your adolescence; it's something mothers frequently do to their sons, you know."

"More and more outrageous," he said, laughing. "We now seem to have established that I should be grateful to you for going."

"That would be uncomplimentary to me and disrespectful to your sufferings," she replied. "Of course you resented my leaving. But now you're old enough to see it may not have been an unmixed evil."

"Did we have conversations like this before you left?" he asked. "I might have missed you less for the relief at not having my ideas turned topsy-turvy every few minutes."

"You don't have conversations with a fourteen-year-old boy," she said. "You listen to his explanations of why you don't understand him."

He laughed again, and then sobered abruptly. "I'm curious about how far you can go with this sort of rationalization," he said. "For the sake of the argument I'm willing to accept the possibility that you did my character a lot of good, and in any case, as you say, that's water under the bridge. But I don't think you can pretend you went off under the illusion that you were doing Dad any kindness."

"Of course not," she agreed.

"You hurt him very badly."

"I told you that I'd fallen in love with Pierre," said his mother. "I had no intention of falling in love with him, but it happened. Once a situation like that comes into existence, people are bound to be hurt one way or another. I don't mean this as a rationalization, Ken, because I'm not saying it affected my conduct, but if I had stayed on here like a dutiful wife, while loving Pierre and wishing I'd gone off with him, your father would have been hurt just as badly and perhaps even more cruelly, since he would have had to live with the symptoms of my discontent."

"You'd have got over that quickly enough."

"Why do you say that?"

"Because it's what they're always telling us," Ken replied. " 'Infatuation; it's only physical, it will pass; time takes care of these things, you'll see.' What I don't see is why these arguments shouldn't apply even more strongly to older people."

"Perhaps they should never be uttered at all," his mother replied. "We look back on our lives, most of us, and we see there was a time when we fell in and out of love violently a dozen times or more, always with the greatest possible anguish yet always recovering in the end, so we speak a little too glibly of puppy love. But things quiet down as we get older. And we reach a state of deceptive calm where our hearts seem to be under perfect control. I'm being quite honest with you, Ken: if Pierre de Saint-Euverte hadn't appeared I might have lived out my life as the most conventional of suburban housewives."

"I doubt that," he murmured.

"The most faithful of wives, then. But Pierre did appear. And I fell in love with him with an intensity which quite overwhelmed the habit of loving your father."

"And that's precisely what I can't understand!" he broke in.

"What is?"

"How you *could* have fallen in love with Saint-Euverte."

"You never met him," his mother observed. "You didn't even reply to my suggestion that you spend last summer with us in Cagnes."

"That wouldn't have mattered," he said. "Oh, I know he was very handsome and attractive and glamorous and all that. A crack sportsman with a title in front of his name. I can imagine a schoolgirl falling flat on her face in front of somebody like that. But you were hardly a schoolgirl, and you were married, and most important of all you were married to Dad. I don't care what you say about Saint-Euverte. I won't believe he was a more decent person than Dad or a finer person than Dad."

"He was entirely different," she conceded.

"Does different mean better?" he asked sarcastically. "To tell the truth, I was shocked by your invitation—as if I could have been that disloyal! But Dad wanted me to go, urged me to go, did you know that? That's the sort of person he is. Do you realize that for six years, in spite of everything, he never said one word about you that wasn't nice? And wouldn't let other people, either."

"I'm well aware of your father's merits," she said, "but I shan't let you make too much of that one. We all know people who rant on about the odious qualities of a former wife or husband who hasn't worked out, but this is sheer vulgarity. You can't insult the memory of a love without insulting your own good taste. I'd be greatly astonished if George *had* been vulgar, so I refuse to admire him just because he wasn't."

"All right, perhaps that wasn't the best example," Ken said. "If you're well aware of Dad's merits, you know what I mean. Nobody could be more tolerant or more understanding. I've seen lots of other fathers in action and there isn't one who can touch him for being willing to listen to the other person's point of view. He looks like a brute and he's the gentlest, wisest, most sensitive man I know. A few years ago I'd gone all the way to thinking he was a saint. I suppose that's an exaggeration: there's nothing goody-goody about him. But comparing him with other men it's not so far from the truth."

"And it's difficult to imagine anyone walking out on such a man," said his mother, lighting another cigarette.

"Very difficult," he said sternly.

"I'm glad you've grown so close to him," she said. "Now you can credit me with appreciating him as much as you do. After all, I've been married to him for . . . twenty-two years, and although I went away for a while I did come back. There were other possibilities. So if I faltered for a time you have to make allowance for a certain waywardness in the female spirit. It can get to be a strain, you see, living up to all that virtue."

"Are you being funny?" Ken asked suspiciously.

"Not in the least. It's true—lamentable, if you like, but quite true. The other person's virtues become your responsibilities, from fear of failing him. Haven't you ever disliked yourself for something you've done, knowing your father would be disappointed in you?"

"Of course, all too often."

"Wondered whether you deserved such a father?"

"Yes."

"Then you have some idea of what I mean," she said. "Feeling always just a bit unworthy can become wearing after fifteen years or so. Being understood *all* the time is no pleasure, especially to a woman—not that we want to feel mysterious, but we need a little privacy. Then, tolerance and wisdom are very admirable, and it's awful that one should get to the point of longing for the sound of a good, healthy irrational prejudice. But it happens. There's a streak of capriciousness in me, or there used to be: I trust I've outgrown it by now. And no doubt it made me susceptible to somebody who wasn't quite so gentle and sensitive."

"Yes, I think perhaps I see," he said.

"As I said before, Pierre was a wholly different sort of man. He had his faults, lots of faults. But he wasn't a saint."

One of the advantages of age, thought George Davenport as he mixed cocktails at the living-room bar, was that even in the grip of a new passion you could accept the physical separations enforced by social intercourse. Probably it was because the sexual drive had become more focused: you knew exactly where you were going, to bed, so the lesser sensualities became less important: there was no need to be touching, constantly touching, or at least the need was satisfied by a glance of intimacy or a smile across the room; parties were a postponement rather than a torment. Whereas with youngsters like Ken and Jessie it seemed a cruelty to leave them sitting yards apart. At that age (George remembered it vividly) sexuality was still diffused and romanticized: there were untold ecstasies in a touch of shoulders, a brush of hands, and to be deprived of these ecstasies was starvation. When Ken and Jessie looked at one another their glances were like long-distance caresses. When Jessie sat expectantly with an unlighted cigarette it wasn't as a girl enforcing her feminine prerogatives but as a girl making an opportunity for the communion of fingertips. The two of them would have been so much happier sitting side by side, where knees might meet in accidental reassurance, where even without touching each would have sensed the other's warmth. But that way, of course, a general conversation would have been quite impossible: you never could have counted on more than the residue of their attention. Presumably this was why Eleanor had chosen to sit in the middle of the sofa, obliging Jessie to sit beside her and relegating Ken to a distant armchair.

Apart from the flow of sensuality between the youngsters, there were other undercurrents in the living room. Ken and his mother were far more relaxed with one another; in fact, the change in Ken was extraordinary. This evening he was visibly delighted with Eleanor, laughing at her, teasing her, and whenever she made one of her more Eleanoresque remarks looking in quick pride to his girl to see if she, too, appreciated the fun.

Jessie's answering glances were always loving and bright, and in all probability this was satisfactory to Ken. George doubted that his son was acute enough, as yet, to perceive that all was not easy between Eleanor and Jessie. Women were born adepts at concealing their hostilities when they chose to, and it took years of experience for a man to learn to recognize the symptoms. When Jessie had hesitated slightly before replying to Eleanor's conventional expression of regret that Laura had been unable to come, Ken would have noticed nothing but shyness or perhaps embarrassment; George had known that his wife's manner, choice of words and tone of voice were all being searched for provocation. So Jessie had come, as was to be expected, with a bit of a chip on her shoulder. As a rule Eleanor could be relied upon to dispel any strain in jig time, but this evening she found a reason not to take the trouble. There was no disdain in her amusement at the youngsters' banter about their tennis rivalry, but a connoisseur of her reactions could be sure she had found something in Jessie's conduct to deplore. He would hear of it later, no doubt.

On the surface, all was amiable. Eleanor had promptly invited Jessie to call her by her first name, and Jessie had responded with a display of good manners befitting a young lady: showing a polite interest in the views of the older generation. Had Eleanor noticed many changes in Bradley's Bluff, she wondered, after such a long absence?

"Not really," said Eleanor. "I can't get excited by the way the Hendersons' split-leaf maple has grown. It's not so much changes that catch your attention as the old familiar things, seen with a fresh eye. The shutters on the houses, for example."

"I know exactly what you mean," Jessie said, defending the freshness of her own eye. "Aren't some of the colors simply hideous?"

"You can find that anywhere," Eleanor said. "But have you remarked that most of the shutters are put up inside out?"

"How can you tell?" Ken asked.

"By the angle of the louvers," said his mother. "If the shutters were ever closed, the sunlight or the rain would come streaming right through into the room inside."

"They're not meant to be closed," George put in. "On some of the newer houses they don't even have hinges: they're simply nailed to the facing of the house. When Paul decided to do his own repainting, I remember he had the devil's own time with the ones on the second floor."

"Oh, I know," said Eleanor. "It's just something you notice when you're accustomed to shutters that work. And it seems symbolic of something or other."

Evidently deciding that the symbolism could not be flattering to Bradley's Bluff, Jessie shifted to inquiring what Eleanor had thought of France. George was pleased with the girl's tact: this was a topic that could keep Eleanor happy indefinitely. Having served all the others, he took a fortifying swallow of his own drink and then mixed up an old-fashioned.

"Where are you going?" Eleanor asked as he started to leave the room.

"To see if I can't lure the Mother Superior from her retreat," he replied. He went through the hall, the dining room (where the table was set for four), and looked into his mother's room. The high-intensity bedside lamp illuminated the lapboard across his mother's knees: she was involved in one of her complicated, multi-pack solitaires.

"It's pleasant to see a human face again," she remarked sweetly. A quick glimpse must have been sufficient pleasure, however, for her attention returned instantly to the cards. "Sometimes I feel that my body could lie here for two or three days before anyone discovered it."

"There's a variety of human faces in the living room," George said. "Why don't you join us?"

"I've better things to do with my time: I am reconciling my soul to God," said Mrs. Davenport, putting a miniature black five on a miniature red six.

"You're premature," said George, "They've just found a wonder drug that cures perversity. I've brought you a drink to celebrate the good news."

"Thank you," she said, taking the glass with a bony claw. "I presume that Ken's bouncy hoyden is out there, but I don't hear the metallic clatter of her mother's executive voice."

"Laura Sydrock couldn't make it this evening. She's dining elsewhere."

"She's dining on sour grapes, I suspect. You should have married that woman when you had a chance, George. She's not Helen of Troy, I admit, but she's more predictable. If Laura isn't at home you know for sure she's at a committee meeting. I should think that a man with your experience would find that thought appealing."

"I'm satisfied with things as they are," said George.

"But will that last?" asked Mrs. Davenport. "With Eleanor, one never can tell just how long she'll be staying."

"You might as well resign yourself to the idea that she's back for good."

"I've tried," said Mrs. Davenport. "The struggle has exhausted me."

"You aren't being sensible," said George. "Lying in bed all the time, like this, is very bad for your circulation."

"It's the lesser of two evils," she replied. "Watching Helen of Troy holding court in my living room would be even worse for my blood pressure."

"But you would enlarge the circle of your victims," he said temptingly, aware that he rarely got anywhere by appealing to his mother's better nature. "This way you have to wait for the flies to come to the spider."

"Seldom has a dying mother been so delicately flattered by her only child."

"Besides, your self-imposed prostration makes a hell of a strain on the household," George said, openly coming to the point. "Martha is beginning to complain."

"Is she?" murmured Mrs. Davenport, giving a little coo of triumph as she turned up a useful ace. "If you are quite positive our good fairy is back to stay, what do we need Martha for? I thought you were keeping her on as a sort of insurance policy, in case Eleanor left for New Zealand with some passing sailor."

"There's a lot of work in a house this size," George said. "If people are going to play at being invalids it becomes intolerable."

"When I was young and we lived in Albany," said Mrs. Davenport, "I attended to a house twice as large and spent my afternoons playing auction bridge. I appreciate that we have fallen upon degenerate times, but even so this place couldn't tax the energies of two healthy women. Am I to infer that Eleanor's only contribution to the household is as a decorative ornament?"

"Of course not. But that doesn't mean that we want to lose Martha."

"I don't know that I agree. If Cathy is any example of what happens to women of that family when they have too much time on their hands, you might be wise to keep Eleanor as busy as possible. Preferably indoors. And refrain from inviting foreign noblemen to the house."

"Your sense of humor will get you into trouble one of these days," said George. "Suppose you were left to Eleanor's mercies. After the welcome you've given her, I wouldn't blame her in the slightest if she left you here to starve."

"There is always the telephone," said Mrs. Davenport. "I could ask visiting friends to smuggle in crusts of bread when they came. That would provide a stimulating new topic of conversation in Bradley's Bluff."

"Mother, I don't think you're taking me seriously," George complained. "If you keep on like this much longer, it's all too likely that Martha is going to quit. I mean it."

"Some French cooking will make a pleasant change," said Mrs. Davenport. "You can tell Eleanor that I am partial to *coq au vin*."

"I finally realize what Saint-Euverte's fatal attraction must have been," said George, losing patience. "He was an orphan."

"Now isn't that exasperating?" asked his mother. "It was going along so nicely, and it's all spoiled by that wretched queen of hearts."

5.

At times the social instinct of the female was a nuisance. As soon as dinner was over Ken was ready to leave—they had eaten so late it was already dark outside—but Jessie's sense of the fitness of things made her oblivious to his pleading glances. First she had to volunteer to help with the clearing up, which was stark madness, since if the offer had been accepted they would have been trapped there for hours. Fortunately his mother declined (permitting Ken to breathe again), and even suggested that they were probably eager to run along. This should have been enough for any reasonable person, but evidently the mysterious rules that girls lived by still weren't satisfied. Refusing to show the least impatience to be gone, Jessie promptly lighted another cigarette, and ten minutes more chitchat had to be endured before she would permit them to make a leisurely, graceful exit.

Once they were out the door, still in the shadow of the house, she spun into his arms and they clung, kissing, making up for the privation of the previous hours. Ken slowly ran his hands up and down her flanks, up her ribs, feeling the sideways swell of the breasts flattened against his chest, deliberately allowing himself no other caresses for the time being, enjoying the small masochism of postponement.

"I've missed you," she whispered finally. "But I've got some bad news."

"What is it?"

"Wait a second," she said primly, leading them towards the car, out of earshot of the house. "I was telling fibs in there," she explained. "Mother didn't really go out this evening; she's at home with a sick headache. So there's not much point in our going back there till you're ready to kiss me good night."

"Oh, damn!" Ken said, stopping short. It was the recurrent exasperation, the reminder that their lives were still not their own. In the world of the automobile there was no shortage of privacy, as such, but apart from its other inconveniences the automobile held a shabby atmosphere of more adolescent grapplings. Bradley's Bluff, landscaped to its last inch, seemed designed for the frustration of young lovers. For comfortable privacy they were still dependent on the comings and goings of inconsiderate parents. "Laura might have gone up to her bedroom," he said, with visions of the large, luxurious sofa in the Sydrock living room.

"We could drive by and see," Jessie said without much hope. "Mummy can't read with these headaches, and I expect you remember where the television set is. Think of trying to seduce a girl under the eyes of *The Man from U.N.C.L.E.*"

"The Club is out," Ken said, reflecting that there was one disadvantage to his mother's return, anyway, in that his own home would be less available than before. "I don't see much point in going to Barbara's. And by now the best seats at the movies are filled with juvenile delinquents with sticky fingers."

"There's the Tavern," Jessie said, "in case you feel like drowning your sorrows."

"Who needs alcohol?" he asked. "My kind of intoxication wears a gray skirt and a red-and-white blouse and a lacy white bra and—"

"A leopardskin chastity belt."

"Genuine leopard?" he asked with interest.

"Nylon," she said apologetically. "Come on, boy, you're drooling. And we might as well resign ourselves to the four-wheeled playground for this evening."

They got into the car and there realized that several minutes had gone by without kisses. They made up for lost time so enthusiastically that Ken, coming up for breath a little later, saw that some sobering distraction was needed if he was to drive away from there without being a menace to evening strollers. "Truce," he said. "In another moment it might occur to someone to wonder why the car won't start."

"Out of gas," Jessie murmured.

"Stop that," said Ken. "Show some respect for the respectability of Elmwood Drive. Nice girls sit at the far end of the seat with their hands in their laps."

"I used to be like that. Somebody corrupted me."

"Behave yourself, we've got to get out of here. Make with the bright chatter, can't you? Tell me what you think of Mother, now you've seen her in the flesh."

"Oh, she's simply fantastic," Jessie said, leaning back. "I hope to God I still look that good when I'm forty."

"Everybody puts all the emphasis on her beauty, and I don't think that's fair to her," he objected. "Looks are just a matter of luck."

"At my age it's luck," said Jessie. "At hers, it's also good management."

"I know what you mean," he said, "but largely it's being born with a good bone structure, and that's nothing but luck. Anyway, Mother isn't *just* beautiful, that's what I'm getting at. She's not someone you just sit and admire and then wince when she opens her mouth, the way you do with Mrs. Yates."

"Mrs. Yates is fifteen-watts," Jessie agreed. "You can't tell whether she misses the point of stories or keeps from laughing so she won't get lines."

"Whereas Mother is an unusual person in her own right," said Ken, starting up the car. "She'll be every bit as remarkable when her looks are all gone. Doesn't she have a wonderful sense of humor? And what I can't get used to is that topsy-turvy way she has of looking at things."

"Well, that's partly exaggeration," Jessie said.

"She doesn't pose," Ken insisted.

"No, but she exaggerates. The way I do when I say there were thousands of people at a party, meaning there were more than twenty. Take that business of the shutters. She probably noticed one house where they were turned around, and it caught her fancy. So it came out that most of the houses in Bradley's Bluff were like that, and there was something terribly symbolic about it."

"No, I don't think so," Ken said. "A lot of women would do that, but Mother has an odd sort of integrity all her own, you can feel it. If she said most of the houses, then I'll bet a lot of them are that way."

"It doesn't make sense," said Jessie. "You'll see in the morning that I'm right."

"You're a stubborn little witch," he told her. By this time they were on Walnut Road, where the houses were not so far apart and were set somewhat closer to the road. On impulse, Ken cut the motor and let the car coast silently to a stop in front of Mr. Thompson's place. They stared at the front of the house. There was some light from a nearby streetlamp, and it seemed reasonable to hope that as their eyes adjusted they would see in more detail, but the shutters remained featureless dark oblongs against the white clapboard. Impelled at the same instant, they slid out of the car and crossed the patch of lawn—just as the front door opened and Mr. Thompson emerged to take his elderly spaniel for its evening airing. The spaniel spotted them at once, and set up an indignant, asthmatic yapping. Mr. Thompson came padding across the grass, peering in the dim light.

"Good evening, Jessie; good evening, Ken," he said hospitably. "Is Halloween early this year?"

"We were looking at your shutters," Jessie explained.

"They are nice shutters," said Mr. Thompson. "They look even better by daylight."

"We wanted to see whether they're inside out or not," Ken said.

Mr. Thompson looked at them. "You're nice kids," he said. "I know this marijuana stuff is in fashion, and it's stuffy to disapprove, but I still don't think it's a good idea."

Seeing no point in giving up now that the worst had happened, Ken reached out and felt. "Mother was absolutely right," he announced.

"Where you are standing," said Mr. Thompson, "is a bed of *anemone japonica* that would have looked nice in the autumn. Of course, planting them there was a mistake if people are going to drop by every evening to fondle our shutters."

"Sorry," said Ken, "but they really are on backwards, you know. See how the slats are angled? If you closed the shutters the sun would still come right in."

"Can either of you think of a single reason," Mr. Thompson inquired, "why anyone in Bradley's Bluff would want to close his shutters?"

"If you were going to be away for a few weeks," Jessie suggested.

"What!" said Mr. Thompson, "and inform every passing burglar that the place was empty? We have one of those electric-eye gadgets that turns on a couple of lamps when it gets dark outside."

"There might be an exceptionally bad storm," Ken said.

"We have triple-track storm windows for storms," said Mr. Thompson, "and venetian blinds for the sun. The shutters are how they should be: if the slats faced the other way the walls of the house would get filthy behind there. I've never heard anything so ridiculous in all my life. Come along, Caesar, walky-walky time."

Man and dog marched off into the night; Ken and Jessie went back to the car feeling that they had survived a grotesque episode without loss of dignity. "At least we succeeded in proving you were wrong," Ken said triumphantly.

"Not necessarily," Jessie replied. "It could just be that Mr. Thompson's house was the one your mother noticed."

"Would you like to try a few more houses?" he challenged her.

"People might think we had a shutter fetish," she said. "I can wait until morning, but I intend to keep count."

"Anyway, I wasn't thinking of shutters when I spoke of Mother's topsy-turvy approach to things," he said, starting the car in motion again. "I tried raking her over the coals this afternoon."

"Your mother? Whatever for?"

"A number of things were bothering me. Mostly about the way she sauntered back into our lives as though no explanations or apologies were called for."

"I thought you rather admired her for that."

"I did and I didn't," Ken said, turning in the direction of the larger properties. "You might have guessed I wasn't satisfied from what I said about our not having been wrong, trying to make a match between Dad and your mother, until Saint-Euverte got himself killed."

"Did you say that?"

"On the terrace at the Club yesterday. You never listen."

"I remember the remark now," Jessie said meekly.

"Well, that made it seem as if she'd been sort of tossed in our laps, willy-nilly. And I couldn't understand why she'd gone off in the first place, if she was the person she appeared to be. Different things. Anyway, we couldn't go along indefinitely pretending that nothing unusual had happened.

Somebody had to do something to clear the air. I was just waiting for a good moment, and this afternoon I tackled her. Perfectly straightforwardly."

"That must have been exciting," Jessie said. "I wish I'd been behind the curtains."

"You wonder how most mothers would react in a situation like that," Ken said speculatively.

"Fortunately, it's not a common problem," Jessie said.

"I imagine most of them would get flustered, don't you? Or indignant at being faced with a lot of impertinent questions. Not Mother. She answered anything I felt like asking, and we discussed the whole affair right from the beginning. She wasn't a bit embarrassed."

"No, Eleanor wouldn't be embarrased," Jessie said. "I'll bet she convinced you that whatever she did couldn't be helped, and if anybody was to blame it was somebody else."

"Why do you say that?"

"Because it's the sort of thing a man would find topsy-turvy. I find it perfectly natural."

"Well, you're giving it the wrong twist, I think. Oh, damn it all!" The dead end of Hickory Lane, where the nearest streetlamp was hidden by a bend in the road, was already taken by a darkened but not unoccupied Chevy. "That's Joe's car. Is he still going with Sally?"

"Not since he discovered that high-school girls will go to almost any lengths for a college man," Jessie said. "Some child is learning the loopholes in the statutory rape laws."

"He's a dirty old man," Ken said disapprovingly.

"The Boyds are in Europe," Jessie said. "Hemlock Terrace ought to be pretty quiet."

"Okay," he said, backing into a driveway to turn around. "No, Mother doesn't waste time making excuses for herself or trying to put the blame on someone else. She faces the responsibility for her actions, and she faces the facts. Perhaps more clearly than most people do. But she can make you see that even the simplest fact can be looked at from several points of view."

"Good for her," said Jessie. "I've been trying to teach you that for years."

"But she's not a spoiled brat who hates to lose an argument. The surprising thing is that with her it's all part of a well-thought-out philosophy. You wouldn't have expected Mother to be someone with a philosophical turn of mind, would you?"

"No," said Jessie.

"Well, she is. Not in the sense of playing with profound theories of the universe. It's a personal philosophy, a philosophy of living, very down to earth and utterly consistent." He stopped the car in a shaded stretch of Hemlock Terrace and switched off the motor and the lights, still deep in thought, trying to sum up the essence of his mother in a phrase and finding it difficult. "Anybody can look for the reasons why somebody acted the way he did. Mother's tolerance goes further than that: she hunts for the reasons why he *didn't* behave some other way, if you follow me. I wouldn't have thought anyone could be more broad-minded than Dad, but I think Mother may be."

"Perhaps her tolerance has to cover more territory," said Jessie. "I have a question."

"Shoot," said Ken, eager to proselytize.

"Did we come here to talk about your parents?"

"What else did you have in mind?" he asked. "I hope you're not one of those unnatural girls who enjoy carnal intimacies."

"To be quite truthful, I can't remember," Jessie said. "So much of my young life has been spent riding around in a car with a young man with a new-found Oedipus complex."

"I talk too much," Ken declared. "I shan't say another word." He was able to keep to his promise for several minutes, until a profound sense of grievance prompted him to say "What the hell?"

"It unhooks in front, you dimwit," said Jessie.

6.

"There!" said Eleanor, returning from the kitchen, leaving the rumble of the dishwasher in the distance behind her. "It's been an instructive day. Cathy was here this morning. I've finally remet Jessie Sydrock. And this afternoon I learned that you are a saint."

George laid aside the evening paper. "It's high time your eyes were opened to the truth," he said. "The coffee's still hot. Would you like a liqueur to go with whatever is left?"

"Some Grand Marnier, if there is any," she said, adjusting an improperly closed curtain.

"I expect there is." He crouched in front of the bar, shifting about the bottles on the bottom shelf. "I gather you've been talking with Ken."

"He taxed me with my sins."

"That was bound to happen. I told you your return couldn't pass without comment. But you seem to have come through the ordeal with flying colors."

"He was terribly sweet about it," Eleanor said. "I see now why you said he's a bit on the earnest side, but I was able to answer most of his perplexities without straining the truth. The only awkward moment was discovering your beatification. I'd hoped the two of you would grow closer together, and I was delighted to see how much he admires you. But I hadn't expected sainthood."

"It seemed like a good idea that he hold onto some illusions about one member of the family at least."

"I didn't disturb them," said Eleanor. "In fact, I'm afraid I may have left him with the impression that my main reason for going off with Pierre was that I had grown to feel unworthy of you."

"I know how that sort of thing happens," George said. "One's determination to be honest with the young breaks down in the face of their idealism." He took her a small glass of the amber liqueur.

"Thank you," she said. "It wasn't entirely untruthful, though. You *are* a bit tiresome, George, the way you persist in seeing the other side of every question and finding good qualities in the most deplorable people. In a sense you are too good-natured. But you are not a saint, and I would think you must have found the imposture wearisome at times."

"It had its inconvenient aspects," George confessed. "Some while back, for example, there was a redheaded divorcée who might have repaid cultivation. But the propriety of my life was too well fixed: there was no plausible way of breaking loose. A devoted son is a more effective guardian than a jealous wife."

"Would this have been early last summer by any chance?" Eleanor asked.

"About then, yes."

"Then she was the reason you were so eager that Ken accept my invitation to come to France."

"I also wanted him to see you again before he got any older," George said. "But I had hopes of putting my freedom to good use."

"You realize that your efforts to persuade him to go were held up to me this afternoon as a particular instance of the nobility of your nature?"

"I'm not surprised," he said. "Once your reputation for saintliness is established, saintly explanations are found for almost anything you do."

"It's more comfortable being an acknowledged sinner,"

Eleanor said, "but there's something capricious about the way these reputations are formed. It was chance that made Pierre a Frenchman, after all, so that my only choice lay between giving him up altogether or tearing my life apart by going off with him. Whereas Peggy Dunstable had a convenient apartment in New York; you could talk of working late and taking imaginary business trips while your affair with her went on for almost two years, without the slighest effect on your standing as a pillar of respectability."

"After all this time I should think Peggy Dunstable could be decently forgotten," George said mildly.

"As we're too grown up for recriminations I don't see why we need to be mealy-mouthed about past history. And Peggy is a part of your history, as Pierre is a part of mine. You were very much in love with her."

"I thought I was," he said.

"It comes to the same thing. I'm not ashamed of falling in love with Pierre, and I think I would be a little shocked if you were ashamed of loving Peggy."

"I haven't your talent for finding that errors are disguised truths," he said, "and I'm ashamed of something or other. Probably that it took me so long to recognize that she wasn't the sort of woman I thought she was."

"That was hardly Peggy's fault," Eleanor observed. "A woman can generally identify the set of illusions her man has fallen in love with, and it's only natural for her to try to please."

"I'm not saying Peggy was to blame for anything," he said with a familiar sense of bewilderment. Conversations with Eleanor had a way of skidding as wildly as a car coming onto an unexpected stretch of ice, until you ended up facing in some surprising direction. They had begun with Eleanor being taxed with her sins and in no time at all, by seemingly logical steps, they arrived at discussing an ancient lapse of his own—so ancient that it rarely entered his thoughts nowadays.

He had been in his late forties: a susceptible age, they said, for well-domesticated husbands. It was terribly flattering to feel irresistible to a girl twenty years younger, a girl just out of college, a ravishing, dark-haired little wench who could have taken her pick of eligible suitors and preferred instead a hole-and-corner affair with him. Nor had there ever been the slightest question that Peggy was out to "catch" him, to break up his marriage. She was too proud of her independence. He had thought of her as a pagan child, deliciously sensual, uncomplicated and happy. It had been an intoxicating, euphoric period. The euphoria was shaken a bit the first time he had gone to her with a worry weighing on his mind: she simply wasn't interested. In fact, she was a little impatient with him for wasting her time with problems that were no concern of hers. The cheerful lover was welcome any time, but not the moody man.

Gradually he came to appreciate that what he had taken for an overflowing love of life was almost the exact opposite. Underneath the pagan was a thoroughly neurotic girl, frightened of responsibility in any form. The appeal of an older, well-married man lay in the very safety he represented: he could make no claims on her, he had to accept whatever she felt like giving. Younger men were more demanding in any sustained relationship; they tended to become possessive, expected her to be intensely interested in them and staged emotional scenes when she wasn't, they become jealous, and sometimes even tried to lure her into that bottomless pit of responsibilities: marriage and children.

Having terrified herself out of any capacity for real emotion she was a natural trap for married men, themselves wary of emotional entanglements. With her healthy sensuality she would have been any man's perfect one-night stand, or an ideal call-girl, but her temperament was too conventional for either of these rôles. She needed to believe herself in love, and the endurance of her affairs gave a certain substance to that delusion. The last time George had run into her she had been involved with a man who was even older than he had been, and so deeply in hock to past wives that he could not possibly have afforded to divorce the present one: the ultimate in safety. This, Peggy had assured him, was the real love of her life.

George found the memory rather embarrassing. He disliked the picture of himself in the early stages of the affair, living as impatiently as any love-stricken adolescent, waiting for the stolen moments he could spend with a creature who existed to a great extent in his own imagination. He liked even less the memories of the long, slow crumble, when he had behaved with the petulance of a man trying to force reality to conform to his illusions. Preferring to forget the whole episode, he thought Eleanor uncommonly tactless in bringing it up.

"Exactly what are you getting at?" he inquired. "Shall we tell Ken all about Peggy Dunstable so he can see that both his parents are equally reprehensible?"

"But I don't think we are anything of the sort, either one of us," she said. "In comparison with most people, I daresay we're unusually tame and temperate. We've never slept around. I think I can speak for both of us on that score. You were so transparent during the Peggy Dunstable era that I'm sure I would have spotted any other major disgressions, and I've never seen you as a man to pick up one of those disposable receptacles when you're off on a legitimate business trip."

"I suspect I'm somewhat undersexed," he said.

"So what it comes down to is that we've each fallen in love once—outside the family, so to speak—in the course of a marriage that's hurrying along to its silver anniversary. Undoubtedly there are more faithful couples, yet ours is scarcely a record of licentious debauchery. The oddest part of it is that with very similar histories you have become a saint whereas I am a fallen woman."

"The histories aren't similar at all," he protested. "I had a respectably sneaky affair which no one was obliged to notice; I showed a proper respect for the hypocrisies from beginning to end. Your course was far too flamboyant. I tried to establish you decently at the bedside of a dying relative, but after six years that story was wearing thin."

"It's a pity you troubled," said Eleanor. "You merely gave Karen Updyke the opportunity to look sly when she congratulated me on my uncle's long overdue demise. Which was slightly annoying. Out of courtesy to you I don't like to wave Pierre's name about like a flag, and at the same time I don't want to subscribe to that preposterous story."

"When I embarked on it I had no idea it would need to stretch so far," George said. "What did you tell Karen?"

"I simply said, quite truthfully, that both my uncles died years ago, and changed the subject. It's quite pointless to tell fibs in a family which includes my sister. The truth appeals to Cathy's sense of humor far more than any fiction, and the trouble with a sense of humor is that it demands an audience. I'm sure that Pierre and I were scarcely out of sight before she thought of some terribly funny remark about us; the remark couldn't be wasted, so she tried it out on the first seventeen people she met. Your version of things never stood a chance of catching up."

"Oh, well, one more prop for your theory of the futility of good intentions," said George. "Is Cathy equally comical about her own misdemeanors?"

"Her sense of humor doesn't extend to herself, no," said Eleanor. "That doesn't happen very often. People who are admired for being able to poke fun at themselves have simply made household pets of their favorite weaknesses."

"But did you speak to her about this flirtation or whatever it is with Fred Palmer?"

"Certainly not. What could I say?"

"That you'd been hearing some gossip about her."

"I haven't been back long enough. People are still gossiping *about* me, not *to* me."

"You must have learned something, just the same," George persisted. "You began by remarking that this had been an informative day, and coupled that with the fact that Cathy had been here this morning."

"And from that you concluded I'd added one more busybody to an over-supplied suburb," Eleanor said, smiling at him. "Cathy will tell me about Fred Palmer when she's ready to, not before. Until then, I'm the dumping ground for her dissatisfactions."

"What are they?"

"Trivialities, mostly, and quite beside the point," she replied. "Those tears the day we arrived were evidence of how run-down she is, you know, and not any sign of joy at recovering a long-lost sister. She's still unsure of how much I may have changed, and she's out of the habit of baring her heart to me. But I did gather that she has some deep-seated resentment against Alan."

"That sounds normal and ominous," said George. "Before a woman makes a complete damn fool of herself she likes to be satisfied that it's all her husband's fault."

"Often she has good reason," Eleanor rejoined. "It's just an idea, but do you suppose Alan could have a Peggy Dunstable tucked away in the city somewhere?"

"No," he said.

"That was the impulsive answer; now try again," suggested Eleanor. "He wouldn't have confided in you yet: that seems to come afterwards with men. The present is private and the past is a source of anecdotes. I've never known a man who didn't have a clear picture of his best friend's sex life."

George scowled, saw that the glass of Grand Marnier was hardly touched, and went to the bar to replenish his own highball. Eleanor was right, as usual. Late-evening conversations over the whisky, when Cathy was out of the room or had gone to bed, had given him some implicitly confidential knowledge of Alan's nature. Alan belonged to that large category of men (sternly disregarded by the moralists) to whom sudden continence quickly became enough of a discomfort to be a distraction. Off on an extended business trip he would always pick up a willing girl; no doubt these encounters were pleasurable, but above all they were therapeutic. Faced with a series of delicate and demanding interviews Alan drank glasses of milk last thing before bed to avert the consequences of an evening's drinking, and just as dispassionately he averted the nagging pressure of his loins. George didn't feel this same need himself, but he had less difficulty than the moralists in believing that it was quite real. So in a technical sense Alan had been "unfaithful" often enough, but in a practical sense, since he wasted no emotion on these hygenic interludes, it could be argued that if his body had strayed his heart remained pure. At home he was well looked after, and had no need of outside diversion. Certainly he had always given the appearance of being a devoted and loving husband.

But had appearances recently become deceptive? That was the question. George could not answer positively on the basis of his own observations: he did not credit himself with the sort of sensitivity that could see through a performance deliberately intended to mislead him. On the other hand, the exigencies of a serious love affair (as George well knew) made demands on a man's time which were far more difficult to conceal than his state of mind, and here he could speak with more assurance. Alan's time was too well accounted for. His recent business trips had definitely been genuine ones, with long-distance calls flying back and forth. Alan almost never worked late at the office, preferring to bring home a bulging attaché case and lock himself into his study. And the state of things at Watson-Briggs made any sort of hanky-panky during working hours unthinkable.

"Could Cathy be holding a grudge over some old affair?" he asked, returning to his chair.

"No," Eleanor said flatly. "She's not that foolish."

"Then it's quite impossible. Alan simply doesn't have the time to spare. Overwork accounts for more virtue than religion does."

"It's something else, then," she said, accepting his word.

"He has all sorts of pressures on him," George added. "Ben Watson has brought his son into the outfit, and Alan is feeling outnumbered these days. With no son of his own, he would like to see Ken go to work there when he graduates."

"I thought Ken was set on teaching."

"Alan is convinced that's just a passing phase which Ken will outgrow when he acquires more self-confidence. He did his level best to talk Ken into working there this summer, but without success."

"Any special reason?"

"Ken offered half a dozen reasons without mentioning the special one."

"Jessie? That's a bit bothersome," Eleanor said, frowning slightly.

"Why?"

"Because it sounds as if he's taking her *too* seriously."

"Is that necessarily bad?" George said. "Nowadays lots of youngsters get married while they're still in college—not, let me hasten to add, that I have the slightest reason to suppose that Ken and Jessie are as serious as all that."

"But it's exactly what we have to worry about."

"Do we? I like Jessie," George said. "She strikes me as a bright, healthy, wholesome, typical American girl with a better-than-average sense of humor."

"She strikes me the same way," said Eleanor. "It's what I object to."

"I could have predicted that reply," George said. "In fact, I invited it. But since there aren't any French girls handy, it's to be expected that Ken will eventually marry an American one. Can you improve on the qualities I listed?"

"Quite easily," said Eleanor. "Your typical American girl depresses me, George. One of the first things that struck me, coming back, was the remarkable number of homely girls there are. Plain girls, fat girls, dowdy girls, girls without a trace of style, girls who are denying their femininity or have long since lost faith in it. You don't see that in France; there may not be as many pretty girls, but there aren't any homely ones. Because they all have a strong sense of their femininity, and are proud of it, and that takes you most of the way to being attractive."

"What the hell does this have to do with Jessie?" George demanded. "She's the prettiest thing in sight."

"She's pretty because she happens to be pretty. She dresses nicely and makes up well because her mother taught her how. And that's as far as her femininity goes."

"Perhaps you haven't noticed her figure. I have."

"She has a lovely body. Have you also noticed how she uses it? How she carries herself? How she sits? How she walks—as flat-footedly as any boy?"

"It's a pity she doesn't twitch her hips like a streetwalker."

"You could try harder to understand," Eleanor said. "I'm complaining of a fundamental lack of pride in her own sex in Jessie. Like so many American girls she has been brought up as a misshapen boy. Her instinct is to compete with her man, not to be a complement to him. She is healthy, yes, and that's for beating Ken at tennis if she possibly can. She's bright, and that's for outarguing him. The sense of humor is for teasing."

"I'm surprised at you, I really am," George said. "If you expect any girl to flutter her lashes demurely and tell him how wonderful he is, you're sadly out of date."

"If I expected anything of the sort you'd have every reason to be surprised," she said. "My belief in a woman's right to her own individuality is well established, I should think."

"It's just the way they have of flirting nowadays," George said. "I doubt if it's any different in France."

"The difference is one of attitude," said Eleanor. "When a girl is truly proud of her own femininity, she hasn't any of the insecurities that need to be satisfied at the expense of a man's ego. She flirts, naturally, but the flirting isn't the first campaign in a lifelong war of attrition. She looks forward to being part of a real relationship, which means that she looks forward to the serious business of being a woman."

"Well, Jessie is still a girl," George said comfortably. "Give her time."

"Time doesn't necessarily help," replied Eleanor. "Haven't you remarked the way American women persist in calling themselves girls until they have one foot in the grave? Womanhood is no admired goal here; it's the irresponsibility of girlhood they cling to. Which is why so many of them discard husband after husband, looking for one who will be content with their bright, healthy, wholesome arrested development."

"I sensed that you hadn't taken a liking to Jessie," said George. "I didn't realize that you'd forecast her career through the third divorce."

"You're wrong, I do like Jessie," Eleanor said. "She's an attractive child, very sweet and with lovely manners—exactly the sort of playmate I'd have chosen for Ken myself. Being in love with her will do a great deal towards civilizing him, and that's all to the good. It's only the danger of his taking her too seriously that makes me uneasy. When it comes to marriage he could do a great deal better for himself."

"Just what do you have in mind for him?" George asked.

"Simply a girl who has it in her to develop into a real

woman. There must be plenty of them about, though he may have to look a bit further afield than Bradley's Bluff."

"I've been listening very attentively," said Geeorge, "and I'm still not entirely clear as to what you mean by a real woman. But I suspect she'd be one who would always retain the right to elope with a transient Frenchman, if the mood seized her. In which case Ken might be happier with a good-natured case of what you call arrested development."

"You're bound to be a bit cynical about women, I suppose," said Eleanor, "but you shouldn't let that influence your hopes for our son."

7.

As the long summer days slipped by, Ken developed a small grievance against Jessie for never having inquired about the state of his ambitions. This was the more annoying because his plans had altered slightly over the winter, veering in a direction which Jessie ought to find highly interesting.

Ken's choice of a career had been influenced, in part, by a consideration of his father's and his Uncle Alan's. When his father duly retired, for example, what would he have to show for forty-some years of work apart from the money he had earned? Not a blessed thing, as far as Ken could see. It seemed a horrible thought that eventually the grave would close over this remarkable man without his having had the least effect on the world he lived in, except as a private person. Uncle Alan's job seemed more stimulating but was open to much the same objections. There must be a certain intellectual satisfaction in bamboozling the public into buying more of this toothpaste than another, but a lifetime of such petty triumphs left the world substantially unaltered.

Before he had any idea what he wanted to do, Ken had determined he wanted something better than this, something to which he could dedicate himself. Lacking any specific talent to give direction to his purpose, he had hesitated among various possibilities for a time, until the day when he recognized that he had an uncommon love of History and could think of no career so satisfying as communicating that love to other young men. He would teach, and he would hope to be one of those teachers who leave an indelible mark on some, at least, of their students.

This had been where his ambitions stood as of last summer. Thinking in terms of an eventual professorship, he had been faced with the prospect of years of postgraduate work. Marriage lay on the far horizon, not so much because he doubted his father's willingness to support two of them for a while, but because he questioned his own ability to keep his nose to the academic grindstone with the distractions of a wife at hand. But the whole shape of the future had changed a few months ago, at college, thanks to a letter from his favorite master at the Courtney School, with whom he kept up an irregular correspondence. Mr. Stafford had applauded his plans of teaching, and asked in passing if Ken had given any thought to returning to teach at Courtney. This causual inquiry had been Ken's light on the road to Damascus. If he fancied himself as a molder of young minds, then how much greater was the influence of a teacher on the preparatory school level, where minds were still receptive and plastic! Remembering the tremendous impact certain of his masters had had upon him, Ken had visions of generations of young men who would look back upon *him* as a vital landmark in their lives. Excited by the idea, he had fired off a letter to the Headmaster, and got back a very encouraging reply, amounting to an offer dependent only upon his final marks. His future was decided. And one of the nicest aspects of it was that he needed only his B.A. to begin. Instead of remotely distant, marriage had become something to which they could set a date—for next spring, if they felt like it.

And if Jessie wasn't aware of this, it was her own fault. She hadn't asked.

She ought to ask. Ken had come to their first meetings this summer brimming with the good news, just waiting for the right button to be pushed to spill over with his excitement. When it wasn't, he volunteered nothing, at first for the pleasure of hoarding his surprise, and later from a sense of injured pride. Did Jessie really take him seriously, or did she not? If she did, shouldn't she show at least a flicker of interest in his ambitions? If she really considered her future bound up with his, mustn't she have some curiosity—just a little—about what her life was going to be?

Apparently not. It was maddening. He made conversational openings for her that an idiot couldn't overlook; she would inspect them suspiciously, as if they were traps, and go off in some other direction. Days went by like this, Ken discovering that a burden of good news became an affliction if you couldn't dispose of it.

Impatience has a way of breaking out at the least opportune moments. When the mind is quite relaxed, half-asleep, drifting, an irritating thought comes creeping in to expand and occupy the void, spoiling the contentment; one is apt to expel the intruder in the shape of words, simply to be rid of it.

"*Why* haven't you asked about my teaching?" Ken asked.

The reply was indistinguishable.

"What?" he said.

"I asked whether you couldn't find something more romantic to say," Jessie replied.

"I'm sorry. I love you madly. It's something that's been bothering me."

"Then you should have spoken up," Jessie said, stretching. "It's what I was waiting for."

"I didn't know whether you were interested," Ken said from the momentum of sulkiness.

"Don't be funny," said Jessie. "Where are the cigarettes?"

"I'll get them." He padded across the room, found the pack and lighted a couple of cigarettes at the same time, trying to reaffirm his gallantry. "You certainly didn't *seem* interested."

"There are times when a girl has to be circumspect."

"What does that mean?"

"The horrors of spring," said Jessie, settling an ashtray between them. "Look, it's not uncommon. A guy goes off in the autumn all fired up to become a doctor and devote his life to suffering humanity. And then something happens. He finds he gets sick if he cuts up a frog, or he flunks Biology, or he listens to his roommates dreaming of the expense-account life. Anyway, he comes back convinced it will be smart to go into Daddy's outfit after all. But if his girl's a dope she's still living in last summer's enthusiasm; maybe she's spent the winter planning to be a nurse so she can work shoulder to shoulder with her mate. So she greets him with prattle of togetherness in the operating room, which is a little embarrassing if he's thinking of wholesale office supplies. All of a sudden he discovers that she has an irritating giggle and that he doesn't like girls with freckles."

"I'd have written if I'd changed my mind," he protested.

"For the past few months you've written of every other subject under the sun, but not teaching. That made me uneasy. And I didn't want to ask, because nothing's more depressing than being reminded of a dead idealism."

"So instead you were tactful," he said, "which is the main source of misunderstandings."

"That sounds like something Eleanor might say," Jessie remarked.

Ken was glad that his blush could not be seen. "The reason I didn't say anything in my letters was that I was waiting to hear what sort of reception I'd get from the Headmaster at Courtney," he explained, and went on with a rekindled fervor to tell Jessie of how his new plans had come into existence, and why they excited him. He spoke of his tremendous luck, in that one of the History masters would be due for retirement next year, while Mr. Remsen, who coached soccer, had reached an age when he would be delighted to turn this extracurricular chore over to a younger man, so that Ken had two qualifications to offer. And to atone for having doubted Jessie, he laid particular stress on the delights of Courtney campus life for a master's bride, as he imagined them.

This time he could not complain of any shortage of enthusiasm from Jessie. She could see almost without prompting how right this sort of life would be for him; she was enchanted by the thought that (unless the Army intervened) it could begin the following year. "But this is absolutely marvelous!" she exclaimed as soon as he began to slow down. "And it's so perfect for you, Ken: something you'll be able to be really proud of."

"That's the one part I'm not quite sure about," he said. "Since I couldn't talk to you, I was talking about it with Mother this morning."

"Oh-oh. What does she have against the idea?"

"Nothing, exactly. But she got to comparing the setup here with the schools in France."

"I'm getting just a bit tired of France," Jessie remarked after a short silence.

"Well, it was interesting," Ken said. "Apparently the school system there is so good that if a kid gets sent to private school it's the same as admitting that he just wasn't able to make the grade in the public schools."

"Very admirable," Jessie said quietly.

"Well, it's the way it should be, isn't it?" Ken demanded. "Courtney is one of the best, but it's not fair that kids go there just because their parents can pay, while much brighter kids have to make out in a ratty high school—and some of them *are* pretty ratty, even around here."

"It's unjust," Jessie agreed, "but there's nothing you can do about it."

"If I'm going to teach I want to be a good teacher," Ken

said, "and if I'm going to be a good teacher I ought to go where I can be the most use."

"That sounds great, but what would it mean in practice?" Jessie asked. "Waiting around in one of the rattier high schools for some bright kids to inspire, and then finding that their parents can't afford to let them go on to college."

"That wouldn't happen often," he argued, "and it still might be better than being part of an expensive conveyor belt for whisking kids into college whether they belonged there or not."

"There will be bright kids at Courtney, too; probably more of them," Jessie said. "Those are the ones who will interest you, and at least you'll know they can do something with their lives later, if they want to. You have to be a bit practical, darling. If the private schools are an injustice, then they ought to be abolished. But you won't accomplish anything by a small, personal, idealistic gesture."

"I know the argument," Ken said. "I just can't decide whether it's good sense or cowardice."

"This is what I don't like about what you call your mother's topsy-turvy ideas," Jessie said. "They don't change anything, they just unsettle people. You'll go to Courtney anyhow, because it's the most sensible and satisfying thing you can do. And because it's also my life we're talking about. But now you'll always feel a tiny bit guilty for having gone."

Ken felt this to be less than fair to his mother, and was mentally organizing an eloquent discourse on the breadth of Eleanor's vision when Jessie inquired idly what time it had gotten to be.

"Wait a second," he said, reaching for his watch and facing it to the dim light. "A quarter to eleven."

"Oh, no!" she said, struggling up. "That meeting's over by now—Mummy will be home any minute. Please, darling, get a move on, get *dressed*."

PART THREE

Iphigenia

7.

"Martha, the dust on top of that bookcase is half an inch thick."

"Can you see that from where you're lying, Mrs. Davenport, or have you been up feeling the furniture?"

"I merely observe the way you whisk through this room nowadays. Very likely that woman keeps you too busy for anything more."

"There's a limit to what I can do if you won't let me bring the cleaner in here."

"People find it difficult to remember there was a day before vacuum cleaners were invented," said Mrs. Davenport, "yet rooms got dusted even then."

"I have a nice feather duster out in the closet," said Martha, down on her knees to maneuver the dry-mop under the bed. "If you want, I could fix the air in here so you couldn't breathe."

"I also seem to notice a deterioration in your usual sunny disposition," said Mrs. Davenport. "I fear you are finding the new regime something of a strain."

"I don't know about the new regime. But I have one sick-room at home to attend to, and I didn't bargain for a second one. That's a fact."

"Ah, yes, poor Joseph. Perhaps for Joseph's sake you should look around for less exacting work. Mrs. Graves was telling me that they are in need of full-time help. A nice, elderly, undemanding couple with a small house, Martha. Mr. Graves is too deaf to hear your radio, and Mrs. Graves is too near-sighted to see the tops of bookcases."

"If I leave here I'm going back to splitting up my time," said Martha. "A couple of hours here, a couple of hours there. That way people don't have any claim on your good nature."

"A very sensible idea. We shall be sorry to see you go, of course, Martha. We had come to think of you as almost a member of the family."

"I'm glad you feel that way, Mrs. Davenport. Because I'm beginning to think Mrs. George is a real nice lady to work for."

"I'm sure you never find her underfoot when there's any work to be done. Still, you have to think of the future. Perhaps you can manage singlehanded now, and that's very courageous of you in a house this size, but it won't be so easy when the nurse moves in."

"What nurse?" asked Martha.

"It can't be long now," said Mrs. Davenport with a sigh. "I've quite resigned myself, naturally, but what worries me is the burden that will fall on you. You can't imagine how fussy these private nurses can be, how much work they create, but I remember from my husband's time. Meals at all hours, and cups of coffee, and their bed linen changed every other day, if you please, and messes everywhere for somebody else to clean up."

"You don't need any nurse, Mrs. Davenport," Martha said stolidly. "Are you ready to move over to the chair so I can fix up your bed?"

"Perhaps you'd better give me your arm, Martha. I find I get a little dizzy when I stand up. That's a bad sign."

"It's a sign you've been lying in bed too long, that's for sure."

"Everybody is so kind about trying to cheer me up," said Mrs. Davenport, perching on the edge of the armchair, "but a woman knows when the end is near. It's the night nurse who leaves the kitchen in such a state you have to spend an hour straightening up before you can start breakfast."

"I guess that's why most people go off to the hospital."

"I have always had a horror of dying among strangers," said Mrs. Davenport. "No doubt it's selfish of me, but I intend to die in my own bed in my own house. I'm only sorry for the trouble it will cause, and I thought it fair to let you know what to expect, so you can decide what would be best for you."

"I'm glad you warned me, Mrs. Davenport," said Martha, grinning at the pillows she was plumping up. "Seems like the Christian thing is to help Mrs. George through your last illness."

2.

All weekend long it had rained steadily, making impossible the garden chores generally saved up for the outdoor days. Now, in the evenings, men hurried to change from city suits into plaid Bermuda shorts and gaudy sports shirts, to sally forth to keep their small domains up to community standards. From one end of Bradley's Bluff to the other, seven o'clock was noisy with motorized lawn mowers. There was a certain hierarchy to these machines, noticeable to Ken as he drove towards his date with Jessie. On Walnut Road, men pushed. On Maple Lane they strolled, merely guiding the self-propelled mowers. And on Chestnut Plaza Mr. Henderson sat sedately in the saddle of his riding mower, steering with one hand and sipping at a martini held in the other.

Even Laura Sydrock was out, crouched on her haunches in front of a flower bed, looking in this posture less like a contemplative toad than most of the mothers of Bradley's Bluff. Laura was a handsome, gentle-eyed woman who had worn well, but her perpetual air of brisk efficiency belied her essential femininity. ("As crisp and wholesome as a Macintosh apple, and just about as seductive," had been one of Mrs. Davenport's crueler descriptions.) It wasn't until you knew Laura well that you realized that the businesslike bustle had once been a defense against shyness and was still a defense against a considerable sensitivity. She was quick to descry other people's bruises, and kept her own well hidden. There was no doubt that she had been quietly hurt by Eleanor Davenport's return, and Ken was guiltily grateful that his own reception in the Sydrock household had not been affected. Some women in Bradley's Bluff, who had not been hurt at all, were still punishing him with sly inquisitive digs.

This evening, however, despite Laura's sensibility, Ken would have preferred to slip by her into the house virtually unnoticed. It seemed feasible: her back was to the street, and she had not seen him drive up. He left the car as quietly as possible, and walked across the grass, avoiding the flagged path, intending to throw out a passing "Evening, Laura," just as he vanished through the screen door.

It didn't work out. Laura looked over her shoulder just as he came abreast of her, greeted him. He paused self-consciously, waiting for the gibe as her glance slid over him. "You look especially handsome this evening," was her only comment, although she smiled. "Jessie went in about half an hour ago, saying she was going to take a shower. I suppose this means that halfway up the stairs is a stair where you'll sit."

He blushed at this evidence of Laura's familiarity with their rituals, and escaped into the house, taking up his post on the landing. Jessie's bedroom was opposite the head of the stairs; with the door ajar they could talk while she was dressing, and this had become a fixed custom. Last summer, when her mother was out, Jessie had sometimes given him a sort of striptease in reverse, allowing him glimpses of her clad first in just a towel, then in frilly underwear, and finally appearing in the doorway with dresses held up against her so that he could make his choice. This year such performances had been abandoned as mere childishness.

"Hi!" he called to the half-open door, since there was no sound of water.

"I thought that must be you," Jessie said. "Anyone else who lets the screen door slam gets a bawling out from Mummy."

"Someday I'll remember," he said impenitently. "What are you wearing?"

"Next to nothing."

"Funny girl! This evening, I mean."

"Well, that's a problem," said the voice from the bedroom. "I've put out my new blue dress. Spectacular neckline, *very* sexy, the sort of thing that draws them like a magnet from across the dance floor. I thought a little competition might be good for your soul."

"Sounds great," said Ken. "I'll take my chances."

"But now I'm not so sure. Maybe I ought to wear something a little more mid-Victorian. Strike a prim and dainty note. Put over the idea that at least one respectable girl is still willing to be seen in public with you."

"Oh, Lord!" he said. "What have I done now?"

"Nothing that's come to general notice, darling. It's not you, it's your family. A really nice girl probably wouldn't associate with anyone from a family like that."

"As of fifteen minutes ago Mother was still safely at home."

"If it isn't one member it's another. Gossip, gossip, all the time. You know what they say about touching pitch. A girl has to worry about her good reputation."

"Lay off," said Ken. "I spent the morning mowing our lawn and the afternoon in my room reading a guy named Steven Runciman, whom you're too ignorant to have heard of. So I've missed out on the tittle-tattle, and what the hell is all this about?"

"There was an exciting party at the Updykes' last night," Jessie's voice informed him. "The local night life is looking up. Rumor has it that your Aunt Cathy belted your Uncle Alan with a poker."

"I don't believe it," he said.

"Neither do I, exactly. But something happened, and it makes you wonder what next week's scandal will be. Will Alan Briggs retaliate by planting Cathy among the tomatoes? Is George Davenport plotting a long-delayed revenge against his erring wife? Any day now I may be interviewed by the tabloids as the girl friend of the victim's son or nephew, and that sort of thing can scar a girl for life."

"What do you suppose really happened?" he asked.

"Hard to tell. It was energetic, anyway. Another account says she slapped his face. The least dramatic version has her throwing a highball glass at his head but missing."

"Without us, Bradley's Bluff would be a drab little suburb," Ken said proudly.

"You've certainly been a conversational godsend this summer," Jessie agreed. "Half the time when I go into a room they change the subject; the other half they keep talking in hopes I can contribute to the dirt. Nobody appreciates me in my own right any more—I'm just a sideshow to the Briggs-Davenport circus."

"There's one advantage to all this," he pointed out. "With everybody gossiping about them, nobody has any time to speculate about us."

"Say, that reminds me," she said in a distorted mumble which informed him that lipstick was going on, "I've decided I want an engagement ring after all."

"Very middle-class of you," he said reprovingly.

"That depends on the point of view."

"You just want something flashy to impress your girlfriends with."

"You're wildly out of date: nowadays an engagement ring is a man's tribute to his girl's lack of virtue," she told him, and he found himself grinning nervously at the brisk approach of her high heels. "And the size of the stone is an index to his appreciation for—Kenneth Fairchild Davenport! *Where is your beard?"*

"You look terrific," he said, gazing up at her in the open doorway.

"I'm in a state of shock and it's no time for compliments. What's going on?"

"I shaved it off."

"It wasn't long enough to get caught in the lawn mower, so I assumed that much. I don't get it. What's she up to? Anyway, I thought lots of Frenchmen wore beards."

"What makes you think Mother had anything to do with it?" he demanded, slightly angry.

"Feminine intuition," she snapped, marching down the stairs and brushing past him without any offering of a kiss. "Last night there was a beard. Your father spent the day on Wall Street. I doubt if you got the idea from mowing the lawn or something you read in a history book. Yet this evening, no beard. I deduce one of those topsy-turvy little conversations with your mother."

He stalked after her into the living room where she dropped indignantly into one corner of the sofa. "As usual, you've got it all wrong," he said. "Mother liked the beard. At least she liked the fact that I'd grown one."

"And she clung to your knees begging you not to shave it off."

"Calm down, can't you? Let's have a drink before we go. You didn't suppose I was going off to Courtney in a beard, did you? That would just be giving the kids an excuse for making my life a hell."

"Courtney is fourteen months away, so what was the rush? Oh, all right—I'll get the tonic." She leapt up again and ran off to the kitchen while he moodily prepared two glasses with gin and ice from the icebucket, thinking how much more gracefully Laura Sydrock had accepted his metamorphosis. "I'm sorry," Jessie said, returning and handing him the chilled bottle. "It came as too much of a surprise."

"I thought you'd be pleased."

"I haven't decided yet. But what made you change your mind all of a sudden?"

"Well, in a way it was Mother, but not the way you think. She never once suggested that I ought to shave it off."

"She begins to frighten me just a little," Jessie said.

"Don't be foolish," Ken said, giving her one of the drinks and settling into the opposite corner of the sofa. "She agreed with me completely about growing the beard. As she put it, once the idea appeals to you you have to go through with it, because if you don't you'll never be sure that it wasn't just cowardice that stopped you."

"Is that why you grew the beard?" Jessie asked. "Out of fear of cowardice?"

"You're pretty good at twisting things yourself," he said. "I grew it because I wanted to. But I was beginning to go along with the idea that it made me look even younger, like a boy in disguise. Remember Bruce Henderson in the school play?"

"I do," said Jessie. "No comment."

"You have to put up with an awful lot of teasing at first," he said. "It's something everybody tries to be witty about. There are only three or four possible wisecracks, but each person thinks he's been so original and funny when he comes up with one of them. You have to pretend to be amused by remarks you've heard a hundred times already, or people will say you've lost your sense of humor. It's a terrible bore."

"But it's what you expected in advance."

"Oh, sure. And there's some satisfaction in defiance. Still, it takes a lot of nerve to go through with it. What was so clever about what Mother said was her pointing out that along with a beard you get a vested interest in the courage it took to grow it. Whether or not it's a becoming beard, it's all you have to show for your suffering. Shaving it off makes a waste of all you've been through, and on top of that you'll have to listen to all the fatheads congratulating you for coming to your senses again. So actually it's a lot harder to shave off a beard than to grow one."

"Yes, that *was* clever of your of your mother," Jessie agreed.

"Very clever. But I think you might have kept me up to date I had a small vested interest too."

"It was meant as a surprise."

"Could you be sure it would be an agreeable one?"

"Well, Mother said any intelligent girl would *say* she liked the beard, but no intelligent girl could be sincere about it."

"Perhaps she understands me better than I understand myself," Jessie said. "That's a little annoying in somebody who doesn't like me."

"Of course Mother likes you!"

"Not really. I can tell."

"You're imagining things," Ken said. "I know what she says about you when you're not around."

"I'm sure she doesn't criticize me. I almost wish she did. It's the thought that she probably praises me that I find so terrifying."

"Why?" he asked.

"Because I don't intend to be shaved off," Jessie said.

Laura Sydrock came in just then and had a drink with them, and by the time Ken and Jessie left for the dance things were all right between them again. Jessie had even conceded that he was handsomer without the beard, and the subject of whether or not his mother disliked her didn't arise again. But it had lodged in Ken's mind as something new to worry about. He thought it probable that Jessie was wrong: his mother's odd sense of humor took some getting used to, and might easily put some people off. Still, he couldn't be sure. Women were supposed to be subtler about these matters than men, and it was perfectly possible that Jessie had noticed something which he had missed.

His first impulse was to tackle his mother head on, but experience had taught him that this approach didn't necessarily lead to the expected results. He might want to talk about Jessie and find himself in the middle of a discussion on French politics. After some consideration he decided that the best move would be to have a talk with his father and see what he had to offer.

3.

Ken's researches into the story of Helen of Troy had brought him upon the character of Helen's mother, Leda, a beautiful woman of singular tastes. Although respectably married to an early king of Sparta, she shared her favors between her husband and a visiting swan. That the swan was actually Zeus in disguise has been asserted though never proven. When Leda eventually gave birth to quadruplets—Helen, Clytemnestra, and a couple of future bully-boys, Castor and Pollux (later to become a constellation)—the paternity of this quartet was vigorously disputed. Homer gave the credit to the royal father, other authorities favored Zeus, some divided the responsibility equally, and a few spiteful neighbors blamed it all on the swan.

No such confusion had attended upon the births of Eleanor of Bradley's Bluff and her younger sister, Cathy. Their mother had been an exceptionally beautiful woman also, but too conventional to indulge an amorous fancy for waterbirds, and too scatterbrained to carry off any other sort of illicit liaison. Their father had been an appellate judge with considerable intelligence, a scholarly disposition and a dry humor. In defiance of the Shavian Theorem, both daughters had outshone their mother's beauty while inheriting a fair share of their father's brains.

Neither legacy had been recognized by the Judge. He would listen complacently while guests exclaimed over his daughters' looks, but had never seen them except as paler copies of the woman whose beauty had captured his imagination as a young man. As for their intelligence, when each girl reached her tenth birthday, obeying some private dogma of his own the Judge would appear bearing a chessboard and pieces, prepared to expound the principles of this noble game. Failing at this, confirmed in his suspicion that his daughters were incorrigibly frivolous, he would retire into his policy of leaving their upbringing to their mother. She, however, although never tired of saying that her life centered entirely about her girls, spent as little time on them as possible, preferring the small social whirl of Alden Park and the prestige of being a judge's wife.

As a result, despite the difference in their ages, the two sisters had been uncommonly close. It was Eleanor, in reality, who had brought Cathy up. Cathy had been doll, pupil, playmate and slave to her older sister, and their mother (as Cathy remembered those early years) had been called into conference only when new dresses were needed. Just at the age when Cathy might have been ready to rebel against this relationship, Eleanor had retired from center-stage—first, briefly, to college, and then into her marriage with George Davenport. Left to the resources of their mother, Cathy had learned to appreciate her older sister all the more, and had continued to look to Eleanor for moral support in the small crises of adolescence and the graver decisions of adulthood.

Eleanor's elopement to France had attenuated this tie without altering Cathy's feelings, for Cathy had thought of her sister as still the same person albeit out of sight, whereas Eleanor's return disclosed the differences that time had made in both of them. The change in Eleanor was more apparent, for six years in an alien environment had given a new slant to her views on almost everything, but Cathy was aware that she herself looked at her older sister with cooler and warier eyes. The old affection was there, and the intimacy of so many shared associations, but they met these days with a certain slight reserve, as of ancient allies each finding that the other has picked up novel and disturbing mannerisms.

"Contrary to anything you may have heard yesterday," Cathy announced a shade defiantly as she swept into the Davenport living room, "I did not attack Alan with a carving knife."

"That version hasn't reached here yet," said Eleanor, putting down her book.

"It will, or something like it," said Cathy. "Mrs. Plummer just looked surprised at seeing me out on bail and asked if Alan was still in the hospital."

"Your temper seems to have become well known. What did you actually do?"

"I threw a matchbox at him. One of the coy ones that Karen has strewn all over the place saying This Was Stolen From The Updykes."

"You missed, of course."

"That's just it," Cathy said, lighting a cigarette. "Normally you'd expect me to knock over somebody else's drink, wouldn't you? All that golf must have improved my aim. I hit him. In the eye with a corner, poor bastard, which was what caused all the fuss."

"Any real damage?"

"Well, he was still ostentatiously bathing in eyewash before he left for work this morning, but that was mostly to make me feel guilty. I don't. He deserved it."

"Do stop pacing about like a tigress with a grudge," Eleanor said. "What had Alan done to deserve the matchbox?"

"Made one of his witty generalizations about women."

"Yes, very exasperating. But it's what most men do when they're caught short for something clever to say. And we can't go blinding all of them on that score."

"He cuts too close to the bone these days," Cathy said. "You know what those generalizations are: there's always a strong implication that a woman's main function in life is making babies. Which is much the same as saying there's something fundamentally wrong with a woman who hasn't made any."

"I'm sure he didn't mean it like that."

"No, you're not, and neither am I. Alan finds a lot of roundabout ways of suggesting that I would be better off spending more of my time at home."

"Could there be some truth to that?"

"Perhaps. There's one thing I've become certain of. I should have gone ahead and had a kid when I had the chance to."

"There were certain obstacles at the time," Eleanor said. "For one thing, you weren't married."

"The wedding could have been moved forward a few months," Cathy said impatiently. "I wouldn't have been the first woman in history whose first baby was a bit premature. A few people snicker at the time but five years later nobody remembers."

"Still, you never even considered those possibilities then, as I recall. Your mind was made up, you simply weren't yet ready to have children."

"That was the official position. You might add that I was madly in love and that Alan was writing my dialogue; whatever he wanted I wanted. And he simply wasn't ready to give up the money I was making. For a few years there it was a lot more than he brought home, you know. So instead of children we have Watson-Briggs."

"But have you any reason for believing that this was why you've not had any children since then?" Eleanor asked. "That woman I sent you to was supposed to have an excellent reputation. What do the doctors say now?"

"That I'm absolutely all right, but what do they really know?" Cathy replied scornfully. "You'll have to admit it's one hell of a coincidence. There was a time when all it needed was one careless moment and I got pregnant. For the past eight years we've been as carefree as rabbits, but without any luck. You explain it."

"Obviously I can't," said Eleanor. "But I wish you'd decide on a chair and sit down. You're making me nervous."

"Nothing makes you nervous; you've always had the temperament of a nursing mother," retorted Cathy, sitting down nevertheless. "What annoys me is that I might have had a taste of that temperament myself, and now it looks as if I never shall."

"That's most unfortunate," Eleanor said. "It's even more unfortunate that you seem to be blaming Alan."

"He has more to answer for than you might imagine."

"That's true of all of us. But what new vices has Alan developed? There must be more than this old misjudgment to account for the way you've been behaving recently."

"So you've heard I've been carrying on with Freddie Palmer—of course you have," Cathy said. "He's very nice and very attractive. And at least he hasn't turned into a smug, self-satisfied drudge."

"Sometimes I feel sorry for husbands," Eleanor said. "When they don't work they're slobs and when they do, they're neglectful. If they despise their work they are hacks or failures, and if they're proud of it they're smug and self-satisfied."

"Are you setting up as a marriage counselor, dear? I don't think you're qualified for the part."

"Why not? My marriage has lasted a good deal longer than most."

"Oh, glory! Only because George had his own personal reasons for not getting a divorce!"

"At bottom, isn't that why most successful marriages survive?" Eleanor asked. "I may have given him some cause for complaint, but at least I never bothered him with flirtations."

"No, you've merely been gallivanting around Europe for the past six years with your lover. There's no comparison!"

"You're right, there isn't," Eleanor said. "My conduct may have been reprehensible from several points of view, but it had the virtue of sincerity. I had fallen in love with Pierre."

"And perhaps I've fallen in love with Freddie Palmer," Cathy retorted.

"I don't believe it," Eleanor said. "You don't fall in love with a second man unless you're out of love with the first, at least for the time being. And you don't give the impression of being out of love with Alan. You're out of sorts with him and out of sorts with yourself, and ready to raise hell. But the fact that you're trying to justify yourself with a fourteen-year-old grievance is proof that you have no real, immediate quarrel with Alan."

"Then you had some real, immediate quarrel with George just when Pierre de Saint-Euverte happened to come wandering by?"

"Yes, of course."

"What was it?"

"A girl named Peggy Dunstable."

"But she was ancient history by then!" Cathy exclaimed indignantly. "You talk of *my* raking up old grievances!"

"She was ancient history in a sense," Eleanor agreed. "That is, I knew there had been some girl, and that the affair was over and done with, and I had closed my mind to it, as one does. But the difficulty was that George is a saint."

"That comes as news. The halo isn't noticeable."

"You should talk to Ken," said Eleanor. "He's quite right:

George *is* a saint. And one thing all saints have in common is a public conscience. Even Simon Stylites made sure his pillar was a tourist attraction."

"Oh, Lord," said Cathy. "You mean George decided to Confess All?"

"Exactly. He had lived with the memory for a while by then, and had worked up a rich sense of guilt. He'd decided he was living a lie by continuing to deceive me. George is quite intelligent enough to know that I might prefer the deception, but his saintly conscience was too strong for him. So one evening when he'd had a highball too many, out the story came. I tried to stop him, but he wouldn't be stopped. I tried to get him to turn it into an anecdotal reminiscence from the timeless past, but he was bound and determined to bare his soul. So he bared it—in unedifying detail. He left out nothing. I think he expected absolution."

"My poor dear!" said Cathy. "You never told me."

"No, I was quite upset, and then events moved rather rapidly," said Eleanor. "But you'll agree it's enough to put one out of all patience with a man, feeling he hasn't the courage to absorb his own remorse. No doubt I would have got over it quickly enough. But, as you say, Pierre happened along just then, when my defenses were at their lowest."

"He *was* attractive," Cathy said reminiscently.

"That he was," Eleanor agreed. "And when you're disillusioned with one set of qualities you're apt to find a particular glamour in their contraries. Pierre was as different from George as different could be. He was dashing, he was adventurous, he was romantic. As a lover, you knew he'd probably be unfaithful but would never have the indelicacy to tell you about it."

"Was he unfaithful?" Cathy asked.

"Very likely. But not too often, I'd imagine, and not very seriously. We rubbed along well together."

"That's a dreary way of putting it!"

"Were you imagining a continual haze of romance?" Eleanor asked in some amusement. "Unfortunately that can't survive past the thirtieth breakfast."

"No, but it *must* have been more exciting than you're pretending," Cathy insisted. "All the people you met! All those places you visited!"

"Perhaps I don't have the temperament of a tourist," Eleanor said. "Certainly I was happiest when we could spend a few months quietly together at the villa, with our own little circle of friends. And, of course, when we went traveling it was generally because Pierre was looking for some dangerous new way of risking his neck, and that rather spoils the pleasure of sight-seeing."

"If you talked to him like this, I'm surprised he put up with you as long as he did," said Cathy. "You must have made a poorhearted companion for a man of that much spirit and bravery."

"Bravery is an admirable quality when bravery is called for," said Eleanor, "but no one was calling for Pierre's. He wasn't even one of those men who constantly need to be proving their courage to themselves. The truth is that Pierre was a person of such limited resources that he didn't find life itself exciting enough. Lacking any real interests, after a few months of peace and quiet he would find things becoming boring, and the only cure for boredom was to take chances, play games with death, stir up his own excitement. Lots of boys are like that before they discover what life is about, and for all his virility and glamour Pierre was a boy who hadn't grown up. In most respects he was less of a man than George is."

"How long did it take you to discover all this?" asked Cathy, much shaken by this view of her sister's grand passion, "and why didn't you come home?"

"Either you've grown more romantic over the past six years, or I've grown more realistic."

"Why do you say that?"

"Because I don't even understand your questions," said Eleanor. "You seemed to think I should have loved Pierre for his daring, which was his least admirable failing, almost a vice. But there was nothing secret about it. I knew from the first that my competition would be his flirtation with death."

"Did you know from the first he was a boy who hadn't grown up?" Cathy demanded.

"That's more difficult to answer," Eleanor said reflectively. "We fall in love with a set of qualities, or even a set of illusions, which appeal to some need in our own nature. Certainly I knew that Pierre was a less self-sufficient person than George; perhaps that gave me the feeling that he would need me more. There was a time when I hoped our life together would prove excitement enough for him, and that wasn't very intelligent of me."

"Yet I'm beginning to think that what I'd pictured as a great romance was really a great disillusionment," said Cathy. "Or are you just talking this way to discourage me about Fred Palmer?"

"Neither one," said Eleanor. "The disillusionment is all yours, apparently, for having highly colored ideas of what an elopement is like. A few months after we arrived in France, Pierre and I might as well have been just another married couple: that's how everybody treated us, and how we thought of ourselves. I'd exchanged the domesticity of Bradley's Bluff for the domesticity of Cagnes-sur-Mer. It was an entirely different life, and I fell in love with that, too, but there was nothing remarkably romantic about it. We were happy because Pierre had a very sweet nature and nothing to distract him from being charming all day long when he was in the mood, as he often was except when he was starting to get bored again."

"And you went on being in love with him?" Cathy prodded. "No regrets?"

"Regrets, naturally," said Eleanor, shrugging. "But I'm a very adaptable person—it's my principal talent, perhaps my only talent. I can concentrate on the best of what I have, and don't waste much energy missing what I can't have."

"That may be the main difference between us," Cathy said. "I suffer from a strong sense of having been shortchanged by life—so far. And there's no point in telling me I really ought to feel myself very lucky. I can count my blessings, and they add up to suburban fever."

"I gather that Alan has been overworking recently."

"Why not? He's got the child he wanted, and he's devoted to it."

'And you have too much time on your hands."

"Oh, I've only one complaint," Cathy said brightly. "On the rare occasions Alan brings home a client, it isn't a French marquis. It's a jerk from Savannah who wants to know why toilet paper shouldn't have a more dignified public image. No!—that's unfair, that makes Fred Palmer sound like a last resort. He isn't, he's a very special person. And quite remarkable."

"I haven't run into him yet," said Eleanor. "About all I know of him is that he's well into his forties and still a bachelor. And I take that as a sign of immaturity, however well disguised."

"That might hold true of men on the middle-class highway," Cathy replied. "Fred has been busy clawing his way up from nothing. He was a slum kid, working on a construction gang by the time he was sixteen, and most of a millionaire twenty-five years later. Now he has a houseful of books and records, gets to the theatre all the time; he's catching up on what he missed. Already he's better educated than most of our Ivy League gentlemen, and more of a gentleman too."

"He's more formidable than I'd realized," Eleanor said. "How serious is this, Cathy?"

"I'm not sure. It could be quite serious. He's more or less asked me to marry him."

"Of course you have to consider whether that's passion or because he sees you as the next step in his education."

"I didn't expect any sympathy," said Cathy. "You've had your fling and now you're all in favor of the quiet life."

"I've always been in favor of the quiet life," said Eleanor. "You'd be wiser to pity my mistakes, rather than copy them."

4.

For six years Ken had had his father's interested attention at his disposal. Evenings and weekends his father had been there to serve as a source of information and experience, as a sounding board, as an opponent, a confidant, a representative of the stodgy generation, an arbiter, a dispenser of pocket money and moral support, a friend, a tyrant and a court of final appeal. If the conversation were one that might be embarrassing in front of his grandmother, there had never been a problem of privacy: the two of them could always retreat to his father's study or the basement workshop. And sometimes at night, after an early date, Ken would look into his father's bedroom if the light was still on; his father liked to read in bed for an hour or so before going to sleep. Ken would sprawl on the second, empty, waiting bed, and the two of them would talk—occasionally until all hours—more like contemporaries, the past year or two, than like son and father.

This had been the pattern, and inevitably the pattern had been shattered by his mother's return: this was to be expected. What surprised Ken was finding it so very difficult to catch his father alone. His mother was always present—or perhaps it would have been more correct to say that his father, when at home, was always wherever Eleanor happened to be, even going so far as to take his cocktail into the kitchen on weekend evenings and perch on the stool there, chatting, while she prepared dinner.

There was no calculated policy in this. Ken knew that if he asked to speak to his father in private the request would have been granted instantly. But such a request would have been tantamount to announcing that he wanted to talk about his mother behind her back, and this he hesitated to do. He tried to create small excuses for taking his father aside, but several evenings of unsuccessful strategy went by before his father, quite adventitiously, came home one day with a large carton containing an elaborate new charcoal-grill-and-rotisserie intended for the back patio. Now no strategy was needed. As soon as his father had cleaned up and changed and fixed himself a drink, he and Ken solemnly went down to the basement to put the thing together.

Ken opened the carton and arranged the various parts on the floor, handing the instruction sheet to his father, and himself opening the plastic bag of miscellaneous hardware and spreading the bits and pieces on the top of the workbench.

"Was this made in the United States?" George inquired after a moment's study.

"That's what it says on the box," Ken said, looking over his father's shoulder.

"How odd," said his father. "I would have said these assembly instructions had been hastily translated from the Japanese by a first-year student of one language or the other."

"You should be used to that," said Ken. "What bothers me is that we have nine extra lock washers, while Bolt P, which seems to hold the whole contraption together, is missing."

"Don't panic," said his father, opening the drawer of the workbench. "We're sure to have something like Bolt P left over from the last gadget we assembled. I'm just as glad your mother didn't follow us down. She asks enough embarrassing questions as it is, and it might have occurred to her to wonder why so many American products, nowadays, leave all the work to the consumer. Here, will this do?"

"Maybe, we'll see. Where do I begin?"

"If this diagram can be believed, which seems unlikely,"

said his father, "those long straight rods must be the front legs. They attach to that curved one with those crossbars. Do not tighten bolts yet."

"I'm glad Mother didn't come down, too," said Ken, setting to work after a glance at the diagram. "There's something I've been wanting to ask you."

"I shall put in the oven thermometer," said his father. "It won't work, but at least it plugs up an unsightly hole. What's on your mind?"

"Not on my mind so much as Jessie's," said Ken. "She's got it into her head that Mother doesn't like her."

"You've come to the wrong person," said his father. "You're not yet accustomed to dealing with two parents, I'm afraid. You'll have to readjust a bit."

"I suppose that means that Jessie's right but you don't want to get involved."

"Not at all. It simply means that I'm taking the first opportunity to warn you against trying to use one parent as a pipeline to the other. You'll find it won't work; we're old hands at this. If you ask Eleanor personal questions about me you'll probably get a lecture on the superiority of French fathers."

"If I ask Mother a question about anything I'm likely to get a lecture on the superiority of French something-or-other."

"You've noticed that, have you?" said his father. "Well, it will wear off in time."

"It hasn't yet, and that's why I asked you. What comes next?"

"Attach E to F. Do not tighten bolts yet."

"Personally, I think Jessie's all wrong," said Ken. "I have a theory. I think it's Mother's sense of humor coming out in some of the things she says. You have to get used to it. I can see how some people might take it the wrong way."

"That's an interesting theory," said his father. "Where's

that screwdriver?—ah, good. The only thing wrong with it is that Eleanor has no such sense of humor. Not a trace."

"You're crazy!" Ken said, startled into disrespect.

"No, I mean it," his father insisted. "I've always found it one of her most restful characteristics. Also, I think it's one of the main reasons she continues to look so astonishingly youthful. Consider your grandmother. She's been a mass of wrinkles like that for the past thirty years or so. Mainly, I'm convinced, from the strain of keeping a straight face after the remarks she fires off."

"So Grandmother's the comedian!" Ken said. "I know Uncle Alan thinks so, but I've never seen it. When she's not outrageous she's just plain rude, and what's funny about that?"

"Now, she's the one who can be taken the wrong way," said his father. "As a young woman she was very, very witty, you know—noted for it in a small way. A bit on the caustic side, at times, as witty people tend to be, but there was a gaiety to her that made her extremely funny by and large. And then my father died. From the way she'd always gibed at him you wouldn't have suspected how much devotion was there, but her joy in life ended with her husband. That made all the difference. The mechanism of wit has persisted, the habit of being witty, but there isn't any gaiety left. The world has become a harsh and outrageous place, and that's how her remarks come out. But she means to amuse. And you'll notice that she's never wicked with anyone who can't strike back."

"I'll take your word for it," said Ken, who had long considered his father's patient affection for Mrs. Davenport one of the proofs of saintliness. "Where do I go from here?"

"Well, you attach that whole mess to the big bowl which they've painted a nice bright yellow so it will look particularly hideous after we've had a few charcoaled steaks in there. Do not tighten bolts yet."

"When do I get to tighten some bolts?" Ken asked.

His father consulted the instructions. "Never, apparently," he announced with delight. "That may leave it a bit wobbly, but things will be simpler if we ever want to take it apart again."

"Pass over that small wrench," Ken said. "What I don't get is why you think Mother doesn't have a sense of humor."

"I didn't say that," his father replied. "I said you mustn't look for it in her conversation. Eleanor can be amused, she has a good sense of the absurd, but she never strives to be amusing. Essentially she's a very serious person."

"But some of the things she says are so comical," Ken objected.

"It won't be a success if you show that you feel that way when your mother is merely saying what she believes. There are a few things that may mislead you. Eleanor knows her own mind uncommonly well and has no hesitation about expressing what she finds there. Neither of these is conventional. And her point of view is intensely feminine, which is unfashionable just at the moment. Together, these factors may give a touch of the unexpected to some of the things she says, and the unexpected often has the effect of seeming comical. But I assure you your mother will be deeply hurt if you go into roars of laughter every time she opens her mouth."

"I don't, of course. And perhaps 'sense of humor' was the wrong way to put it. Certainly some of her opinions are unexpected enough to put somebody off at first. Has she always been like this, Dad, even before she went to France? I can't seem to remember."

"Oh, yes. France merely added a new dimension to her disapproval of the world we live in."

"That sounds unfair," Ken protested. "Whatever Mother is, she's a realist."

"She calls herself a realist," said his father, "but in all the years we've been married I've never been able to make out exactly what she means by the word. With most people it would connote a certain willingness to come to terms with reality. In your mother it seems to mean a clear-eyed determination that reality will come to terms with her."

"Come to think of it," said Ken, "I've noticed a certain manic levity in your conversation ever since Mother came home; no doubt you'll sober down eventually. What now?"

"I've been waiting for this: 'Invert sub-assembly, insert axle and attack wheels.' Since they don't specify, I presume you can choose your own weapons. There, now!—that's precisely what I mean. Can you imagine your mother adding that last, frivolous remark? She wouldn't, and you know it. She's far too serious-minded."

All of which was most informative, to the extent that one could rely on George Davenport's perceptiveness as a judge of character, but it brought Ken no closer to the question of how his mother felt about Jessie. This thought bothered him on and off all through his date with Jessie that evening (when he felt guilty for not having tackled his mother head-on), and troubled his efforts to get to sleep later that night—or, rather, early the next morning.

On the basis of past experience, his father's evasiveness could be taken as an indication that Jessie was right. His father was notably a tenderhearted man; if Ken was upset and his mind could be put at rest by a word, his father would not have been likely to withhold that word out of mere principle—assuming, of course, that the word was true.

On the other hand, past experience was no longer a reliable guide, and this in itself was a disturbing recognition. Ken felt (a bit belatedly) like a player who discovers not merely that the rules of a familiar game have all been altered, but that the old rules, to which he had long been accustomed, were essentially false. There was nothing natural about the intimacy he had long enjoyed with his father, though it had come to seem the most natural thing on earth to him. The truly natural shape of things would have been an intimacy between George and Eleanor, with Ken somewhat excluded, although having his own close relationship with each of them. His mother's return had introduced a normality to which Ken was a stranger, ill at ease. His old memories of family life were useless, for the adaptations of a fourteen-year-old were no help to an adult. He simply had to accept the fact that he didn't yet understand the new rules, as evidenced by his surprise at the difficulty in seeing his father in private. It was entirely probable that there were established customs, standards of behavior, known instinctively to all his friends who had grown up in more conventional families, but still a mystery to him. And this could mean that he had committed some frightful breach of etiquette in asking his father what his mother thought of somebody, while his father's response, far from being an evasion, had been a courteous and delicate lesson in the proprieties.

So he had made no progress. In fact, he might even have taken a step backwards. It was possible that his offense had been so gross that his father would have remarked on it in the course of the evening: "Can you conceive of such a thing, Eleanor? Ken actually came to *me* to ask *your* feelings about Jessie!" "My God, George! Is he lost to all sense of decency?" Well, his mother probably wouldn't put it quite like that, yet she might well be waiting to take him to task for his misconduct when he raised the subject.

This apprehension could not deflect him from his purpose, but it did make him procrastinate through much of the next day, while he rejected one opportunity after another as not entirely propitious, and then carefully chose the worst moment of all: just when his mother was readying the downstairs for a large cocktail party. He hoped to get off more lightly if she was somewhat distracted.

"I'd like to ask you something," he said.

This blunt announcement was what he had finally settled on after thoughtful consideration of a dozen more devious approaches. There was a great deal of appeal to the idea of striking up some innocuous conversation into which Jessie's name could be introduced casually, allowing him to inquire, in passing, "You *do* like her, don't you?" The trouble with such an offhand question was that it might bring an equally offhand reply. His mother might say, "What a delightful girl she is!" and change the subject in all innocence, and he would have learned absolutely nothing.

A more oblique attack, such as remarking that his grandmother had nothing good to say of Jessie, might bring him another discourse on his grandmother's personality, and he was having difficulty enough assimilating the last one.

More fruitful, unquestionably, would be to lead his mother by logical steps into an objective discussion of Jessie's character, but he had not yet perfected the technique of leading his mother anywhere. The most logically planned progressions had a way of ending almost anywhere but the intended destination. Not because his mother was illogical, not because she was discursive, but because she was unpredictable. Ken might be sure that a remark was virtually rhetorical, admitting of only one possible response which would take him tidily to the argument he was trying to advance, and it would be at this very point that the conversation would calmly turn a corner and continue down a side street. This wasn't capriciousness, Ken was sure; it was simply the way his mother's mind worked. If invited to agree that American highways were better than French ones (which was indisputable), she would promptly ask what good were highways which never told you where you were or where you were going, and which were cluttered with signposts which had to be read before you could determine whether or not they applied to you, instead of symbols which could be recognized instantly and dismissed or obeyed as the case might be. So that instead of scoring an unanswerable point you suddenly found yourself trying to defend an untenable one.

"I'd like to ask you something," Ken said, having decided that a direct, unambiguous approach was the only one that offered *any* hope of success.

"Ask away," said his mother. "Let's see how this table looks over there."

"It's silly, I expect, but Jessie's convinced that you don't really like her."

"That's odd," his mother said vaguely, studying the new arrangement of the living-room furniture. "Does she often get such ideas about people?"

"Oh, no," said Ken, horrified by the suggestion that his love might be suffering from paranoia. "This is the first time. It's just you."

"Then she must put me into a special category. Have you given her any reason to think of me as a potential mother-in-law, for example?"

"Well, yes, of course," he admitted.

"Then that's the answer: naturally I make her somewhat nervous. No, I think the table is better off back where it was. How far have your plans progressed, or is that still a secret?"

"I suppose we'll be formally engaged by the end of summer. There's no real rush. We shan't be getting married till next spring."

"Next spring?" said his mother. The tone of thoughtful questioning could have applied either to her survey of the room or the immediacy of this prospect; Ken, defensively, chose the latter interpretation.

"That's right," he said firmly. "Any objections? I know all the arguments against early marriages."

"Someday you must tell me what they are; I can't imagine,"

she replied. "Early marriages must be absolutely delightful. It's early divorces that cause all the trouble."

Ken laughed aloud, wondering how his father could ever have questioned his mother's sense of humor, and then abruptly silenced his laughter, realizing that in fact his mother's remark could have been deadly serious. His next feeling was of regret for the discussion with his father, since it seemed to be making him awkwardly self-conscious in his dealings with his mother. "Anyway, you're in favor of the idea?" he asked hopefully.

"Myself, personally?" she asked in surprise, starting for the kitchen. "Well, no, I find it absolutely terrifying—but then it's none of my business."

"Of course it is!" he protested politely, trailing after her. "At least you have to tell me why you used the word *terrifying*."

"I don't have to do anything of the kind," she said. The kitchen table held florist's boxes and waiting vases; Eleanor began taking out the flowers a couple at a time, slicing a neat half-inch from the bottom of each stem, and putting the flowers at random into the different vases. "Even if I'd been around the past six years and had a better notion of your capacities, I wouldn't be so presumptuous as to try to influence you on such a matter. I have no respect for mothers who meddle in the lives of their grown-up children."

"You're not meddling," he argued. "Isn't it your duty as a mother to give me the benefit of your experience?"

"Oh, you're welcome to that any time," said his mother. "In this case I don't think it will be of much help. I married an established businessman seventeen years older than myself."

"If you weren't going to explain, you shouldn't have said what you did," Ken complained.

"That's probably true, but you asked how I felt, and I'm not in favor of lying, either."

As his mother simply went on placidly arranging flowers,

Ken was obliged to conjecture what she could have found so frightening about his prospective marriage. "We're not planning on having children right away," he offered. "Not for several years, in fact."

"Naturally I'm pleased to hear that," said his mother. "It's all those squirming little children underfoot that make an early divorce so messy. What's worse, they often make the divorce as impracticable financially as it is desirable from every other point of view."

"We seem to be at cross purposes," Ken said. "Jessie and I are only thinking of getting engaged; we haven't started discussing the divorce yet."

"It's just when the circumstances are so unfavorable that one recognizes what a good idea trial marriages would be," said his mother. "Young people ought to be able to say they're sorry it didn't work out, and go their respective ways with good humor and dignity, instead of being dragged through the sordid unpleasantness of the law courts."

"You must be thinking of some other young couple," said Ken, still inclined to be diverted by his mother's way of putting things. "I'd say our circumstances are about as favorable as could be. I have the offer of a congenial job that will support us perfectly comfortably. I don't expect to ask Dad for help, but it would be no great calamity if I did, and Laura Sydrock isn't exactly broke either."

"Those are arguments that might persuade a bank to give you a loan," said his mother. "They have very little to do with holding a shaky marriage together."

"What's going to be shaky about it?" Ken demanded. "Jessie and I have known each other all our lives, so there won't be any horrid surprises. We've been in love for ages, and it gets better all the time. We're compatible as all hell. I suppose there'll be some stresses and strains in the process of learning to *live* together, but that's true for everybody."

"I admire your self-confidence, I really do," said his mother.

"Those stresses and strains which you mention so lightly are what destroy so many marriages and spoil most of the others, and you're prepared to undertake them at a time when you won't be able to cope."

"Because I'll be learning my job?" Ken asked.

"That's understating the problem. You don't really know a thing about teaching; you'll have to find out as you go along, repairing your blunders as best you can. And at Courtney you won't just be teaching the boys: to an extent you'll be living with them. In class and out they will present you with a hundred new problems every day, and you'll have to solve them one by one because you won't have the past experience that provides so many solutions ready-made. Every difficulty will be fresh and agonizing to you. I can scarcely think of a more demanding situation—not that I doubt your ability to measure up to it. Of course you will. But I'm awed by your courage in facing the most delicate phase of a marriage at the same time. Jessie will have her own adjustments to make, and her own strains and stresses—and this means her own claims on your patience and your sensitivity even on days when the boys have done their best to reduce you to a nervous wreck. As I said, I find the prospect absolutely terrifying. But quite possibly I'm underestimating you, and in any case it's none of my business."

"For somebody who can't imagine the arguments against early marriages you seem to have covered the ground rather thoroughly," Ken remarked.

"It's at times like this that I really miss Marie-Odile," said his mother. "She could go into the garden and pick handfuls of flowers here and there and turn out the most exquisite arrangements every time. It's a gift that I simply don't have. There, that's the best I can do, and I'm not proud of it. Put this one on the table by the fireplace, will you?"

Ken carried off the vase of flowers and was halfway to

the living room when he realized that once again a conversation with his mother had been one long detour. "Hey," he called back, "you never did say whether you liked Jessie."

"Don't be silly," said his mother. "Look and see if I remembered to fill that silver cigarette box."

5.

As sometimes happens, their last departing guest was a woman who had spoken scarcely a word during the party and then had discovered her voice on the doorstep. A slow-witted woman, whose thoughts never formulated themselves till the conversation had moved on to a different topic, she would be left at the end of a party with a whole collection of unexpressed opinions. Rather than waste these altogether, she made a Parthian shower of them for her host and hostess.

In general, George would have been fretting with impatience, but this evening he was rather grateful for the delay. He knew that Eleanor was in a state of quietly suppressed outrage, and as soon as they were alone he would be the victim of it. During the party she had suffered from much misapplied tact. Several of the guests had felt called upon to make some comment on Eleanor's prolonged absence, without touching on the cause of it, and had resolved this problem by congratulating her on her courage in remaining abroad so long. These were people who had "done" Europe in a fortnight or two and had brought back vague but ineradicable impressions of picturesque poverty, overly spiced foods, rapacious natives, outlandish tongues, dangerous drivers, and a general lack of suburban amenities. Accordingly, they thought it the height of delicacy to suggest that only force of circumstances could have caused Eleanor to remain in such uncongenial surroundings, and they took for granted her relief at getting safely back to God's country.

This was bad enough. Even worse was the woman who had shown an irritating partiality for the phrase "a high standard of living": a phrase which nowadays had an unfortunate effect on Eleanor's disposition. In a smaller gathering she would have spoken her mind without hesitation, but today the obligation of playing hostess to so large a number had kept her on the move, able only to throw out a sweeping, unsatisfactory dissent before turning her attention to a new cluster of guests and some fresh indignity.

Throughout the party George had sensed the accumulation of repressed indignation in Eleanor. Now, when the front door finally closed behind their dallying guest, he spoke up promptly. "You've been on your feet for hours, do sit down," he told her. "Let me bring you a drink for a change, and let me remind you that I didn't make any of those remarks."

"Dear George!" she said in weary amusement. "Have you been expecting me to rail at you?"

"Well, not exactly," he said, looking around. Their imprisonment in the hallway had given the couple who had catered the party (Martha's sister and brother-in-law) a chance to clear the livingroom of its debris, and now they could be heard chatting comfortably out in the kitchen while they cleaned up. Familiar with postparty depression, they had thoughtfully left a tray with a couple of clean glasses, half a pitcher of drinks and an assortment of tempting canapés; George carried this over to the coffee table in front of the sofa. "I could feel you seething, and I figured all that steam pressure would have to go somewhere."

"Well, it is exasperating," Eleanor admitted. "They are so smugly positive that Bradley's Bluff is the last word in comfort and progress, and they're so ignorant. When Marie-Odile comes to visit we'll have to do a lot of explaining to convince her that she hasn't stumbled into one of the more slummish outposts of civilization."

"Now that's a splendid exaggeration!" said George. "And who is Marie-Odile?"

"You say I'm exaggerating because you more than half agree with them," she accused him.

"I try to be reasonable," he said mildly. "I know a few weeks in a hotel in Nice doesn't make me an authority on anything. But we got around a bit, and I wasn't all that impressed."

"You were looking for the things you're accustomed to," she replied. "That's how this 'standard of living' nonsense gets started. Who decides? An American counts television sets and Cadillacs, finds we have more than anybody, and declares we have the highest standard of living. A Frenchman has just as much right to count bidets—and then France has the highest standard of living and we come nowhere at all. There's not a single bidet in Bradley's Bluff—yet—and that makes it a pretty backward area to a French point of view."

"It's a matter of custom," George said.

"It's a matter of cleanliness," Eleanor retorted. "We wash the parts of us that show. And I'd like to know when Mr. Smith will be coming to install *my* bidet."

"The trouble is, that's a real project and he has to fit it in," George said. "The bathroom floor has to be ripped up and the plumbing reorganized, and then the floor will have to be retiled, of course. And I've tried my best, but I can't get Mr. Smith to see it as an emergency."

"Tell him your marriage is hanging in the balance."

"I'd like to understand that last remark," said George with pretended calm. This was the first time since Eleanor's return that she had said anything that hinted at their future, and he wasn't going to let the moment pass without comment—if only to show that his devotion was nailed to the mast. "Does it mean that you've finally decided to stay—provided I can lure Mr. Smith into coming before your patience gives out?"

"You can tell him that I'll certainly leave unless he comes soon," said Eleanor. "Further than that, my dear, I'm still not ready to be pinned down."

"I'm going to feel like an awful damn fool with that thing sitting in the bathroom if you go off again."

"Civilization isn't going to arrive in Bradley's Bluff with one bidet," said Eleanor. "You can't seem to appreciate the difference in atmospheres, George. There isn't even a book store! A rental library in back of the card shop, but no book store. In fact, I've not found one within twenty miles."

"There's one in Alden Park."

"There's a stationer's that claims to sell books. They have eight Bibles, two dictionaries, an atlas, and four of the current best sellers. Every village in France has its book store. Every town of any size has at least half a dozen. There was an American journalist staying with Eric last summer who'd been researching an article for one of the big magazines; he'd turned up the surprising fact that there are more proper book stores in Paris than in the entire United States. We couldn't believe him, but he had the figures to prove it. Doesn't that embarrass you just a trifle?"

"Wait till they get more television sets," said George. "The book stores will die like flies."

"Don't you believe it," said Eleanor. "Marie-Odile is part of the generation that grew up on television, and she's a voracious reader. Both in French *and* English. And how am I going to feel when she's in a mood to browse through a book store and I have to confess that the nearest I know of is in New York City?"

"I have no idea," said George. "Who the devil *is* Marie-Odile? I've heard the name."

"Of course you have, I've spoken of her dozens of times. She's the young cousin of Pierre's I'm so fond of."

"And she's coming for a visit?"

"We've discussed that, too."

"As I recall, it had been mentioned as a vague possibility for some unspecified future time. Now I gather it's become more definite than that."

"Possibly," said Eleanor. "I cabled her this afternoon, and already I'm beginning to wonder whether I was smart. For five years I've been trying to convince the child that Faulkner's novels should not be taken as a literal portrait of life throughout this country. Marie-Odile is fond of me, but like so many kids over there she adores Faulkner, and she's always suspected that my protests were patriotic bravado. When she discovers that I have to drive seventeen miles to get an edible loaf of bread, she'll be sure of it."

"I had a feeling that bread was going to turn up on your list."

"That's only the beginning," Eleanor assured him. "Bread, bidets and books. Would you like me to go on to C for cooking, or D for doctors, or E for education?"

"Not really," said George. "For the sake of argument I'll concede that Bradley's Bluff is a frontier camp, liable to be attacked by redskins at any moment. I'm much more interested in this Marie-Odile, and why you suddenly cabled off a summons."

"I'm not sure she can come, of course," said Eleanor. "Her last letter did sound as if she was at loose ends, though, so I took a chance."

"You've also taken a chance on driving Martha out of the house, do you realize that? She'll never stand for a guest room, too, while Mother is playing invalid."

"If Marie-Odile accepts, I'll get your mother back on her feet."

"How?" George asked.

"I don't know yet. But I'll think of a way."

"And all this happened this afternoon," George said musingly. "If you'd waited till after the party I'd have understood it better: you might have felt in need of someone to sympathize with you about the squalid, impoverished life you're leading. But this afternoon? How old is Marie-Odile, by the way?"

"Twenty or twenty-one, I forget. Her birthday is in August."

"And attractive, I presume, since there aren't any homely girls in France."

"She's not a raving beauty. But fairly pretty and quite enchanting."

"An idea is creeping up on me," said George. "I'm slow, but I get there in the end. Were you talking with Ken this afternoon? More specifically, did he mention Jessie's suspicions that you aren't as captivated by her as you might be?"

"The subject came up," Eleanor admitted.

"And you changed it."

"We were sidetracked by my discovery that those innocent children think of themselves as engaged. And are planning on making it formal by the end of the summer. Were you aware of all this, George? That it had gone this far?"

"No, I wasn't," he said. "These days you don't go prodding, you wait to be told. But I can't say I'm surprised, and on the whole I'm delighted."

"That's your guilt speaking, for the shabby way you dashed Laura Sydrock's hopes."

"What absolute nonsense!" George said indignantly. "I never encouraged her hopes, and there's no way to stop a woman from hoping short of retiring to a monastery. I don't feel at all guilty."

"You must," said Eleanor. "It's the only way I can account for your belief that the Davenports owe the Sydrock household a wedding. You are sacrificing your son to the workings of your own conscience."

"Tell me, does Ken know that he's just a sacrifice?"

"Of course not. He fancies that he's head over heels in love, just as he should. It's not for him to recognize that they're both much too young, and that next year he'll need to be concentrating on the apprenticeship to his career instead of the delights and difficulties of marriage. It's our responsibility to think of things like this. You may prefer to shirk it, but I can't."

"And your way of facing up to the responsibility was to send for Marie-Odile?"

"You can look at it like that, if you wish," she said after a pause. "Even if she can come, it may not make the slightest difference. But it seemed sensible to invite her."

George looked at his wife (as serene as ever) with a mixture of awe and dismay. Experience had taught him to be cautious in leaping to conclusions about what Eleanor had in mind. No course of action was necessarily as simple as it seemed. When another woman gave you a handful of jewelry to be cleaned you could reasonably assume that she wanted her jewels cleaned; with Eleanor it could mean that she was planning to elope to France the following morning and these were jewels which she considered Davenport property rather than her own. So in this case George did not draw the facile conclusion that Eleanor was simply trying to install a rival to Jessie in their house. That might be the essence of it, but there would be wrinkles not so easy to recognize. What fascinated him was the swift ruthlessness with which Eleanor could decide something should be done, and do it. The doubts and uncertainties that tormented him, the paralyzing inability to be *sure* what was best for somebody else, seemed to be no part of her nature. She acted as if she possessed some source of inside information on the difference between right and wrong. Often George found this an admirable quality. This time he was less certain.

"It would be nice to have a clearer notion of what you are

scheming," he said. "I presume that Marie-Odile is on her way to becoming what you describe as 'a real woman.'"

"That's my impression of her," Eleanor agreed.

"Then let me ask you a hypothetical question. You make a great point of how young Ken and Jessie are. If he was thinking of marrying a girl like Marie-Odile would you be so concerned about their ages?"

"I would certainly be less so," Eleanor said. "You see, a girl like Marie-Odile would take it for granted that a man's life-work takes first place. She would school herself to play second fiddle for a while; she would be satisfied, for the time being, to make herself a source of strength and a refuge from the anxieties outside."

"It seems to me that Jessie is quite sensible enough to do all that," George said.

"Of course she is, and her intentions would be excellent, but all her instincts would betray her. Playing second fiddle would soon become an affront to what she doubtless calls her 'integrity.' She's been brought up to an equality of expectations, and she'll think her husband's principal business is to live up to her expectations."

"You may be right," George said doubtfully. "I've seen more of Jessie, and I can't agree, but then I don't have your gift for lightning appraisal of character. It's also possible that you are prejudiced."

"Entirely possible," Eleanor said. "Which is why I wouldn't dream of interfering."

"That's not the only reason," said George. "You also know that a hint of open opposition would merely add that dash of defiance their romance has been lacking. So you won't interfere. Instead you'll just install the prettiest wench you can locate in the bedroom next door to Ken's. Did you say her birthday is in August? Will she get a gold wristwatch if he's sleeping in the guest room by then?"

"Really, George!" Eleanor exclaimed in amused surprise. "Your lapses into vulgarity are so rare that they always come as a shock."

"Forgive me," said George, not at all contrite. "I find this whole operation so highhanded that I can't make out where duplicity ends and good taste begins."

"Now you're the one who's exaggerating," said Eleanor. "There is no duplicity, and I have no scheme, as you mean it. Quite sincerely. I have invited a girl I'm very fond of for a visit. Naturally I hope Ken will like her too. That's all there is to it."

"Not quite all, I'm sure," said George.

"Essentially all," Eleanor insisted. "I do feel that Ken's acquaintance with girls has been sadly limited, and it's high time he discovered that his little tennis partner isn't the last word in femininity. But what scheme did you imagine I had in mind?"

"You could be hoping for a more sympathetic daughter-in-law. You virtually said you were."

"I was answering a question that pretended to be hypothetical," Eleanor said. "As far as Marie-Odile is concerned you're simply not being realistic. I don't want to hurt your feelings, and my love for Ken is quite as strong as yours, though a trifle rusty. But he's only a college boy at one of those colleges where the boys are encouraged to romp about playing games when they're not studying."

"That's an unmaternal way to describe the activity of next year's captain of the soccer team."

"An honor which may impress Jessie and will amuse Marie-Odile," said Eleanor. "There's not a hope that she'll find him mature enough to take him seriously, you needn't worry about that. I expect she'll flirt with him, as she'll doubtless flirt with you, much as a pianist keeps his fingers supple."

"If Ken is as callow as you make out," said George, "isn't it a cruelty to expose him to the heartless flirting of such a high-voltage creature?"

"That remark will embarrass you when you meet Marie-Odile: she's very sweet and very gentle. Yes, there's the off-chance that Ken will lose his heart to her. I see no harm in that. The experience would be educational, and Marie-Odile would see to it that he didn't get hurt too badly."

"And if Jessie gets hurt, that's just her hard luck."

"In the long run I'd be doing Jessie a kindness," Eleanor declared. "After all, there are real women at large in this world. It's entirely possible that Ken will find this type more attractive than any other. Surely it's better that he make such a discovery before he gets married rather than afterwards."

"I hope Jessie shows a proper gratitude when she loses her boyfriend."

"What makes you think she will? Ken may not take the least notice of Marie-Odile."

"If you decided it was your duty to bring this creature flying from France, I doubt if she's somebody who is easily overlooked."

"It's our duty to show a child the difference between the real thing and the imitation, but the choice will always be his. I don't know why you're so confident about what will happen."

"That's not confidence," said George. "It's sheer panic."

"Even from your point of view there's probably no need for panic," Eleanor said. "When people grow up on ersatz they often seem to develop a preference for it. Otherwise, how could so many loaves of bread be sold in this country?"

6.

Under the circumstances, which were socially somewhat unusual, there had been no real communication betwen the Davenport and Sydrock households on the upper, or parental, level. Not that there was any rift between the families. On the contrary, the decencies were carefully preserved: invitations were offered, excuses made, rain checks accepted. On both sides there was a tacit assumption that after an interval of some awkwardness, which had to be lived through, the friendships would gradually revert to normal.

Not long after Eleanor's return, she and Laura Sydrock had encountered each other in the local supermarket, under the eyes of half a dozen Bradley's Bluff matrons who pretended to study cans of cat food while hoping for food for gossip. The two women had put on a performance that was a model of its kind. Laura had briskly made it obvious for aisles around that Eleanor's reappearance was the happiest event of the summer. Eleanor had acted the part of one who, if she had not been encumbered by a head of cauliflower in either hand, would no doubt have rushed into Laura's arms.

One evening a few weeks later George and Eleanor had been having a drink in the lounge of the Country Club when Laura arrived on the arm of Colonel Dawson. There were exaggerated wavings and blowings of kisses across the crowded room, intended more for the attention of interested onlookers than to signal that the parties had noticed one another, and a little later Laura had stopped by the Davenport table for a moment's public chat. George had boomed out a jocular inquiry as to whether Ken was still in good health, since the boy spent more time at Laura's than at home; and Laura recognized that Eleanor's dress could only have been made in Paris, and declared that she had never seen anything so becoming.

Such meetings, however, while serving to frustrate the natural malice of Bradley's Bluff, were useless for any exchange of opinions between the families. The appearances of friendship were maintained, but the rapport of friendship still waited on events which had not yet occurred. One of these days they would meet at a convivial party, and unaffected, sympathetic conversations would smooth over the awkwardness, and things would get back to their old footing. But for the moment there was no way for Eleanor to know that the impending engagement she so much disliked was equally disapproved of by Laura Sydrock, although for entirely different reasons.

"To tell the truth, I'm surprised at both of you for even considering the idea," Laura announced over cocktails one evening when Ken was staying for dinner. "Your generation is supposed to sneer at such formalities. Long engagements ought to be square, or whatever the new term is."

"One of our charms is that we're old-fashioned," said Jessie. "We don't like rock and roll and we do look forward to a long engagement. Of course that will come after Ken has taken you aside and asked your permission to propose to me."

"That you're an idiot I've always known," said her mother. "But you, Ken! How did she talk you into going along with such nonsense?"

"You both make it sound as if it's going to stretch over most of a decade," Ken said. "It's only till next June, after all."

"Even so, it's preposterous," said Laura. "It's an anachronism."

"Somebody has to uphold the fine traditions against the

frivolity of the older generation," Jessie declared solemnly. "Decorum is being trampled underfoot. Youth must make a stand."

"Historically there must have been a justification for engagements," Laura said. "I suppose there was a good logical reason, once, for the publishing of banns."

"I'm in favor of that," said Jessie. "What are they and where do we get them published?"

"Even into the middle of the last century the custom made sense of a sort," Laura said, "when young men were going off on jobs that could keep them away for several years. But nowadays? It's an outdated custom kept alive by the diamond industry."

"Speaking of diamonds, I expect a large one," Jessie said. "It's getting larger all the time."

"You heard that, Ken?" said Laura. "Surely by next June you can find a girl who isn't so rattlebrained and mercenary. Excuse me a moment."

She went off to the kitchen to see how the dinner was coming along, and Jessie promptly bounced into Ken's lap. A moment later she leaned back and looked at him reproachfully. "There was something I had to tell you, and now you've distracted me."

"You're rattlebrained," he explained. "Even your doting mother says so."

"No, I'm not: I've remembered. It's Betty's swimming party—she's changed it to next Friday. That's okay with you, isn't it?"

"Sure," he said. "No, wait, maybe not. That just may be the day Saint-Euverte's cousin is arriving, I forget. Mother wants me to drive her to the airport."

"Coming for a *visit?*" Jessie asked incredulously.

"The rest of the summer, I gather."

"Sometimes I think your father is out of his mind," said Jessie. "After his experience you'd expect he'd want to keep that pack of Don Juans at the other side of the Atlantic. Instead he rushes out with the Welcome mat. He doesn't learn, does he? I suppose this one keeps a string of polo ponies and flies his own airplane."

"Possibly, but I doubt it," said Ken. "This one's name is Marie-Odile."

"A female of the species!" exclaimed Jessie, her eyes narrowing a trifle. "Say, this is awfully sudden, isn't it? There wasn't any mention of an expected guest the other evening."

"I only heard about it yesterday. But from the way Mother spoke, it was something she'd been planning for some time. I know she's very fond of Marie-Odile."

"Marie-Odile," Jessie repeated. "That's a middle-aged sounding name. I picture her as gray-haired, quite stout, and bothered by rheumatism."

"Try again," invited Ken.

"I'm not sure that I want to," Jessie said. "Could it be that your mother is importing a *girl*?"

"It could, but you needn't make it sound as if Mother's involved in the white-slave trade."

"That's not as far from what I had in mind as you might think. How old is she and what does she look like?"

"I've no idea what she looks like and I couldn't care less," Ken said. "I imagine she must be about your age, more or less; Mother said something about her having to be back in Paris for the start of classes."

"Has your mother suggested this will be a good chance to practice your French?"

"No, Marie-Odile speaks English. But Mother did say she might want to borrow me for a few evenings to squire her about a bit until she's had a chance to meet people."

"That won't be necessary," said Jessie. "The evening she arrives I'll throw a party for her and I'll invite every heart-free young man within three suburbs."

"That's a terrific idea!" said Ken.

"I wonder if Eleanor will think so," said Jessie, slithering back to her end of the sofa just before her mother returned to the living room.

"All that's needed nowadays," said Laura, resuming her own line of thought, "is sufficient warning for friends and relatives so they can rush into the city and buy elaborate wedding presents which you'll never use anyway. If you announced your engagement during the Easter holidays that would give ample time to everybody."

"I can't see that it really makes so much difference," Ken said.

"It probably wouldn't make any difference," Laura said, "but it just might. Everything's going so smoothly now. Why not just leave things the way they are?"

"There's a lot to be said for getting a man firmly nailed down," said Jessie.

"Engagements don't nail anybody down," Laura replied. "They just create a situation that's a little more awkward to back out of."

"I'm all in favor of that, too," said Jessie.

"I know I'm sounding stuffy, but that's one of the penalties of being sensible," Laura said. "A year is a long time. Of course you're convinced your feelings won't change, but you're both smart enough to know that they *could*. Jessie will be meeting new men. Ken, you'll be meeting new girls."

"Sooner than you might imagine," Jessie muttered.

"You should both be free to go on looking around, seeing what the world has to offer, without feeling guilty if you kiss the wrong person good night," Laura argued. "As soon as you're officially engaged you begin to feel you've committed yourself, and there's a sense of pressure. Especially for a man. If it goes on too long you can start feeling trapped."

"I already do," said Ken. "I've felt that way for years. It can't get worse."

"But it can," said Laura. "At the moment there's absolutely nothing to prevent you from shaking hands good-naturedly with Jessie and walking out of here."

"Nothing except the knowledge that there'd be a knife in my back before I reached the door."

"Right," said Jessie. "I could stand your walking out but that good-natured handshake would be too much for me."

"Sometimes I wonder why I go through the motions of being serious with you two," Laura said. "It's a waste of breath. There's nothing so cocky as youngsters before life has pulled the rug out from under them once or twice. Can't you understand that if your feelings don't change, it doesn't matter when you get engaged? But there's always that chance in a million that something will go wrong. A broken engagement means a certain amount of public embarrassment, and the risk is so easily avoided."

"I suppose that sort of tawdry prudence is natural to middle age," said Jessie. "I'd hate to think that Ken had such a chickenhearted streak in him."

"Come to think of it, Laura is probably right," said Ken. "It isn't fair to expose you to the spiteful mockery of your catty little girl friends when you get jilted."

"I won't have to listen to it," said Jessie. "I'll be busy explaining to the judge that everything went black."

"As a mother, I'm a complete failure," declared Laura. "I had hoped to instill . . . oh, bother!" She broke off at the sound of frantic buzzing from the kitchen, and hurried from the room.

Jessie was just starting to reach for a cigarette; she arrested the motion and looked suspiciously at Ken. "Have you said anything to your mother about the engagement?" she asked.

"Well, yes," he admitted.

"You weren't planning to, yet."

"I didn't volunteer anything. Mother sort of guessed, and there didn't seem much point in lying about it."

"When was this?" Jessie asked very casually.

"A couple of days ago."

"A couple of days ago. And yesterday, out of the blue, this Marie-Odile is coming for a visit."

"I don't see any connection," said Ken.

"I do," said Jessie. "In the days before telephones and telegrams it might have been a coincidence, but even then it would probably have been witchcraft."

"What would?"

"I told you your mother didn't like me," Jessie said impatiently. "You blurt out our plans and now at high speed your mother's importing a girl she does like."

"You do have a persecution complex!" Ken said with astonishment. "This is a hell of a discovery to make! Next thing you'll be suspecting me of being unfaithful every time I look at a girl. The engagement is off."

"This is the first time I've realized that probably half the people who get locked away for delusions of persecution are absolutely right."

"You're not right," said Ken, "you're all confused. It's not *my* mother who is opposing this engagement, it's *yours.*"

"We don't have to worry about what Mummy says," Jessie replied. "She just has a horror of long engagements, and she has a reason. When she was still a kid she was engaged to a boy who eloped with somebody else at the last possible moment, after most of the wedding presents had arrived. So it was heartbreak and a mess to straighten out, and the humiliation on top of everything was just too much. If she's prejudiced, you can hardly blame her."

"I'm not blaming her," Ken said. "I merely pointed out that she's the one person who has spoken up against our getting engaged. Mother hasn't. Her attitude is that it's none of her business."

"That's no comfort," said Jessie. "Your beard wasn't any of her business either, and look what happened to that!"

"This is nonsense," Ken said irritably. "It's stupid to have mother-in-law problems before you have a mother-in-law."

"The odd part of it is that I don't have any doubts about getting along with Eleanor once we're married," Jessie said. "It's reaching that point that's beginning to worry me."

"I don't see why," he grumbled. "This isn't like you, Jessie. When you were down in Bermuda you knew I was going out with Frank's sister. And though she's a little sexpot if there ever was one, that didn't seem to bother you a bit."

"It didn't—much," she said. "Whether you realize it or not, the game's got rougher since your mother came home."

"Only in your imagination. Because you've persuaded yourself that Mother doesn't like you. Which simply isn't true."

"I've never said she *dis*likes me," Jessie said. "She's always pleasant, she's even casually affectionate, as if you'd brought a cute puppy home with you. But I know damn well I'm not what she wants for a daughter-in-law. For one thing I suffer from the ghastly disadvantage of not being French. You're about to discover that they turn out a superior style of girl over there."

"Oh, no I'm not," Ken said. "And I can think of lots of better reasons why Mother invited Marie-Odile for a visit. She probably wants someone who will sympathize with her for living among a bunch of barbarians."

"You may be right, but I don't believe it," Jessie said. "My persecution complex tells me that Marie-Odile is a razor in disguise."

7.

Most weekday mornings George Davenport and Alan Briggs caught the same train; they would ride in side by side, companionably but not communicatively. Each carried an attaché case of papers pertaining to the day's work ahead, each had his copy of the *Times* to be digested, and their business interests overlapped but little. Occasionally one might remark on an unexpected death in the business community, and the other would grunt a response, and that would be the extent of the morning's colloquy. In a sense they rode together because each could rely on the other's silence, which was less certain in a stranger.

On the homeward trip in the late afternoon, relaxing after the day's decisions, they were much more expansive—but they rarely met. There was a choice of several trains leaving at short intervals, and sometimes a scramble for seats, so they left these encounters to chance. Often it would be on the platform at Bradley's Bluff that they found they had traveled back together but separately.

This afternoon, however, George was sure he had spotted Alan far ahead of him in the station. Feeling sociable, and aware that he had rather neglected the friendship since Eleanor's return, he walked through the train until he found Alan sitting in a window seat in a half-empty car, staring morosely out at the platform. George pushed his attaché case onto the rack and sank into the adjoining seat. After a moment Alan turned with the blank, incurious expression of one whose gaze would skid over unfamiliar features and focus on some point beyond, denying all human contact; then his face lit into a wry grin.

"Hail, Menelaus!" he said.

"I have a new insight into that old story," said George. "Nobody's ever thought of it before. But when Helen finally got back home she spent the first six months holding forth on how much better everything had been in Troy."

"You're undoubtedly right," Alan said.

"I can almost hear it," said George. "The slaves were more obedient, the children were better behaved, the chariots didn't rattle as much and the bread was ten times as good."

"Yes, but the best of the joke is that *she* was undoubtedly right, too," Alan said.

"The bread may have been terrific, but the Trojans lost the war, didn't they?" George said.

"Wars may be sophisticated but they can't be civilized," Alan said. "Other things being equal, a war will be won by the country with the greater supply of barbarians. Troy was a civilized place.

"Did they have bidets?" asked George.

"The Greeks get all the publicity," said Alan, "so we tend to forget that Troy was an old and thriving city when the Greeks were a lot of rowdy upstarts. It commanded the trade routes from the Aegean into the Black Sea and stayed rich for five centuries or so by taxing the passing merchants."

The train lurched gently into motion. Despite vacation time, their car was almost full now, and the din around them was composed of shoptalk, baseball arguments, dirty stories, and theories about the day's juiciest news item: a nineteen-year-old lad having wiped out the family of six next door "just for the hell of it." George felt mildly self-conscious, a bookish conversation of this sort seeming so out of place in a commuters' train, but Alan, as usual, was oblivious of his surroundings.

"The Trojan War was actually fought by the Greeks to

break this monopoly," he went on, "but if there really was a Helen they used as a pretext, and she was hauled back to Sparta by some semisavage princeling, I don't doubt that she spent her time complaining of the decline in her standard of living."

George was surprised, never having noticed this familiarity with the classics in his friend. "Have you been doing some homework?" he asked.

"Of course," said Alan. "Ken's conceit amused me, and I brushed up a little to see what had caught his fancy. And then I became morbidly interested. The parallels go further than the boy realizes."

"Really?" said George. "If I'm the semisavage princeling, who are you?"

"Agamemnon," said Alan.

"I remember him," said George. "A great and noble warrior. You're not the type at all."

"My battles are fought on Madison Avenue, but they can be surprisingly bloody at times," said Alan. "Still, Helen had a sister, Clytemnestra, and there I am: husband to Clytemnestra and the father of Iphigenia. Do you remember Iphigenia?"

"I majored in economics," said George. He was grateful now that they had been provided with these classical sobriquets, for there was no way of telling whether they might be overheard by some other resident of Bradley's Bluff, unlikely as this seemed as long as they kept from shouting at one another. "My memories probably date from some children's version of the legends."

"The Greek armies assembled in Aulis to set sail for Troy," Alan said, "but for weeks and weeks there was no wind, and the men were growing restless. So Agamemnon consulted the oracles, and acting on their advice he sent for his daughter, Iphigenia, and sacrificed her to the gods. And that same day a fair wind sprang up, and the fleet sailed off to war. There's a feeling around the house, these days, that I sacrificed our own Iphigenia for a favorable wind."

"Oh, Lord," said George, instinctively concealing his prior knowledge.

"Clytemnestra wasn't happy with the way her daughter had been disposed of," Alan continued after the tumult of people crowding off at the first stop had subsided, "and she took herself a lover. They had a fine time while the war lasted, and the day Agamemnon returned from Troy they teamed up and killed him. In the bath, according to some sources. Personally I prefer showers, and I've taken to locking the door."

"It must be hell to be imaginative," George remarked.

"You don't think my Clytemnestra and her lover are murderous types?" Alan asked. "I'm inclined to agree with you, but I'd be put out if we were mistaken. So I'm always just a little nervous returning home from the daily war."

"Rubbish," George said firmly, unable to determine how serious Alan was being. "To begin with, I don't believe for one moment that your Clytemnestra has a lover. In the second place, in spite of the fancy names, I think you're being damned indiscreet."

"I thought the husband was always the last to know," Alan retorted. But he fell silent, looking moodily out at the overcrowded countryside, until a few more stops had gone by. When he resumed, the car was almost empty, with nobody recognizable within earshot. "Are you being protective, George?" he asked. "Or is it possible that the gossip hasn't reached to Elmwood Drive?"

"Oh, the gossip!" said George. "Think of those hundreds of women waiting for us to come home: they all read the same magazines, watch the same television programs, go to the same parties. Conversation would die altogether without gossip. To give them credit, much of it is highly imaginative."

"In this case, allowing for a certain exaggeration, you can take the gossip as pretty accurate. She's running around with the bastard, no question about that."

"Perhaps so," said George. "But there are plenty of harmless explanations before you get to the one you've chosen."

"Are they credible, though?" Alan asked calmly. "This is something I've never understood. When the lady down the street spends half her time with a stray man we draw the rational conclusion that she's getting laid. We might be wrong, but the probabilities are high that we're right."

"I don't know that I'd go along with that," said George.

"In the teeth of your experience you're still a romantic," Alan said. "It's the national disease. When it's *our* wife or *our* daughter or the heroine of some bloody comedy we want to believe in some innocent, platonic explanation of her misbehavior. That's why I've never been able to stand comedies. At the last moment we're told that she was just doing it to make her husband jealous, or something equally fatuous, and we're supposed to clap like crazy and go home convinced that our daughters are virginal and our wives are chaste."

"Are you happier convinced of the opposite?" George asked.

"Well, I feel more sensible, anyway," said Alan. "Less like a yokel. I know the chances are that Clytemnestra is getting laid, I accept it, and I find that the idea doesn't horrify me quite the way it ought to. The problem is, where the hell do we go from here?"

"Does that mean you're thinking of a divorce?" George asked.

"I?" said Alan in surprise. "God, no! What put that in your head?"

"If you don't especially care how she's behaving. . . ."

"I didn't say that," Alan replied. "Naturally I care. I don't like it a bit. But apparently I'm not one to smolder with jealousy; I can see that there's some poetic justice to the situation; I can even accept my share of the blame for past mistakes. If she has to get a fling out of her system I won't enjoy it, but I can suffer through it. If that's all it is. The trouble is that I like that girl and I liked my life the way it was. It's a mess you should have some sympathy with."

"Oh, I do," said George. "You're beginning to be afraid that it's getting out of hand?"

"I'm beginning to have a horrid feeling that she's one of these old-fashioned girls who believe in the double standard," said Alan. "She takes it for granted that I, as a man, can sleep around a bit without getting involved emotionally."

"I hope you haven't made the blunder of rubbing her nose in that," said George.

"No, but I know she suspects, and it's never worried her. But for her to do the same thing would be all wrong, from her point of view. It's that God-damned double standard. She's a nice girl, and nice girls have to fall in love to justify the behavior of their bodies. On this score I'm bound to say that her older sister set a deplorable example."

"For six years you gave the impression of admiring Eleanor for having had the courage of her convictions," George pointed out coldly.

"George, I was wrong and I apologize," said Alan. "That was before I appreciated what a pernicious thing the double standard is. And of course the circumstances were different: I was misled by the superficial glamour of someone running off to another country. But I was wrong; I admit it. It's outrageous the way women mess up good marriages just for a roll in the hay. We should have a right to expect the same emotional self-discipline they expect of us."

"I'm inclined to agree," said George, "though if Eleanor were here I suspect she'd find a flaw in your argument."

"Where would the world be if we fell in love every time we got an erection?" Alan demanded. "Society is held together entirely by our self-control, while the women are becoming more and more irresponsible. There's something radically wrong with this country if wives can't be discreetly unfaithful without always making it into a grand passion."

"It's a pity Eleanor is missing this," said George. "She'll never have such an opportunity for telling us how much more elegantly the French handle the problem."

"I don't especially want to be quoted," Alan said, "but I wouldn't protest if Eleanor could knock some sense into her sister's head. Somebody has to, and I feel maddeningly helpless. For the time being she's stopped listening to me."

"Have you been trying to reason with her?" George asked. "That's probably a mistake."

"In the name of sanity, what do you expect me to do?" Alan rejoined. "I'm damned if I'll carry on like the tenor in a second-rate Italian opera. I'm not pretending to be without jealousy: of course I'm jealous, but I'm ashamed of it. It's a grubby feeling, getting upset because you can't have exclusive possession of somebody else's body—like a child wanting to smash up a toy if he can't have it all to himself. The only fidelity that really matters is emotional fidelity, and that's what I'm afraid of losing."

"It's a highly civilized point of view," said George, "but by your own theories it's possible to be overcivilized. If it lost Troy the war it might lose you your wife."

"Just what are you suggesting?" Alan asked. "That I should go home and punch Cathy in the nose to prove the depth of my affection?"

"Well, hardly. But it does seem to me that your attitude of lofty sufferance could be mistaken for simple indifference."

"As a sympathetic listener you're unbeatable, George. As an adviser on how to keep a straying wife in line, unfortunately, your background doesn't inspire confidence."

"For all I know, it might be good advice," said George. "I never even got the chance to put it into practice."

8.

"I suppose you've heard about our guest," Eleanor said.

"Indeed I have," said Mrs. Davenport. "What's more, I've been expecting your visit. It won't work."

"We seem to be at cross-purposes before the conversation has begun," said Eleanor. "What won't work?"

"I don't intend to be evicted from my deathbed just so that Martha has more time to devote to a French hussy."

"I should hope not," said Eleanor. "Marie-Odile is a properly brought up girl and quite capable of tidying up after herself. There won't be any extra work for Martha."

"That's difficult to believe," said Mrs. Davenport. "I still remember the state in which dear M. de Saint-Euverte left the bathroom on the rare occasions he troubled to take a bath."

"He was accustomed to servants," said Eleanor, "but Marie-Odile is just a poor cousin. She's a Verdurin, from the strict and serious side of the family. She's very sweet and rather shy. If you don't frighten her off you'll find her extremely charming."

"There's little harm in that, since I'm not likely to run off to France with her," said Mrs. Davenport. "You may need to keep a sharp eye on George, though. This house has become a terminus for flights to the Continent."

"George has been vaccinated," said Eleanor. "I'm less sure about Ken."

"He's so infatuated by that graceless hoyden of his he wouldn't notice if you packed the entire Folies Bergère into the guest room."

"Yes, and that's partly your doing," said Eleanor. "You have a lamentable influence on Ken. On the whole, I'm pleased to hear that you're not planning on getting up and about just yet."

"It's clever of me to exert any influence at all on someone I scarcely see," said Mrs. Davenport. "As a matter of courtesy he drifts in and out of here daily, and pretends to talk to me, but nothing whatsoever penetrates that besotted haze he's in."

"I wish that were so," said Eleanor. "You keep trying: you lie here thinking of new ways to tease him about his little love affair. When you remark that tennis does so much for a girl's figure, all of it disastrous, he hears you. And he goes off more determined than ever to see that graceless hoyden, as you call her, as the most exquisite creature on earth."

"If he can believe that, there's no hope for him," said Mrs. Davenport. "He should have inherited better taste from our side of the family, but there were other factors involved."

"There's always hope until they actually get married," said Eleanor. "Unfortunately, an engagement seems to be in the offing."

"That doesn't surprise me," said Mrs. Davenport. "We mustn't forget that the poor boy spent his most formative years in one broken home. No wonder that he's impatient to start another of his own."

"Surely it isn't fair that Ken should be punished for my misdeeds," Eleanor said persuasively, "and you and I appear to be agreed that Jessie would be just such a punishment. Now I'm giving Ken a chance to discover there are more attractive girls in the world, but if he goes around breathing defiance all the time I'm afraid he won't even notice."

"Are you planning to push Ken into the arms of this French wench?" asked Mrs. Davenport.

"Well, only in a manner of speaking," said Eleanor. "After all, the other girls in Bradley's Bluff are only paler versions of Jessie. Marie-Odile is entirely different, and we can hope that Ken will find the contrast appealing. You could help by fighting down the temptation to be witty at Jessie's expense. Nothing blinkers a man like chivalry."

"May I ask whether my son is aware of what you have in mind?" said Mrs. Davenport. "The last I knew he was still showing an uncritical fondness for Jessie."

"He hasn't changed his mind," said Eleanor, "but he sees the logic of expanding Ken's horizons before it's too late."

"Nothing addles a man's wits like uxoriousness," said Mrs. Davenport. "Has George led such a contented life that he thinks you the ideal person to pick a bride for his son?"

"I don't understand," said Eleanor. "I took it for granted you'd be in sympathy with my idea. You are no more enchanted by Jessie than I am."

"I'm the wrong age and the wrong sex," said Mrs. Davenport. "That doesn't mean I want to see my only grandson snared away by a foreign trollop."

"You're quite unfair! Marie-Odile is a charming girl."

"I don't doubt it," said Mrs. Davenport, "and this household has suffered enough at the hands of French charmers for one lifetime. Better the hoyden I know than a hellion I don't."

"Well, I can't ask for anything more than your sudden preference for Jessie," said Eleanor. "That can't do any harm."

"Anything to oblige," said Mrs. Davenport. "You won't care if I tell Ken exactly what you're up to."

"Not in the least. He already expects an outrageous twist to anything you say, so he won't believe you. But you'll focus his curiosity on Marie-Odile very nicely."

Mrs. Davenport blinked reflectively for a few seconds. "There is a pathos to the helplessness of a dying woman that seems to escape your notice," she said finally. "Possibly Ken will be more observant. I will have the suggestion of a death rattle in my voice when I dig up the old gossip that Jessie wasn't really Brian Sydrock's daughter at all."

"I never heard that story," said Eleanor.

"Perhaps I just invented it, perhaps not," said Mrs. Davenport. "But it's a splendidly Victorian reason for opposing their engagement with what little strength I have left. And it will make Jessie into such a romantic figure that Ken won't pay any heed to this Parisian streetwalker you're bringing into our once-respectable home."

"I wonder that I could have expected a little cooperation," said Eleanor.

"Are you leaving?" asked Mrs. Davenport. "Ken must be due back soon; you might remind him that he's not yet paid me his daily visit."

"No, I think not," said Eleanor. "I get the distinct impression that your condition has taken a turn for the worse, and that visitors are too much of a strain."

"Are you the sort of woman who would deny me the comfort of my only grandchild?" asked Mrs. Davenport. "I suppose that's a foolish question."

"I'm thinking of your welfare," said Eleanor soothingly from the doorway. "The hearty bumptiousness of the young doesn't belong in a sickroom. Ken is no more selfish than most young men, but I'm sure he'll be relieved to hear that his courtesy visits are too exhausting."

"Just a moment," said Mrs. Davenport. "You've brought home to me the folly of leaving two defenseless men exposed to your mischief-making. Especially now that you're bringing in reinforcements from abroad. I shall be getting up—even though I strongly suspect that this has been your design all along. But I cannot permit you a free hand in mutilating the lives of *all* my descendants, even though it means giving up my hopes of dying in peace. Starting tomorrow Martha can set the dinner table for five."

PART FOUR

La Cousine de Paris

7.

Self-consciousness was not one of George Davenport's weaknesses. He had long since come to acceptable terms with himself, and rarely worried about what sort of impression he might make on other people. When he did, it was on the level of reminding himself to eschew facetiousness in the company of Mr. Murch, who had very little sense of humor at best, and none at all where the stock market was concerned. Certainly George never gave special thought to his personal appearance except to make sure, when he went out with Eleanor, that he was wearing one of the neckties she had given him, since she considered his own taste in haberdashery to be deplorable.

Yet this hot summer evening, after a quick shower on returning home, he found himself hesitating among his collection of short-sleeved shirts, wondering what sort of first impression he wanted to make on Marie-Odile Verdurin. The arrival of this temptress from overseas, this representative of the country his wife so admired, had come to seem a small crisis in the household. George was of several opinions about the visit, all of them unfavorable in one fashion or another. He had to fight against a wild temptation to put on a torn shirt and faded dungarees, and let himself be discovered in this outfit sitting on the front step, bare-footed, scratching at his crotch and chewing on a turnip.

Lacking the courage to go through with this scheme in the full view of Elmwood Drive, and doubting that the larder would provide a turnip anyway, he looked for other ways to live up to the image of the Ugly American. Surviving from some forgotten Caribbean cruise were russet slacks and a shirt printed with purple and orange flowers, bought in a moment of tropical aberration and preserved for the annual charity costume dance at the Country Club. If he could just turn up a fat cigar to complete the picture, he should satisfy whatever preconceived notions Marie-Odile might be bringing with her. If Marie-Odile began contemplating her flight back to civilization as soon as she crossed the doorstep, George's feelings would not be hurt in the slightest. The obvious drawback to this whole idea was that Eleanor might not be amused. He was going to have to treat their guest with careful courtesy, however he might feel, or risk his wife's indignation—and this he could not afford.

So he put on a dark blue shirt and light-weight gray slacks, feeling cowardly as he did so and somewhat resentful, suspecting that regardless of what he wore he could be seen as a dressed-up peasant whose shanty offered inedible bread, an insufficiency of books, a scandalous lack of bidets and God knew what other deficiencies besides.

The dressed-up peasant trudged down the stairs to make himself a much-needed drink. Just as he was taking out the bottle of bourbon the front door slammed, and an instant later Cathy Briggs appeared.

"They're not here yet?" she said. "This place has come to be the suburban waiting room for planes from France. Fix me a martini standing up, George."

"Are you here to inspect the French pastry?" George said. "The plane was late, and now they're trapped in the evening traffic."

"Is this the child's first visit to the States?" Cathy asked.

"Why do you call her a child?" George asked irritably. "I have every reason to suppose Marie-Odile is a fully grown maiden, chronologically if not morally."

"Eleanor speaks of her that way. Is it her first visit?"

"Of course," said George. "Who needs to go slumming a second time?"

"I seem to detect a certain lack of enthusiasm for your little guest."

"Not at all," George said hastily. "After a bad day at the office I'm grumpy until I get my evening tipple. Where's Alan, by the way?"

"Who knows, who cares?" Cathy said. "There was some story about a Chicago client who had to be wined and dined and then poured aboard one of the Queens. It's dull enough to be true."

"You don't even have the excuse of a bad day at the office for the way you sound," said George, vigorously stirring her martini. "We have to cheer one another up or we'll make a rotten welcoming committee."

"Cheer me up, George," Cathy said. "Tell me funny stories: tell me the real reason you never divorced my sister. These days I'm looking for some good, solid arguments against divorce."

"There's only one," he said. "The grass on the other side of the hill is seldom as green as it looks from a distance."

"I'm also tired of potted wisdom. I get enough of that at home."

"If you're looking for originality about marriage you're several thousand years too late," said George, handing Cathy her drink and picking a seat that gave him a view of Elmwood Drive through the picture window. "Cheers!"

"After all this time you'd think we'd try a new system," Cathy said. "Marriage is like democracy: everybody knows that neither of them works, but nobody's come up with anything better."

George glanced thoughtfully at his sister-in-law poised on the edge of the sofa, looking, as almost always, on the point of departure to someplace more amusing. Apart from their physical beauty, Cathy and Eleanor had always seemed to him as dissimilar as two sisters could be: the one serene and serious, the other high-strung and volatile. He would have thought the first essential for a successful model was a phlegmatic calmness, to withstand the ennui of waiting around and the tedium of posing; yet Cathy's career had proven how mistaken this idea could be, for she was nervous, impatient, and temperamental to a fault. And where Eleanor's opinions were usually slowly formed and intensely individual, Cathy showed that brittle sophistication which spoke (to George's way of thinking) of too many New York cocktail parties. She would say whatever might flash into her mind, provided it could pass for being "clever." George considered her delightful company for brief periods and could not imagine being married to her, but those very qualities which would have exhausted and exasperated him, Alan found stimulating. Alan delighted in his wife's vivacity, he needed someone who could match the restlessness of his own mind, and Alan was the one who counted. Cathy's chatter about divorce was disquieting, and George wished that Eleanor were there to carry the burden of this conversation.

"There's nothing wrong with democracy," he said, "except the notion that it can be conducted by a bunch of politicians with no required qualification but a love of office. It's much the same with marriage: all we demand of people is some urge to go to bed together, and we're surprised if this isn't enough for a lifetime."

"That may hold true for youngsters," Cathy said. "When we become older we have a clearer idea of what we want from a marriage."

"Perhaps," said George. "But are we any likelier to get it?"

"I should think so. When romance doesn't dazzle us so much and we can see the other person for what he is, and recognize the qualities we're really looking for."

"I suspect that's the worst delusion of them all," said George. "Every quality that attracts you has a drawback you hadn't bargained for: there's no virtue without its thorns. Marry a man for his charm and you have to live with his selfishness, marry him for his strength of character and you'll live with his lack of charity, marry him for his modesty and you're liable to find it's well justified. The first five years of any marriage are spent learning to live with the dark side of the very qualities you most admired. And if you haven't got out by then you're either happier than you realize or you're remarkably slow-witted."

"It was fifteen years before Eleanor ran for it," Cathy said. "Do you think her as slow-witted as that?"

"Eleanor took a recess," he replied. "She needed a holiday. It's a humbling thought, but perhaps all wives should get an occasional holiday."

"Yes, I know you always took it for granted she'd return," said Cathy. "But that hope must have worn thin. I'm surprised you didn't start a divorce, at least: it just might have jolted her into thinking of coming home."

"I didn't want a divorce," George said. He paused to organize his thoughts, not with any intention of baring his own soul, but with the hope of shaping an argument that might help dissuade Cathy from taking an irrevocable step. "You see, I wasn't a youngster when I married, I was thirty-five," he started, prepared to be eloquent with wisdom, and found that he had lost Cathy's attention even before he had begun. She was looking not at him but beyond him, with an expression of wonderment. He turned, and was astonished to see his mother, fully dressed for the first time that summer, advancing in slow, cautious steps across the carpet. "This is a pleasant surprise," he said, leaping up to offer her his arm "You must be feeling better, Mother."

"Must I? Well, I'm not," said Mrs. Davenport, lowering

her fragility gently onto an armchair. "But I understand that we're due for a foreign invasion, and the menfolk of this house are easily outnumbered. My place is at the barricades. I only regret that I have but one life to give for my country. Make me an old-fashioned, George."

"I'm beginning to feel sorry for Marie-Odile," said Cathy. "She's going to get an odd first impression of American hospitality."

"Once upon a time this house was hospitable to excess," said Mrs. Davenport. "We even lent one of our wives to a passing tourist; it was years before we got her back again and she'd been turned into a tiresome expatriate. That sort of thing leads to xenophobia. Chastity begins at home."

At the bar George was suddenly discovering that he would have preferred to have his mother safely back in bed again, out of the way. Somehow it had not occurred to him (had it occurred to Eleanor?) that she would emerge from her bedroom up in arms against the intruder. There was a real danger that his mother's scathing tongue could reduce a girl to a pitiable state, especially a girl whose English might not be equal to the onslaught, and any normally chivalrous young man was certain to gallop to the defense of a maiden in distress. "Calm down, Mother," he advised. "Marie-Odile is probably quite harmless."

"I am sorry to hear you say that," said his mother. "It reminds me that you used much the same phrase about Saint-Euverte six years ago. 'He seems like a harmless young man,' you announced, and with your usual perspicacity went on to express the hope that Eleanor wouldn't find him too much of a bore. But I fear I interrupted a chapter of your fascinating autobiography, George. Don't let me stop you."

"He was about to explain why he never divorced Eleanor," Cathy said with malicious amusement.

"Excellent," said Mrs. Davenport. "If he has a coherent explanation, I never managed to elicit it. Of all people, a stockbroker should know the meaning of 'cutting one's losses,' but not George. I dare say he has beggared half his customers by urging them to cling to bad investments."

"On the contrary," said George, handing his mother her drink, "I've made them rich by stopping them from dropping sound investments just because the market looked unfavorable for a while."

"If Eleanor is your idea of a sound investment," said Mrs. Davenport, "I can understand why you waited so long for a senior partnership. She's a two-legged speculative risk."

"There's the car," said Cathy.

"Stand by to repel boarders!" said Mrs. Davenport.

George turned to see that Ken had sensibly stopped in front of the house, where it was easier to unload in good weather, rather than having to carry luggage up from the garage. George joined Cathy at the window to watch, while his mother sat where she was, chanting scraps of patriotic verse modified to the occasion. "Listen, my children, to this report, of brave old Emily Davenport. . . ."

"Plenty of luggage," remarked Cathy. "Oh!—she's a tiny little thing, isn't she, George?"

"Nothing's been left out, though," he said, grudgingly admiring the lines of a slender but perfect figure.

"Shoot if you must this old gray head," declaimed Mrs. Davenport.

"But she's not nearly as pretty as I expected," George added with relief.

"You think not?" said Cathy. "My God, George!—what *were* you expecting?"

This question remained with George throughout the evening. What, indeed, had he been expecting? Obviously some flamboyant, big-bosomed creature, extravagantly attractive, exuding sex appeal from every pore. Eleanor could scarcely be blamed for this flight of his fancy: she had spoken of someone gentle and shy, she had warned that he would be embarrassed by some of his anticipations, and as a rule Eleanor's statements could be taken quite literally. Yet in this case he had chosen to disbelieve her. He had allowed his imagination to run riot, he had built up a figure of such ravening, prowling seductivity as had probably never existed outside Hollywood or some adolescent daydreams.

And now he felt foolish. Marie-Odile was just as Eleanor had described: a sweet girl, somewhat shy, moderately attractive. His first impression that she was not pretty at all—almost plain—did not survive for long. To someone accustomed to another style of good looks, Marie-Odile's features at first seemed exaggerated: her eyes too far apart, her nose too pronounced, her mouth too wide, and except for some subdued shadowing around the eyes she appeared to wear no make-up. Perhaps an hour or so went by before George caught himself appreciating what an attractive girl she was, positively admiring her. It was hard to account for this change, for Marie-Odile had none of that remarkable animation of expression which can sometimes give charm to the homeliest face; she had a rare but delightful smile, and otherwise was apt to express herself with gestures rather than grimaces. George was forced to believe that he had been blinded by prejudice, for once he had discovered that Marie-Odile was pretty he was never again able to see her as anything else.

But her most striking characteristic in the hours after her arrival was the perfect poise of her silences. George had not realized what a loquacious family the Davenports were: it seemed they never stopped talking. Amidst this babel of voices Marie-Odile was a contrast in quietness, answering with courteous brevity the questions fired at her about the flight across or her reactions to the sight of New York—even contenting herself with monosyllables when a monosyllable was sufficient, something no Davenport had ever been known to do. Later on it was evident that this initial reticence must be attributed either to shyness or uncertainty while her ear became attuned to the flow of nonstop English, for by the next day she proved capable of upholding her end of any discussion, and by the end of the week was chattering away like the rest of them. But that first evening she listened, and spoke mostly when she was spoken to, occasionally turning to Ken for a low-voiced consultation about something that puzzled her.

The rapid familiarity between this pair startled George until he realized that nothing more need be seen in it than the natural alliance of young people against the middle-aged world. Coming into a strange environment, Marie-Odile would look automatically (without any sinister prompting) to the person whose age alone should make him sympathetic to her timidity. Ken responded fraternally. If he made any comparisons between Marie-Odile and his prospective fiancée, he would find all the superficial advantages on Jessie's side, for she certainly was the more strikingly attractive and had the more positive personality, more sparkle and more vitality. Marie-Odile's appeal was softer and more insinuating but not without its effect, for Ken was already easier with her than he usually was with strange girls, whom he generally treated with polite indifference or heavy-handed, bantering flirtatiousness, depending on whether he found them alluring or not. He treated Marie-Odile with such relaxed indulgence that you would have thought he had brought a favorite younger sister back from the airport.

The most extraordinary reaction to the newcomer was Mrs. Davenport's. Her warlike attitude vanished the instant Marie-Odile crossed the threshold. While continuing to subject her family to her customary acerbity, Mrs. Davenport behaved towards their guest with an unexpected and uncharacteristic grandmotherly solicitude. On no evidence that George could see, she decided the girl was a frail and sickly creature, probably suffering from anemia, and quite unable to withstand the rigors of a flight across the Atlantic. Marie-Odile's gentle reassurances carried no authority. Mrs. Davenport spent much of the evening denouncing her family for tiring Marie-Odile with their foolish questions, and urging that the poor, poor child be sent directly to bed.

George was inclined to feel that some of his wife's unpredictability was rubbing off on the other members of his household.

2.

On the centermost of the three mats he had spread at the pool's edge Ken lay stretched out contentedly, waiting for the girls to emerge from their locker room. Now that he had adjusted to Jessie's jealousy—half joking and half deadly serious—he was enjoying it. He rather liked the sense of being fought over, even if the fighting was all on one side. His only anxiety was that Marie-Odile (who hadn't a clue as to what was going on) might get scratched by an inadequately sheathed claw, but he relied on Jessie to be too clever for that: she would never give her supposed rival the chance to seem victimized. She was like a tigress politely indicating the boundaries of her private hunting ground, merely hinting at the fate trespassers could expect.

Jessie was the first to appear: quite a lot of her. She had acquired a new bikini for the occasion, and it seemed probable that she had looked for the skimpiest she could find, then chosen a size too small. The effect was stunning. Scrawny Mrs. Fitzpatrick, at one of the umbrella'd tables, might snort and comment audibly about the rules of the Club being stretched too far, but her husband (the Chairman of the House Committee) showed no sign of being offended. Ken, philanthropically disposed, didn't mind at all. This was his, all his, and if Jessie felt like improving the scenery he would bask in the envy of less fortunate men.

"Very nice," he congratulated her. "No one would mistake you for a boy."

"I'm furious," she muttered, dropping to her knees beside

him. "I've been outwitted. She stalled until I'd changed, and then produced the most demure little one-piece you ever saw. Now I'm going to feel brazen and exhibitionistic."

"Don't. Think of all the pleasure you've brought into a lot of drab lives."

"I wasn't planning to be a civic service," she said "Do *you* like it?"

"The more of you I see the happier I am," he replied. "If I were any happier this afternoon Mrs. Fitzpatrick would call the cops."

"You *don't* like it!" she said accusingly.

"But I do, love, I swear I do," he said. "If there weren't so many people around I'd find other ways of showing my enthusiasm."

"And you don't think it's exhibitionistic?"

"Oh, come on," he said. "If you didn't want your figure to be noticed and admired, then you made the weirdest purchase of the summer. There's Marie-Odile, and I don't think 'demure' was quite the right word."

The French girl's bathing suit was one piece, certainly, but a cunning pattern of black and white stripes enhanced the lines of her body, and when she turned to watch a youngster dive off the high board it was apparent that the suit had virtually no back at all, and Marie-Odile had a lovely one. She carried a string bag of impedimenta, and as soon as she reached them produced a bottle of suntan lotion and began anointing herself.

"The sun is formidable," she explained gravely. "I peel easily."

"I would have suspected that," said Jessie. "It can lead to trouble."

"Not if you take precautions," said Ken.

"You can never be safe enough," said Jessie. "Marie-Odile must be prudent about peeling."

"Eleanor gave me this," said Marie-Odile, looking at the bottle. "She said it was very good. Ken, you will do my back, please?"

"With pleasure," he said.

"With efficiency would be more to the point," said Jessie, lying back to dissociate herself from this performance. "The important thing is to cover the territory briskly, without dawdling or detours."

"I'm an old hand at this," Ken said. "Nothing slapdash about my workmanship."

"It is annoying," said Marie-Odile, "but I cannot become tanned like you and Jessie. Jessie is even darker than you are."

"She works at it," Ken said.

"We have a fairly private sun porch," Jessie said.

"There's a touch of the nudist about her, in case you hadn't noticed," Ken said. "Jessie is responsible for most of the low-flying planes over Bradley's Bluff."

"Thank you," Marie-Odile said to Ken. She recapped the bottle and flipped over on her stomach; the three of them lay side by side, sharing the ashtray that Ken had filched from one of the tables. "It is a charming swimming pool, this. With the terrace up there, the colored umbrellas, the tables with people drinking, it reminds me a little bit of Eden Roc."

"Where's that?" Jessie asked.

"On Cap d'Antibes, not far from where Ken's mother lived. A lovely place. But the pool is mostly for children and old ladies; one swims in the sea. There are diving boards out over the water, and a raft. And water-skiing too, if you want, but that is expensive."

"Don't tell me Mother went water-skiing," said Ken, shaken by this picture.

"Oh, no, she only had lunch there sometimes," said Marie-Odile. "But I was swimming there almost every day last summer, when I was staying with my . . . with your mother. She was very disappointed that you could not come."

"My God, this is last year's plot!" said Jessie. "She doesn't give up easily, does she?"

"How is that?" asked Marie-Odile.

"Day by day I am learning to appreciate Eleanor," said Jessie.

"Yes, she is ravishing, isn't she!" Marie-Odile said with enthusiasm. "Do you say that? So delightful, so original. I adore her, she is one of my favorite people. One never knows what she will say next."

"You think she has a sense of humor, don't you?" said Ken, who was conducting his own poll on this question.

"But certainly!" said Marie-Odile. "Always she has been very dry, very droll, as long as I have known her. Even at first, when she scarcely could speak French, she always made me laugh."

"My French would probably make you hysterical," Ken said.

"No, you do not laugh at my mistakes in English, do you?" said Marie-Odile. "That would not be gallant, and you are very gallant. It is that the things Eleanor says are so unexpected. I still remember the first time I met her. She and . . . does it embarrass you if I speak of my cousin Pierre?"

"No, not at all," said Ken, feeling that family history had made him sophisticated.

"It was Eleanor's first winter there," said Marie-Odile, "and they stopped by to visit us on their way to Austria for the skiing. Pierre was telling about his plans and suddenly he stopped in the middle of what he was saying and looked at Eleanor and asked 'But what will you be doing with yourself all day while I am skiing?' One could see he had not thought of that before, sometimes he was very selfish. Eleanor smiled. 'What will you be doing all day while I wait for them to carry you home?' she asked. 'Rushing around countryside that

God intended for chamois and children on sleds. I will occupy myself no less sensibly.' It was not Eleanor's mistakes in French that made us laugh, I assure you, it was Pierre's expression. He had never heard skiing spoken of so disrespectfully."

"Until just now your cousin has never been entirely real to me," Ken said. "He's been a name in a legend, like Paris."

Marie-Odile looked bewildered. "Paris?"

"Not your home town," Jessie said. "The character who ran off with Helen of Troy. She probably nagged at him to stay indoors while javelins were flying about."

"Yes, I see," said Marie-Odile. "And you are right. Eleanor has a great love of living, and she could never understand why Pierre had to flirt with death to be happy. He was a strange man, with so much charm on top of melancholy. His father and two older brothers were all killed in the war, and I thought, myself, that perhaps he always felt guilty for having been too young. Well . . ." her face lit suddenly into a smile, "I am Paris's cousin, the cousin from Paris, and I am too hot." She got up gracefully and went to the pool's ladder, where she climbed down into the water and swam about with a gentle breast stroke, keeping her hair from getting wet.

"It's curious," Ken said reflectively. "Mother has spoken of Saint-Euverte a number of times. Yet somehow he's never come alive to me before."

"Is that so surprising?" Jessie asked. "I don't suppose most mothers chat about their extracurricular love life to their sons. In this case it's almost unavoidable, but even Eleanor must feel a sense of constraint."

"In front of Dad, maybe, out of politeness," Ken argued, "but why with me? I'm not a kid."

"No, but you're devoted to your father," Jessie said. "I can give Eleanor credit for ordinary tact, even if I feel left out of the fan club you're forming with Marie-Odile."

"There's nothing exclusive about it," Ken said. "Anyone can join."

"I'm not qualified, darling: I don't find Eleanor droll enough. But I'm glad you've found something in common with your little houseguest. You can share your Oedipus complex with her, and save the rest for me."

"She's a sweet kid, isn't she?" said Ken. "Nothing to ruffle your paranoia."

"Her perceptiveness unnerves me," said Jessie. "She's been here a couple of days and already she's uncovered facets of your character I'd never noticed. Since when did you become so very gallant?"

"Since I explained to her that she mustn't take Grandmother seriously."

"I dearly wish I could arouse this protective streak in you," Jessie said. "Perhaps I'm not coy enough. Would you do me a teentsy-weentsy favor, Ken?"

"Not if you ask for it that way."

"Just a little favor. Please?"

"Name it."

"Grow your beard again . . . ."

"What?" he cried. "Spend the rest of the summer feeling like a hedgehog? It feels horrible when it's just getting started, and it looks worse."

"*I* wouldn't mind," she said earnestly. "I'd promise not to mind."

"Well, I would," Ken said. "It's too hot, and I don't feel like going through all that teasing again. Besides, it wouldn't be polite."

"You might have left out that last objection," Jessie said. "Never mind. It was just a crazy idea."

3.

Possessed of a true ear and a booming baritone, George Davenport in his collegiate days had enjoyed a small glory as a singer. In the late hours of a fraternity-house party there would be demands for George's rendition of one of the sentimental ballads of the previous century, which by then had come to seem hilariously comical. And even nowadays, once in a long while—usually, as this evening, in the shower—he would be in a humor to let loose with as much as he could remember of some of those far-off, beery triumphs.

Oh, comrades! fill no glass for me
To drown my soul in liquid flame,
For if I drank, the toast should be,
To blighted fortune, health and fame. . . .

The maudlin words, and the mock-lugubrious tune echoing so satisfactorily off the tiled walls, were no index to George's state of mind. On the whole, he was quite pleased with life. The first fortnight of Marie-Odile's visit had slipped by with nothing to indicate that Ken was liable to become infatuated with their guest; she was proving a pleasant addition to the household, good company for Eleanor (the two of them chattered French by the hour), and no threat to the future as George preferred to imagine it.

Then by a mother's sacred tear,
By all that mem'ry should revere . . .

Having safely negotiated the high note, he stepped out onto the bath mat and began toweling himself off. It was a mixed satisfaction to realize that he and Eleanor would shortly be dispossessed from their own bathroom for a while, Mr. Smith having sworn by all that was holy that he would be coming in next week to rip up the floor and reorganize the plumbing.

Though boon companions ye may be,
Oh, comrades! fill no glass for meeeee.

He finished the song, and slipped on a robe to protect himself against the sudden chill of their air-conditioned bedroom.

Eleanor looked at him from the mirror of her dressing table. "You have the most mournful way of celebrating your good moods," she remarked.

"That was my greatest success," he boasted. "Sung with a straight face and a slight tremolo here and there, it was guaranteed to reduce a roomful of drunken young men to helpless laughter."

"For someone faced by an edgy evening with Cathy and Alan, you're remarkably lighthearted," Eleanor said. "Has the stock market been behaving the way you intended it to?"

"No, no—I'm just being completely selfish for a change," he said, wandering around the room assembling the clothes he planned to wear. "I refuse to worry about potential upheavals at the other end of Bradley's Bluff; I have enough problems to keep me preoccupied at home. But I begin to think I can see sunlight ahead, and I shan't let you discourage me."

"I wouldn't dream of it," said Eleanor. "I'm happy myself, that Mr. Smith has finally managed to fit us into his schedule."

"Yes, I take that as a good omen where you're concerned," he said. "Merely an omen, yet I do get the feeling that you're more at home all the time, you're settling down again. You still find things to disapprove of, but then you always did: it's something of a hobby of yours." In all truth, this was a quality of Eleanor's he had always appreciated. Her way of turning the obvious inside out was a safeguard against taking things for granted; there could be little fear of growing staid and stuffy while she was around. "But the tone of your disapproval has altered over the last month: nowadays you sound more like an indignant native than a critical outsider. That pleases me. And I'm delighted that you've presented Ken with a kid sister. He can have all the sisters he likes, as long as incest doesn't creep into the picture."

"You are more in Ken's confidence than I am," Eleanor said, examining her nails to see if they were dry. "Has he spoken of these brotherly emotions, or are you drawing your own conclusions from his behavior?"

"I've had a fair amount of practice at that," George said. "If there had been any change in his feelings towards Jessie, I would have noticed it."

"No doubt you're right," said Eleanor. "Yet there's not been any further talk of the engagement."

"There never *was* any talk of the engagement that I know of, apart from what you wormed out of him one afternoon. But that doesn't mean anything, anyway. I gather from Ken that Laura has her own reasons for urging them to put off the formalities until one of the vacations. They may have decided to humor her."

"What a sensible woman Laura is!" said Eleanor. "I look forward to being back on friendly terms with her again."

"So the two of you can discuss all her daughter's deficiencies?" George asked. "I'm surprised at your stubbornness, actually. I expected your opinion of Jessie to improve as you saw more of her."

"Perhaps it has," said Eleanor, "but my opinion of Ken has also been improving all the time. I can't pretend to be impartial, but he strikes me as an uncommonly decent young man. And that means he's more vulnerable than most."

"He can look after himself," George said comfortably.

"How?" Eleanor asked. "What defenses does a young man retain when he falls in love? By nature, Ken is one to fall in love wholeheartedly and unreservedly; like you, he has a deep sense of loyalty. I wouldn't want to see him any other way, but it puts a lot of responsibility on the girl A thoroughly self-confident girl can cherish such a love; a more insecure girl will be uneasy with it. Quite unconsciously a girl can come to despise a man for putting a higher value on her than she puts on herself."

Quickly dressed, George stretched out on the chaise longue to wait for Eleanor to be ready. "I can recognize some of the faults you find in Jessie," he said, "but I'm staggered to hear her accused of any shortage of self-confidence."

"Are you?" said Eleanor. "Yes, because she's pert and bright and flirtatious you take her at face value. Yet how can she possibly be self-confident? She's an only child, brought up entirely by her mother; she hasn't a shred of firsthand knowledge of what a marriage ought to be or ought not to be; she's had neither a good example to learn from nor a bad example to be warned by. In fact, she knows even less about the problems of living with a man than Ken knows about teaching."

"If the prospect frightens her, I give her credit for keeping her fears well hidden."

"Of course it doesn't frighten her," Eleanor said. "What you mistake for self-confidence is simply a healthy child's conviction that the unpleasanter rules of life will be suspended on her behalf. Divorce is rather like sudden death: they both exist, but as misfortunes that overtake other people. Jessie's marriage is sure to be a blissfully happy one for the simple reason that she is Jessie: no other reason is necessary. It won't be until something goes wrong that her insecurity will appear. She won't have the foggiest notion how to cope, she won't even be convinced that she ought to cope with anything so unjust, and somebody will have to pay for her inexperience. Why Ken?"

"Why not?" asked George. "It occurs to me that his own exposure to matrimony leaves something to be desired. Perhaps the two insecurities will cancel out one another."

"Darling George, sweet George!" said Eleanor affectionately as she prepared to slip out of her dressing gown and into her dress. "Your reproaches are always put so gently."

"No reproach," he protested. "It's just that we tend to overlook the blemishes in our own children."

"Quite true," she said. "Ken may well have a lifelong distrust of foreigners. He may regard all house guests with a jaundiced eye. He may dislike letting his wife go down to the corner for a pack of cigarettes for fear that she won't come back. It's not agreeable to realize that his wife may suffer on my account, but you're perfectly right."

"Have I won an argument?" George asked, bewildered by this sudden collapse of resistance.

"Well, not exactly," Eleanor said, giving her hair a last touch of the comb. "You've reminded me of one more reason why Ken's wife will need as much well-founded self-confidence as possible. There!—I'm ready. And we ought to get moving."

They went downstairs. The young people were already gone; Mrs. Davenport sat alone in the living room with the evening newspaper George always brought home with him. He bought it for the closing prices and the business gossip; his mother gleaned the front pages for stories of murder and rape, having discovered that Eleanor was easily needled into deploring the country's atmosphere of violence.

"We'll say good night now, Mother," George declared, hoping for a quick escape. "You should be asleep by the time we get back."

"They're still carrying on about that enterprising young

man who exterminated the family next door," said Mrs. Davenport, holding up a withered cheek to be kissed. "It's all hypocrisy: with more lads like that we wouldn't need to worry about the population explosion. He came from a broken home, incidentally. His mother ran off with a Polish acrobat."

"Unless the family next door was Polish, I don't see the connection," said George.

"Everybody thought he was such a good-natured, friendly young man," said Mrs. Davenport. "Nobody suspected what was festering beneath the surface. Don't you ever worry about Ken?"

"Constantly," said George. "Each morning before I go to work I count the neighbors. Sleep well, Mother."

But as they continued down the stairs to the garage, George sensed Eleanor's abstraction and could have cursed his mother's mischief-making sense of humor. He was tired of hearing Eleanor build whole sociological theories on these freaks of savagery, and determined, this time, to seize the initiative himself. Accordingly, as soon as he was at the wheel of the car, backing out into their driveway, he said: "It's a bad legacy from our pioneer heritage. Ugly, admittedly, but it's easy to put too much stress on that ugliness and forget that it's just the dirty side of the coin: the obverse of much that is best and most vital about this country."

"You do insist on the silver linings, don't you, George?" Eleanor said. "Even where mass murder is concerned."

"Violence is not a decadent characteristic," he said. "It's a sign of immaturity, if you like—but immaturity, for all its disadvantages, is a stage of growth and promise and discovery." This was an argument George had given much thought to, in an effort to find some logical way of answering his wife's dissatisfactions with the land he loved. He had learned that the more obvious arguments simply would not do, arguments based on the country's prosperity being especially treacherous, since they left out of account so much that was taken for granted in other countries.

For example, Bradley's Bluff tended—if only out of snobbery—to send its children to private schools. So school taxes were an abomination, the public schools were held to a starvation budget and had become quite bad, and you had to go along with the crowd or penalize your child. Ken's schooling, by the time it was finished, would have cost George upwards of forty thousand dollars, probably closer to fifty. This was a considerable sum to put aside after taxes, and how families with three or four children managed, even in this relatively well-to-do community, George could not imagine. Clearly a European who could count on the best schooling available without being out of pocket was in an enviable position. When you added in medical benefits, hospitalization, freedom from worry about the lingering terminal illness which could plunge a family up to its ears in debt, it was obvious that a Frenchman earning half George's income could actually be better off.

When backed into a corner, George couldn't insist that an accumulation of dishwashers, deep freezers and color television sets was *better* than a good public school system, so he had had to go looking for some other proof of his country's superiority, and had found it in the very immaturity Eleanor sometimes complained of.

"Our past has been one of adolescent growth and change," he said now, "and we're damned lucky to have no other. We have no remnants of feudalism to escape from, no class system, no dead hand of tradition. We don't pretend to know all the answers, but we're looking for them. The older countries may be more civilized in one sense, but in another they're finished: they've found their solutions and they're stuck with them, they aren't going anywhere. We're still floundering. But there's no criticism you can make of this country that thousands and even millions of Americans aren't making at the same moment. We're still hacking out our future, and by the sheer nature of things some of the solutions we find will be better than anything the world has seen before."

"You're very eloquent, George," said Eleanor, "but the eloquence sounds as if it might have been left over from the turn of the century."

"Giants take a bit longer to grow up," he replied. "In a small country it's easier to isolate a problem, and limited resources will determine how you solve it. Here we can afford to look at the problem from fifty points of view and experiment with fifty solutions. The waste may be appalling and the progress slow, but the possibilities are unlimited. This is where the action is, Eleanor, the adventure and the excitement. Like it or not, this is where the future is being manufactured."

"Perhaps," she said. "It's the romantic argument, certainly. You can't expect it to carry much weight with a realist."

"I have always respected your individuality," said George, "but I wish you hadn't so much faith in your private pipeline to realism."

"What would you prefer that I call myself?" asked Eleanor. "I act on the assumption that I have one life to lead, and the more active half of it is already behind me. The thought of adventure and excitement doesn't stir me in the slightest. I'm not the stuff that pioneer women were made of; I'm not an idealist. I'm a cat who wants the most comfortable home she can find."

"Then I'll just have to look for arguments with more cream in them," said George.

"I don't know that I come and go by arguments," said Eleanor. "I suspect not. Isn't most logic the self-justification of romanticism?"

4.

Something odd about the atmosphere of the living room nagged at the back of Ken's mind, but for quite a while he could not determine what it was.

Certainly not that his grandmother was complaining of life's indignities: this was a part of his oldest memories. "You cannot imagine what a bedlam it was," she said accusingly to George, as if he were at fault for spending the day at his office while his bathroom was being torn apart. "Only two men were up there, but it sounded as if seven of them were demolishing the house with sledge hammers. Ken was actually driven outside to do some work in the garden, and you know what a rare phenomenon that is."

"It was a scorcher, too," said Ken. "The lawn mower needs a new spark plug."

"The noisy part of the job is finished," his father said. "The rest shouldn't be too bad."

"Everybody else could escape," said Mrs. Davenport. "Martha shamelessly announced that the basement needed cleaning, and disappeared to the only refuge in the house. I was left to suffer alone, as usual."

"I'm surprised the girls aren't back by now," George remarked. With the excuse of needing a new dress for the Hendersons' annual party, Eleanor had taken Marie-Odile off to the city for a day's sight-seeing.

"There are several possibilities," said Mrs. Davenport. "They may have been picked up by the Vice Squad. Or they may still be comparing all the ways in which New York doesn't measure up to Paris. I must say, when the noise here finally stopped this afternoon I found the house curiously restful. Quite like the good old days."

And here, Ken suddenly realized, was the oddity that had been puzzling him. For six years this grouping of his grandmother, his father and himself had constituted the normal household: this was the family portrait of his adolescence. With the return of his mother, and his grandmother's retreat to her bedroom, the grouping had vanished for a while, not to reappear until this particular late afternoon. And in the interval, brief though it had been, the portrait had faded, become a souvenir of the past. This threesome was no longer an entity; in fact, it was surprising now to think that it had seemed an entity until so recently. Now they were merely a part of something that waited to be completed. The sense of this swept over Ken with a rush of irrational panic: he imagined the traffic accidents that might occur between the city and home, leaving them incomplete again and all the more bereft after this interlude of entirety. Up to this point he had been coping with the incidental embarrassments of his mother's return (for though he might delight in her presence there were still the pussies of Bradley's Bluff to drop snide remarks within his hearing); now he faced the idea of losing her again, and saw that the thought was intolerable.

"I much prefer things as they are," George said to his mother, and then very casually added, "How about you, Ken?"

It was the first time his father had openly invited his opinion. "We shouldn't have let her go off this morning," Ken blurted. "She's still not used to the car, Dad; she complains that you aim it instead of steering it."

His father looked amused and pleased. "I expect she'll be able to aim it homeward."

"The highways are much too safe," said Mrs. Davenport. "A

preposterously high percentage of people get to their destinations every day, dashing the hopes of their loved ones."

Only a moment or so later the slamming of car doors in the garage below punctured Ken's new-found anxiety and gave his grandmother fresh cause for discontent. "There they are now," she said. "Peace has ended. We will have to listen to all the reasons why New York City is a disappointment."

But on this score Mrs. Davenport was a false prophet. Marie-Odile returned from the day's outing bubbling over with enthusiasm. Evidently they had had great luck with traffic and parking, and had made a real tourist's circuit of the city from The Cloisters to Greenwich Village. Somehow they had managed to fit in a glimpse of Lincoln Center, a trip to the top of the Empire State Building, a quick bite at the Automat ("I decided that came under the heading of sightseeing," Eleanor explained), several hours of shopping and even a brisk trot through the Museum of Modern Art. Eleanor admitted to being exhausted, but Marie-Odile was ebullient, professing herself enraptured by everything she had seen. Nowhere on earth could there be such an exciting city; the vitality was formidable; everybody, but everybody, was in a hurry! So many old buildings being torn down, so many new ones going up! Such a lot of elegant department stores, and then she had almost been terrified by the enormity of Macy's.

"Enormousness," Ken corrected her.

"Thank you," said Marie-Odile. "Best of all I adore the skyscrapers. One has seen them often at the cinema, but it is different when you stand there yourself, looking up and up. And the panorama from on high is absolutely magnificent! You have seen it, of course, Ken?"

"I was taken up once when I was a kid," he said. "It was a misty day, and you couldn't see much. There were promises of another visit, but nothing came of them."

"Don't interrupt with your juvenile frustrations, Ken," said Mrs. Davenport. "It has been a long time since I have heard a good word spoken about this country, and I am enjoying it. Please go on, Marie-Odile. The more fulsome the compliments, the better."

"No, I am talking too much," said the French girl, instantly self-conscious. "I know how boring it is when our cousins from Toulouse come for a visit and insist on telling us all about Paris. And I am dying of thirst. Some beer, I think . . . Eleanor?"

"A lovely idea," she replied, and Marie-Odile had darted off to the kitchen before Ken could get to his feet.

"What a pleasant change," said Mrs. Davenport. "Evidently people from abroad can see more of our attractions than someone who has merely spent a few years there."

"You have to make some allowance for the French notions of *politesse,*" Eleanor said. "Marie-Odile considers herself a guest here, quite properly, and would think it bad manners to make any critical observations. What she'll say when she gets back home is another matter."

"Not necessarily," George disagreed. "We grow blind to the things we take for granted, and when we get a chance to make comparisons we tend to be struck by the novelties that appeal to us. She may go back with a wholly favorable impression, not having had a chance to notice the deficiencies you're so aware of at the moment."

"I know one thing she's noticed," Ken said, grinning. "Girls in Bermuda shorts—and the French *politesse* went right out the window. She insisted it must be a school uniform created by some man-hating nuns."

"There are some criticisms that cannot be quarreled with," said Mrs. Davenport. "If she spoke out about the hats men have taken to wearing recently, I could be offended only by the moderation of her language."

"Things like that are fair sport," said Eleanor, "but you couldn't lure her into serious fault-finding if you tried. I wish as much could be said of us when we go abroad."

"I wonder if you're right," said George, just as the French girl returned to the room with two glasses of beer. "We've been talking about you behind your back, Marie-Odile."

"Oh, yes?" she said, undismayed, handing one of the glasses to Eleanor.

"You've been here long enough to look around a bit," said George, "and we get the impression that you are enjoying yourself—"

"Very much, yes," put in Marie-Odile.

"—but you must have noticed some things that struck you unfavorably, and we were curious as to what they might be."

"What sort of things?" asked Marie-Odile.

"I have no idea," said George. "Has anything disappointed you or shocked you?"

"Ah, I see," said Marie-Odile. "Yes, this morning, not long after we got into New York. We were driving about, and Eleanor was confused by which way the streets went, and we stopped to ask directions from a policeman. He was not at all polite. He did not salute and he did not even say good morning. I was very shocked."

"If he'd done either, Eleanor would have been more shocked, and she was driving," George said. "She might have crashed the car. But that's not exactly what I meant. You only had a glimpse of New York, after all, but by now you can compare the way of life around here, in Bradley's Bluff, with what you're accustomed to. Something must have disturbed you."

"Disturbed me?" said Marie-Odile, seeming to find this an odd concept. "There is much that is different, naturally, and still much that I do not understand. That is part of the fun, is it not? But one is not disappointed in what one doesn't understand, and sometimes I remember to ask Ken to explain."

"Well, what sort of thing don't you understand?" George asked doggedly. "Preferably something that Ken hasn't already made clear to you."

"Oh . . . ," said Marie-Odile, looking about her for an illustration. "I cannot, just at the moment—yes, the windows! I have wondered about them."

"Do you mean the shutters?" Ken asked.

"No, no, the windows, the big windows," Marie-Odile said, gesturing, and turned to Eleanor for help. "Comment s'appellent ces grandes fenêtres?"

"Picture windows," said Eleanor.

"Yes, picture windows, thank you. These I find curious, but I forget to ask. In back of every house there are trees, lovely gardens, grass, flowers, bushes—all so pretty. But these picture windows are always in front, where you look at the other houses and the cars going by in the street. That I do not understand."

Ken was amused by the observation, and even more by the reactions to it: his father looked utterly nonplussed, his grandmother was blinking furiously. It was his mother who finally broke the silence. "Well, you begged for it," she remarked.

"I'd simply never thought of it before," said George, as if the question had suddenly become troublesome. "It *is* peculiar, isn't it?"

"There must be a reason," Marie-Odile said anxiously, obviously fearing that she had been tactless.

"Of course there is, my dear," said Mrs. Davenport. "You must realize that houses like these are not designed by proper architects but by building contractors. And from a building contractor's point of view, it is natural to be terrified of who might be arriving at the front door."

5.

George had been toying with the idea of a private talk with Marie-Odile long before he persuaded himself that it could probably be managed without embarrassment on either side.

He had more confidence in the girl's composure than he had in his own. She obviously saw nothing remarkable in the fact that for six years she had known Eleanor as her cousin's mistress, and now was visiting Eleanor in her husband's home —and perhaps in Marie-Odile's experience there *was* nothing unusual about such metamorphoses. She seemed to have a practiced delicacy in dealing with the subject: she would speak of her cousin in passing, casually but unaffectedly, and she would reminisce about the times she had spent with Eleanor, but without any reference to a relationship between the two. When Marie-Odile spoke of Pierre and Eleanor together it was always as part of some larger gathering, to which they might have come independently; there were no explicit reminders that they had been living together, neither was there any sense that the implicit truth was being coyly strained or evaded. George admired the girl's easy dexterity. And he had noticed that she spoke of Pierre affectionately but objectively, without a trace of hero worship, even critically. She had spoken with scorn of his indifference to such serious matters as politics, she had called him "selfish," and she had several times called him "frivolous"—an ambiguous word, but one which the earnest younger generation never used in a complimentary sense. So it was likely that if George himself raised the subject, Marie-Odile would satisfy his curiosity without the least hesitancy.

Disclosing this curiosity, however, was another matter.

There was something humiliating in admitting, out loud (and to a girl!), to being curious about one's wife's lover. Yet there were a number of unanswered questions about Eleanor's elopement, and George had had to live with them for six years. Her running off had staggered him, but for all the wrong reasons. He had known that Eleanor was very much out of sorts with him for the time being. With the episode of Peggy Dunstable behind him, he had appreciated that after a dozen years of even the best marriage there could come a faltering of the enchantment and a susceptibility to other attractions. If Eleanor had thrown herself into an affair with almost any other man on earth, George would have been offended, hurt, indignant, but much less surprised. It was her eloping with Pierre de Saint-Euverte, specifically, that had so shocked him.

As his mother pointed out, he had expected the man to bore Eleanor. Obviously, unless you were a morbidly jealous person, you didn't evaluate a visitor by wondering whether this was a man likely to captivate your wife and run off with her; at most you asked yourself if he would prove sympathetic or not. In this case George had thought not very, but had hoped that Saint-Euverte's undeniable charm would make up for the rest.

Even afterwards, faced with an accomplished fact, George had refused to believe that his judgment had been so completely mistaken. The most painstaking reappraisal of Saint-Euverte's character still led to no understanding of what had happened. Yes, without a doubt the man was uncommonly good-looking, had a magnetic virility and great charm of manner. Yet any suggestion that Eleanor had been bowled over by this combination of attractions (which must have been the quick, popular explanation), left out of account the fact that Eleanor was Eleanor: the first person to look beyond such superficialities, and the last person to be impressed by them.

Saint-Euverte could be interesting when he talked about himself. He had kept them fascinated one evening with the story of a mountain climb he had done the previous summer. The challenge and exhilaration of it were infectious as he spoke: he had led them with him up that face, describing the difficulties and the techniques of overcoming them so vividly that they had triumphed together on reaching the summit. There had been no braggadocio about him. This was just something he had done and enjoyed doing, and he took it for granted—boyishly—that anybody else would have enjoyed the experience equally. His had been the luck of the opportunity, but he gave you a vicarious share in that luck generously, graphically and amusingly. But when the conversation moved along to a more impersonal topic, Saint-Euverte had simply lost interest until he could make it personal and amusing again. Mention of international affairs would not arouse him till he remembered that an uncle of his had once been ambassador to Russia: a source of diverting anecdotes, well told and beside the point. And the ubiquitous book stores Eleanor spoke of could hardly have profited much from Saint-Euverte, for any talk of books led him straight to his friendship with Hemingway, whom he had known in Spain, who had been responsible, in fact, for Pierre's first appearance in the bull-ring. . . .

What was there in such a man—shallow, self-absorbed, confined to his own small pursuits—to bewitch Eleanor? She was scarcely a Desdemona to be stirred by stories of peril and derring-do: indeed, she was far more likely to make fun of them. And while she might not be as much a realist as she claimed to be, she was a serious and very feminine woman with a strong sense of the fundamentals of living. Someone as frivolous—that *was* the right word—as Pierre de Saint-Euverte should not have appealed to her at all.

So for a long time after the elopement George had remained convinced that what had happened was all a dreadful mistake: Eleanor had acted out of impulse, and sooner or later would come to her senses, would return home. Eventually, of course, it had become apparent that this interpretation simply would not do, yet George had continued to cling to the shadow of hope, out of a mixture of bewilderment, stubbornness and inertia. Perhaps if he had moved in a larger world he might have encountered some woman who could supplant Eleanor in his imagination, but in the pattern of life he had established for himself, the shuttle between his office and Bradley's Bluff, there was no such woman. A few trivial office-based affairs had led only to disenchantment. Laura Sydrock was the pick of the local possibilities, and Laura aroused him no further than friendship. He would have had to upset his life to go exploring further afield, and that without the least confidence in finding the equal of what he had, so incomprehensibly, lost. He had felt himself too old to go chasing after disappointments; it had seemed simpler to go on hoping, however unreasonably.

Now that a throw of the dice had made his hopes come true—or so it seemed, anyway—perhaps he ought simply to shut his mind to the past, concentrate on smoothing out the present and trying to lash down the future. This he would have done except for the appearance on the scene of Marie-Odile: someone who might shed some light on the mysteries that had tormented him for years, and conceivably might even offer comfort to his longing to believe that Eleanor's return was not quite so much the result of chance as it appeared. The last was the frailest of hopes, probably to be disappointed, based only on the cavalier way Marie-Odile spoke of her cousin, mentioning his faults without fear of Eleanor's disapproval.

There remained the necessary courage to expose himself to humiliation, and this George found by reminding himself firmly that Marie-Odile was no part of his life. In another few weeks she would be returning to France, not to be seen again, presumably, for some indefinite period. If she took with her the opinion that George Davenport was an oafish creature with a streak of prurient curiosity, that would be no great misfortune.

Having decided this much, George waited patiently for a moment when he and Marie-Odile were alone together, and unlikely to be disturbed for a time. This came one evening when he was superintending the roasting of a chicken over the new charcoal grill. Marie-Odile had come asking if she could help, and remained, stretched out on a patio chaise, to keep him company.

"I'm afraid I've been remiss about expressing my regrets for your cousin's death," George began formally. "Under the circumstances, it's been difficult to know what to say."

"It is also difficult to know what to feel," she replied. "When a man spends his adult life trying to suicide himself, one thinks perhaps he found what he was searching for. I cannot imagine what Pierre would have done with middle age."

"That's something young people can rarely imagine, even about themselves."

"Yes, but the idea is not frightening, and for Pierre it *was* frightening, I think," said Marie-Odile thoughtfully. "He said last winter, after the skiing, that he could sense his reflexes were no longer so fast as before. Each year that would have been worse. In the end I expect he would have become a gambler, just to have something to risk—and *that* is a sadness, is it not? Think of gambling with plastic chips against those wrinkled old ladies after you have gambled with life itself! So perhaps it was for the best."

"I have been curious about . . . Pierre," said George, busying himself with the basting brush, meticulously swabbing the rotating bird with seasoned melted butter. "That sounds like a foolish thing to say. Perhaps you feel I'm being rude."

"But why?" Marie-Odile asked gravely from behind him. "To me it seems very natural to be curious."

"He was here for a few weeks," George went on awkwardly, as if addressing the chicken. "I was busy much of the time, preoccupied . . . my impressions of him were superficial, I dare say. And it's always hard for a man to tell what a woman sees in another man. I mean, of course your cousin was exceedingly attractive and charming and all that. I'm putting this clumsily, and I don't know whether you're following me. But the point is that I was surprised."

"That is an English understatement, I think," said Marie-Odile.

"No, you don't understand," said George. "It would be arrogant of a portly, middle-aged man to be surprised at the success of somebody younger, much better-looking, much more charming." The heat of the glowing coals on that sultry evening was making George sweat like a pig. "Just the same, I was surprised—by Eleanor," he finished weakly.

"But I understand very well," Marie-Odile insisted. "For other reasons we were all surprised too. We did not think of you, we did not know you. But we were surprised that Pierre had found someone so sensible to look after him. Before it had been silly women, caught by what you said: the charm, the glamour. For Pierre's sake we were very pleased."

Driven back to his perch on the wall, mopping his face with a handkerchief, George stole a glance at Marie-Odile. She met his eyes gravely, sympathetically. Yet even as he felt assured that there would be no embarrassment in talking to her, he felt uncertain of the clarity of this exchange. Marie-Odile could trick you by accident: seeming to choose her words so carefully, but translating as she went, she could say something to one side or the other of what she meant. "Did Pierre need someone to look after him?" he asked.

"He was a proud and lonely person," she replied. "He had so many friends, but he seldom felt close to anybody, never easily. Perhaps this was because he had not known his mother; she died when he was born. But always there had been an emptiness in his life, and then suddenly it was filled up. He adored Eleanor, you know, absolutely adored her. I do not think he had ever really been in love before, and then he felt as complete as he was capable of feeling."

"Naturally I can understand someone falling in love with Eleanor," George began, and then stopped short, realizing that his next question had been forestalled, answered as well as it was ever likely to be answered. Pierre de Saint-Euverte's attractions might be called superficial, but the impact of such a man falling head over heels in love—and this at a time when Eleanor was dissatisfied—would have been overwhelming. Throw in the suggestion of an appeal to Eleanor's maternal instincts, her unconscious need to be needed, and there was no reason to ask why she had loved in return. To a degree, given the right circumstances, love was a communicable disease. Perhaps the answer was still more complex, but this was as near to the truth as he needed to get, or as Marie-Odile could be expected to lead him "Yes, I see," he said, "or up to a point I do." By which he meant that he could understand the beginning and not the continuation, yet it seemed too impolite to suggest that Eleanor must have found out she was wasting herself on such a man. "I'm still surprised that it lasted so well," he added tentatively.

"Did it?" said Marie-Odile. "I was never sure. And last

summer it seemed that Eleanor was under a cloud, you know? All the time, and I found that very natural, because Pierre was racing. She hated that, but he could not bring himself to stop. It must have been very frustrating for her. She is a woman to make somebody happy, but Pierre could not be happy for very long. Happiness made him restless and guilty."

"Then why the hell didn't she come home?" George demanded brutally.

"Truly, I am not sure," said Marie-Odile, shrugging. "There could be so many reasons."

"Could there?" asked George, feeling stupid at not being able to think of one of them.

"For one thing, Pierre was so dependent upon her, you cannot imagine. If she had left him, he might have tried to ski down the face of Mont Blanc or killed himself driving at Le Mans or something just as foolish."

"That's blackmail," said George.

"It is blackmail if you make threats and of course Pierre would never make threats," said Marie-Odile. "But Eleanor would know just the same, it was something she had to know. And then she had grown very fond of the life in France, I believe."

"No argument there," said George.

"Yes. And also there is the pride of someone who has taken a radical step."

"Pride?" he questioned.

"You think pride is only for the men?" asked Marie-Odile.

"No," said George, whose reaction had been that Eleanor was too sensible to be influenced by such a sentimental consideration. "Perhaps I don't understand."

"There is a sort of social pride especially for women," said Marie-Odile. "I have a good friend, Amélie; she is older, but we are very close. She fell in love, and her parents detested the man. They said he was no good, worthless, and with us the family is very important: it is not easy when their disapproval is strong, and it was *very* strong. But Amélie was determined, and she married anyway. She was wrong, her parents were right. Her husband is a beast, and she is miserable. Yet she can do nothing. Her parents were too severe: they made her guilty for disobeying, and now she is too proud to admit the mistake."

"I see your point, but it doesn't really apply to Eleanor," George said, privately amused by this girlish analogy. "She always knew she was welcome to return home."

"Perhaps. But you made it very difficult for her," the girl said unexpectedly.

"I could scarcely have made it easier,"

"You could have given her the divorce. She wanted it."

"Oh, no!" he moaned.

"Oh, yes!" Marie-Odile insisted. "When one has hurt somebody and been wrong, the pride is strongest. With the divorce, Eleanor could have come as a free woman, with dignity, is it not so? Without the divorce she would just be a naughty wife asking to be forgiven. That is hard."

"I'm a simple man," said George. "I would have thought a divorce was a sign that you wanted to be free of a woman. Not that you were smoothing the path for her homecoming."

"Possibly I am wrong," Marie-Odile said meekly. "It was an idea I formed from something Eleanor said one time."

"Then no doubt you are right," said George. "She has a genius for proving that any action her husband takes is a blunder that can be held against him."

"I think not," said the girl. "And one must be philosophical. In the end it has all worked out for the best."

"Has it?" he asked gloomily.

"Yes, I believe so," said Marie-Odile. "Partly that is why I came. I am curious too, you see, and I am very fond of Eleanor. She has been good to me, and I wanted to feel that she was happy. You understand? And now I am content. She is more . . . relaxed than I have seen her in a long time. That is good. One can sense that she has come home again."

Moved, George had returned hurriedly to his basting, heat or no heat. "I wish I could be so sure," he said. "She is still terribly fond of France."

"To me that seems natural, of course," said Marie-Odile. "But not of the first importance. I cannot imagine the woman who rules her life by geography."

George mulled this over thoughtfully for a moment. Finally he asked the chicken: "What *is* of the first importance, then?" There was no reply. When he looked around he saw that he and the chicken had the patio to themselves: Marie-Odile had slipped quietly away, perhaps feeling that she had given him enough to think about. She was a remarkable girl. George could appreciate now, finally, why Eleanor thought so highly of her. He tried to imagine having this sort of conversation with any other girl he could think of—Jessie Sydrock with her wisecracks, for example—and shuddered.

6.

As yet, the annual party at the Hendersons' was the closest thing to a community tradition that Bradley's Bluff possessed. The Hendersons might not be the richest family—there was much speculation about this—but they were certainly the oldest: Phyllis Henderson being a lineal descendant of that Ephraim Bradley whose legendary courage in a game of five-card stud, with the six, seven, eight and ten of diamonds showing and the eight of hearts in the hole, had won him the rolling, rocky, run-down farmland that today formed the greater part of the prosperous suburb.

Even the Hendersons' back lawn had its limitations, would hold only so many tables, so the party had a certain exclusiveness. The younger set was barred, as were recent arrivals, the unpolished or unprosperous or unpopular, and anyone outspoken about voting the Democratic ticket. Accordingly, the privilege of eating an alfresco buffet dinner on rickety folding chairs under Japanese lanterns, while providing dinner for the mosquitoes, had become a sign of one's social standing in Bradley's Bluff. Invitations were schemed for shamelessly; any charity that had Phyllis Henderson's blessing could be sure of a heavy subscription from hopeful newcomers and the lately married; and many were the disappointed households where couples assured one another that it was a dull party, a wretched party, a stupid party, and the real fun would be at the Country Club's costume ball, scheduled for the week following.

By the established families it was regarded as a crush, somewhat redeemed by the excellence of the buffet, which was provided by an outfit from the city and made a welcome change from the familiar repertoire of the local caterers. Moreover, the party served certain minor functions, such as letting you be safely cordial with people you didn't wish to trouble about the rest of the year, and giving you the chance to inspect others, without obligation, who lay outside your usual circle. It was here that Eleanor encountered Fred Palmer for the first time, during cocktails.

Between intervals of the usual chitchat ("Yes, isn't it remarkable what luck they always have with the weather!") George observed this meeting with mixed emotions. At first he was amused. Palmer was a blunt and rugged man who wore his poise like a challenge; it was a delight to see the way Eleanor slid past the slight stiffness of her sister's putative lover and set him to talking naturally. But later, watching them from across the lawn, as deep in conversation as two old friends, George felt a faint uneasiness. He repudiated jealousy; life with Eleanor would not be worth living if he were to get nervous every time she smiled at another man. It was just this combination of reputations (he told himself) that unnerved him. Palmer had to be considered a prowling predator, Eleanor's immunity to this type remained unproven—and it was difficult to believe that they had so much in common to chatter about.

"In one respect you were lucky, George," said a voice beside him, and he turned to find that Alan Briggs had joined him, puffing at a pipe and looking at that corner of the lawn which George's gaze had just quitted. "At least Paris caught the first ship for Troy; he didn't hang around where you'd keep stumbling over him among the canapés."

"I thought you were above such considerations," said George.

"In the abstract, perhaps," said Alan. "In the concrete—and

he does look as if he was roughly molded out of concrete, doesn't he?—he's a blot on the landscape. I can think about him philosophically, but actually seeing him stirs up the primitive man."

"Have another drink," said George.

"The primitive man is a terror," Alan said admiringly. "He doesn't stand around talking. He marches up to his rival, fells him to the ground with one mighty blow, and then kicks him to death with highly polished black oxfords."

George glanced at his friend's lanky, sedentary build and shook his head. "On second thought, don't have another drink."

"Oh, I know," said Alan. "I would find myself lying flat on the ground while the women made a fuss over his bruised knuckles. I can understand the popularity of dueling: swords must have gone a long way to even out inequalities of physique. With a dexterous turn of my wrist I would parry his clumsy thrust, then lunge with catlike swiftness and skewer him through his black heart."

Seeing Eleanor throw back her head and laugh with pleasure at something Fred Palmer had said, George could almost approve of this picture. "Civilization has gone too far," he said. "We are emasculated by the fear of making fools of ourselves." He refrained from adding that he would have been glad to interrupt that little get-together across the lawn if he could have thought of a graceful way of doing so.

"We make fools of ourselves anyway, passively if not actively," Alan said. "A cuckold may rationalize his position, but he can't find much dignity or satisfaction in it."

"I could have told you that six years ago," George said. "I dare say I did."

"You don't know what suffering is," Alan retorted. "If Phyllis Henderson's sense of humor runs true to form, I'll find myself at the same table with the son of a bitch, obliged to be amiable and cheerful under the knowing scrutiny of the others. You can't imagine what that's like. I'll do it, but the primitive man will rebel: he'll flatly refuse to digest the dinner, and I'll lie awake all night with heartburn."

Whether this prophecy was fulfilled George never knew, but he had his own experience with their hostess's well-known notions on how to make these parties entertaining. She was supposed to spend the preceding month gleefully planning the arrangement of her place cards, ensuring the closest possible proximity of neighbors who had fallen out, women who had developed an unconquerable aversion to one another, and men in bitter competition for the same promotion. So it should have come as no surprise to George, after he had filled a plate at the buffet and been directed to table fourteen, to discover that he was seated beside Laura Sydrock. Any hopes of spectator sport from this juxtaposition, however, were thwarted. Laura had had ample time to recover from the disappointment of whatever hopes she might have cherished, and George, who had never admitted the legitimacy of such hopes, was glad of the chance to dispel a lot of feminine nonsense, as he considered it.

"Good evening, my dear; you look flourishing," he greeted her as he sat down. "Do these parties grow larger each year, or is old age making me unsociable?" He smiled genially at the other couple at their table—a woman Laura had ousted from the Hospital Committee, and a man who regarded all stockbrokers as tools of an international Jewish conspiracy —and dismissed them from his mind. "Mother is displeased with you," he told Laura. "You never came to visit her during her lie-in strike."

"It's been a hectic summer," she said briskly. "The most reliable people on three of my committees all picked this year to go to Europe. I don't know when I've been so busy."

"Bradley's Bluff has been doing well by the airlines," George agreed. "I started it all in the Spring, and since then there's been a lot of traffic in both directions." This remark was quite deliberate, since he felt that any conversation pretending that Eleanor didn't exist would be a waste of time. Laura took the hint. Dropping her voice to a dry murmur, she recounted amusingly some of the more bizarre forms gossip had taken after Eleanor's homecoming; then, looking George squarely in the eye, she declared that he seemed like a new man and that she was very happy for him.

"And for Ken, too," she added in a more normal voice. "By avoiding the difficult years, Eleanor has gained a more appreciative son than most of that age. At least he never stops rattling on about her."

"Yes, that's worked out well," said George. "And I even have hopes that Mother will come around in a year or two."

"I really should stop by," said Laura. "I've felt guilty about neglecting the old lady. But she's up and about again now, isn't she?"

"To tell the truth, it was more peaceful while the reign of terror was confined to her bedroom," said George, "but I don't know how to ask her to go back. We'll have to fix a date for dinner. If you can pin Jessie down, we might enjoy our son's company for an entire evening. Incidentally, I gather you were the one who put a stop to that notion of a premature engagement."

"Was I?" said Laura. "I no longer presume to take the credit for these things. Naturally I pointed out the dangers of binding oneself to anything as speculative as the future, thereby making a bore of myself. If they've leaned in a sensible direction, it was probably for a totally different set of reasons. But I have no idea how things stand."

"I've heard nothing more of it," said George.

"Neither have I," said Laura, "but I don't think I'm in Jessie's confidence just at the moment. She's been moody and uncommunicative recently. I must say, Ken is very sweet and handles her perfectly: he simply refuses to pay any attention to her sulks, and he can always think of some nonsense to start her laughing. But something is troubling her, just the same."

"All I can offer is that it hasn't infected Ken. So it can't be serious."

"Probably not," said Laura. "I've wondered once or twice if there might be some jealousy of the French girl who's staying with you. Jessie has let slip a few remarks that had more bite to them than humor."

"If it's that, she's being unusually foolish."

"Can you be sure?"

"I can," George said firmly, having come to think of Marie-Odile as his own protégée ever since their conversation on the patio. "Marie-Odile is an exceptionally level-headed young woman. I know for a fact that she likes Ken all the more for being so serious about Jessie, having got a poor impression of the casual promiscuity among vacationing youngsters last summer. If Ken so much as leered at her she'd be sadly disillusioned, but in practice he treats her like a younger sister who needs protecting. Considering that in most respects she's more mature than he, the spectacle is somewhat comical, but nothing to get jealous about."

"Then it's odd," Laura said. "Jessie isn't one to get jealous about nothing."

Like most such arbitrarily assembled parties with no natural conviviality but the random effects of hard liquor, this one had a mixed success. The bores enjoyed themselves as usual, while those trapped in their presence longed to escape to other tables where everybody appeared to be having such a good time. Phyllis Henderson's malicious groupings had less than their usual effect, in that no fist fights broke out, and the man whose face got slapped, it was generally agreed, might have deserved it for a variety of reasons. A few people went home with thoughts of a new love affair, while others left choleric with rage. A greater number of guests, the easily satisfied and the fortunately situated, felt that they had spent a delightful evening, and nearly everybody took away fresh material for gossip. The homeward-bound cars radiating outward from Chestnut Plaza were murmurous with comment: appreciative and caustic, confiding and conjectural, contentious and concordant.

"I saw you patching up the friendship with Laura," Eleanor said. "It had crossed my mind that Phyllis would probably put the two of you together."

"Laura was in fine form," George said. "I made a tentative date for next Saturday; you'll have to confirm it."

"Well done," said Eleanor. "These mob scenes do serve a purpose, though I'm not civic-minded enough to undertake one myself."

"A number of purposes," said George. "You seem to have made a new friend."

"Fred Palmer? Yes, I'm sorry I hadn't run into him before. I *do* like him, George."

"I feared as much."

"He's *human,*" Eleanor explained.

"Undeniably," agreed George, "but I suspect that means you're putting most of the inhabitants of Bradley's Bluff into some other category."

"Could you tell the Hogans from the Greens with your eyes closed?" Eleanor challenged him. "Fred's opinions and interests aren't predictable statistics, he's not a product of the mass media, he's his own man and most amusing. We ought to see more of him."

"We're bound to bump into him with some frequency," George said. "I don't know that I'm so eager to have him to the house, if that's what you're thinking of."

"Why not? Does my enthusiasm put you off? I hope you aren't going to develop a streak of jealousy; your self-confidence has always been one of your strongest attractions."

"Just at the moment it's in a stage of convalescence," George said. "But I had other social hazards in mind. Cathy and Alan are always dropping in without warning. It could be unfortunate if they found Fred Palmer there. He brings out the primitive man in Alan."

"I shouldn't think that nonsense would last much longer," Eleanor said. "It's obvious now that Cathy is quite the wrong person for Fred."

"You give a perverse twist to everything," George complained. "Since your sister is already married to a man we both like, it should be enough to say that Palmer is the wrong person for her."

"I have no convictions about that," said Eleanor. "Fred is a strong and gentle man—rather like you in a number of ways—and for all I know he's done her a world of good. But you've always said that if you had to live with Cathy her brittleness would rub you raw in no time, and I'm sure the same would be true of Fred."

"You may have put your finger on the way to put an end to that romance," George said. "Point out to Cathy these resemblances between Palmer and myself. Your sister still has a deep admiration for you. She'd never dream of eloping with the sort of man you eloped away from."

"In all justice you have to be given a fair chance to get remarks like that out of your system," Eleanor said, "but I think you might begin struggling against temptation. It's hard to look to the future, as you want me to do, when you're constantly reminding me of the past."

"You're absolutely right," George said contritely. "The subject will never be mentioned again."

"That's an exaggeration," said Eleanor, "unless you are contemplating matricide."

7.

There was a baseball game on television that afternoon, and Marie-Odile's education in Americana was being hilariously extended. Part of the hilarity came from the French girl's puzzlement over a sport where most of the players spent most of the time waiting for something to happen, and part from Mrs. Davenport's mischievous amplification of Ken's explanations.

"Is that a home run?" Marie-Odile asked.

"Just a long fly," said Ken. "Now watch the runner on third. He's tagging up and he'll try to get home after the ball is caught. There he goes."

"Oh, he fell down!" said Marie-Odile.

"He slid like that on purpose; it makes it harder to tag him. But he's out anyway."

"Then why is he waving his arms and throwing his little cap on the ground?"

"He's tired of playing," said Mrs. Davenport. "He's trying to tease the umpire into sending him to the showers."

The telephone rang but they paid no attention, daytime calls usually meaning household problems that Martha would have to deal with in any case. But a moment later, while Ken was still explaining the significance of the play that had just finished, Martha stuck her head into the room.

"That was Miss Jessie," she said to him. "She's down at the Parlor and wants you to pick her up."

"Okay, thanks," he said grumpily. He couldn't imagine how Jessie had got into Bradley's Bluff's tiny shopping center without a conveyance to get her home again, and was annoyed at being imposed upon for nothing when he was enjoying himself. Sure that Jessie expected him alone, he asked Marie-Odile if she would like to come along, but she shook her head.

"I think I am beginning to understand this game," she said. "Besides, sometimes when no one else is around, Mrs. Davenport is very severe with me, and then I feel like one of the family."

"The man coming up to bat is the pitcher," said Mrs. Davenport, promptly taking over the rôle of commentator. "He will strike out. Pitchers have a professional, nonpartisan alliance: they try to inspire respect for their art by striking out at every possible opportunity. If by accident a pitcher hits safely he is fined fifty dollars by the pitchers' guild. . . ."

Ken went off no happier for knowing that Marie-Odile's idea of the great American sport would be deformed forever unless he spent another afternoon undoing his grandmother's damage. His resentment was directed against Jessie. Dragging him out on this wild-goose chase was just the latest symptom of her recent moodiness, and he had long since decided that jealousy wasn't as entertaining as it had originally seemed, although there didn't appear to be much you could do about it except wait for it to wear off.

Bradley's Bluff had half a block of small shops mostly devoted to services that the big shopping complexes along the highway didn't satisfy: filling prescriptions, repairing shoes and watches, and delivering booze at midnight when you ran short in the middle of a party. Right in the center of this short main street was the ice-cream-and-candy store known as the Parlor; Ken was lucky to find a parking place not too far away. He peered through the plate glass, hoping to find Jessie on the lookout. On one side stood glassed shelves of the homemade candies and petits fours needed for bridge parties and the like, but the real activity, during the summers anyway, was at the long soda fountain opposite and in the room behind filled with leatherette booths, each with its own link to the jukebox. This was the young teen-agers' social center, and Ken hadn't been inside for years. Today there was no choice. He opened the door, wincing disdainfully at the cacophony of raucous voices within, and pushed his way through the children.

Jessie sat on a stool halfway down the marble-topped counter, nursing a short Coke. She looked at him in the mirror, over the frieze of inverted sundae glasses, and it was obvious that she was not pleased with life. That made two of them.

"What in the name of God?" he inquired.

"I'm drowning my sorrows," she said. "Peter Rabbit is dead."

This inane remark, overheard by a gaggle of nymphets, started off a shrill of giggling that set his teeth on edge. He reached past Jessie for her check. "You've had enough to drink," he told her. "Try to make it to the door without staggering." She came obediently, and as they waited in line to get to the cashier he asked, "How on earth did you get down here?"

"I walked," she said simply: a reply which could only have been intended to exasperate him further. In the first place, walking to the Parlor was for kids who hadn't yet attained the right to the family car; in the second place, assuming that Laura was out with the car, it made absolutely no sense for someone to trudge most of a mile on a sweltering afternoon for something that stood in racks in her refrigerator at home.

"I'm glad you're feeling so fit again," he said sarcastically, as he opened the door for her. "When you wouldn't play tennis the other day I thought you might be coming down with tired blood." But once they were in the car he loosened the control on his indignation: "What the hell *is* this?"

"I'm sorry if I spoiled your afternoon," said Jessie. "Did I interrupt a delicate moment?"

"That joke's getting tiresome!" he snapped, and then realized that this squabble was attracting the attention of a couple of brats on the sidewalk. By the time he'd started the car and backed out into the traffic he had cooled down again. "Forget it, love, I'm sorry. Is something the matter?"

"Mummy is out for the day and I had to make a phone call to Alden Park," Jessie said, lighting a cigarette from the dashboard lighter. "That's a toll call, and if all went well I didn't want it turning up on next month's phone bill. You know Mummy, the frustrated bookkeeper: she hunts through the list for errors and if she finds a number she doesn't recognize she checks her address book and then calls the Business Office. So she'd have been down on me, wanting to know who Dr. Menzies is over in Alden Park and whether I'd called him and why."

"Why?" asked Ken, with a sinking feeling that his world was about to fall in on him.

"I was over there the other day," Jessie said. "The afternoon I broke our tennis date, in fact. I gave my name as Joan Shelby, and they took a sample. They shoot it into a rabbit, don't they? And if the rabbit dies, it's positive?"

Self-preservation enabled Ken to pull the car over to the side of the road and cut the motor. "I think they use frogs nowadays," he mumbled.

"Well, there's one frog who won't a-wooing go."

"So that's . . . Why didn't you tell me?"

"Because I hoped I was just being a hysterical idiot," Jessie said. "No point in giving you that to hold over me if I didn't have to."

"Sure," he said numbly. His mind didn't seem to be working very well. He supposed there were responses he ought to be making, things he should say or do to comfort Jessie, but the suddenness of this news had paralyzed him for the moment. When Jessie had spoken of going to a strange doctor he had had a fleeting, sickening vision of obscure malignancies—but not this, which should have been impossible. "I don't get it, Jessie," he said. "I thought we were foolproof."

"That's right, we were," she said. "But your girlfriend is worse than a fool."

"Aw, stop it!"

"I mean it," Jessie said in a hard, bright voice. "Much worse than a fool: she's a spoiled brat and a bitch. I don't much like it, but there it is. Anyhow, you had to know, and there's something else I want you to know, right from the start. I'm not going to let you be hurt by this. That has to be understood. It's not your worry, and I mean that very seriously. You're out of it."

"Hey, now look!" he protested.

"No, don't look," said Jessie. "I've made a mess of things and I'm sorry, but I'm a big girl and I don't expect anybody else to pick up the pieces. That would just make everything worse, and it's bad enough as it is. And now I wish you'd take me home."

Ken was lightheaded. He felt strange, he didn't know how he felt. Not exactly frightened, not exactly confident—but different. Changed by the knowledge that nothing was ever going to be quite the same. Perhaps this was how adulthood really arrived: on a darkening afternoon with Jessie sitting beside him, not touching him, weeping.

PART FIVE

Helen's Grandchild

7.

"Well, well," said Eleanor with a faint smile. "It doesn't seem so very long since you tried to call me to account for *my* misdemeanors."

Ken braced himself defiantly to the onslaught he had been expecting for most of a day. His parents' initial reaction to his thunderbolt had not been any worse than he'd expected: he hadn't thought either one of them would start bellowing with moral indignation. His mother had taken the news with perfect calm, turning instinctively to his father, as if he were the one who was likely to be upset, in need of comfort or reassurance. And, indeed, it was his father who had seemed shocked and had fired off a few scathing remarks about folly and irresponsibility before Eleanor could calm him with the argument that what was done was done, and recriminations wouldn't help.

This crisis could be said to have brought his parents closer together. After hearing what Ken had to say they had tended to consult together without any further reference to him. Throughout the evening (with Marie-Odile and his grandmother present) they had treated him, he felt, with a shade more austerity than usual, and had retired early, presumably to discuss ways and means in private. A tap at their bedroom door had elicited a muffled baritone suggestion that he take a cold shower and go to bed with an uplifting book.

An attempt this morning to point out to his father that he, Ken, was an essential part of this situation, had brought upon him the gruff observation that he had played his part most effectively and it was time for older and wiser heads to take charge—the stuffiest and most unsympathetic remark Ken had ever heard his father make, but his father's abrupt departure for the office had prevented any further discussion. Ken was becoming fretful, even angry. He deeply regretted what had happened, of course, and was desperately anxious to get things straightened out, but he saw no reason why this unlucky proof of his manhood should relegate him to the position of a child whose opinions needn't be consulted. By the time his mother saw fit to seek him out with her flippancy about her own wrongdoings, Ken was in a mood to defend himself with some heat.

"Have I committed a misdemeanor?" he asked.

"I don't know yet," said his mother, turning his desk chair to face the bed, where he had been sprawled out reading. "I only meant that it seems as if we take turns considering one another's disregard for the proprieties."

"There's no comparison," Ken said. "*I* haven't hurt anybody at all."

"You've done no great harm yet," his mother conceded, "but the possibility of somebody getting hurt is considerable."

"Well, I'm glad somebody has decided to discuss that much with me," Ken said. "I was beginning to think it was all going to be settled behind my back."

"That seems impractical and sounds just a bit sulky."

"You see! I *am* being treated like a child," Ken cried. "First I'm left out, and when I don't like it I'm accused of being sulky. That's not a word you use to adults. How far would I get if I said you or Dad were being sulky?"

"I should hope you'd have no occasion to," said Eleanor. "Personally, if I knew my concerns were being discussed behind my back by people who loved me, I'd assume there was some good reason for it. In this case there were several."

"What were they?"

"Your father, quite naturally, is very upset," said Eleanor. "If I hadn't been here, you'd have had to bear the brunt of that yourself, and I don't think you would have enjoyed it."

"What does he have to be so upset about?" Ken demanded. "He's not the father of that baby, I am. I'm upset! Was he shocked because Jessie and I have been sleeping together?"

"He was surprised."

"And you weren't?"

"Not in the least," said Eleanor. "But I'd been away; I came back to find a grown man. When I saw that you and Jessie were so much in love that you were planning to get married, naturally I thought you were sleeping together: anything else might have shocked me. But George hadn't the advantage of that objectivity; he's watched you changing day by day, and to him it was just a little while ago that you were still a schoolboy. I think he pictured you as stuck in the stage of tender romance and puppy love."

"He has more sense than that," Ken said scornfully.

"It isn't entirely a question of sense," said his mother. "However, none of that had to do with his being upset. His illusions may have suffered a slight jolting, but he hadn't too much difficulty reconciling himself to the fact that you are normally male. What *did* upset him was the element of carelessness, which smacks of irresponsibility. And also the impression he got that you were trying to put the blame on Jessie. He considered that unmanly."

"What the hell was I supposed to do?" Ken growled. "Strike a noble pose and say that it was all my fault? When it wasn't?"

"Whether or not it was a fault, you had your share in it."

"Look, I want some credit for knowing which end is up," Ken said. "I've been well informed about the facts of life for as long as I can remember, and I'm in no hurry to contribute to the population explosion. I'm not a slob, and I don't believe in taking chances. Birth control is no mystery these days. But that was *Jessie's* department."

"We deduced as much," said Eleanor. "That was just the trouble. If you're so well informed about birth control you must know that accidents *can* happen, even to the most prudent. But your attitude appeared to be that since you couldn't be blamed for the accident, you could wash your hands of the responsibility."

Ken howled softly. He was righteously aware that he was the only person whose behavior had been blameless and honorable throughout, and he nevertheless kept finding himself in the falsest of false positions. Belatedly he sympathized with Jessie's argument that so-called delusions of persecution might be entirely justified. "Who's washing his hands of anything?" he asked. "I'm the one who wants to get married as quickly as possible! And who the hell said anything about an accident?"

"Your father took that for granted," said Eleanor. "I wasn't so sure, myself. What did happen?"

"I don't know what happened," Ken said querulously. "Jessie wouldn't talk about it. All I know is that she insists it was all her fault. She made some sort of an idiot of herself, okay. If that's the case why should I go around in sackcloth and ashes?"

"You must know more than that."

"Why must I? Jessie was mad at me. She wouldn't talk."

"What on earth had you done to make her mad at you at such a moment?"

"What had *I* done?" Ken echoed bitterly, beating one fist against the bedspread. "It has to be my fault somehow or other, doesn't it? Can't you understand?—I was in the dark myself until half past three yesterday afternoon. Jessie had been bitchy for a few days, but there were lots of ways to account for that: it might have been the curse coming on for all I knew. When a girl calls up and asks you to pick her up at the Parlor you don't leap to the conclusion that it's to tell you that she's pregnant, for God's sake! All right—I was in a bad mood when I picked her up. I'd snarled at her a few times before she had a chance to drop her little bombshell."

"Oh, the poor child!" exclaimed Eleanor. "Just when she most needed your sympathy!"

"I know, I know," said Ken. "I felt like a bastard, sure. But you don't go pussyfooting through life just in case somebody has bad news up her sleeve."

"It was most unfortunate, anyhow. I can see why she was hurt and angry. But I can't believe that she simply gave you the news and let it go at that."

"Just about," said Ken. "I tried to cheer her up, naturally. I said at least we'd managed to do away with any objections to our getting married—but this only made matters worse. She got furious. She told me I was an insensitive clod and she certainly was *not* going to marry me—not now, anyway—and that was final."

"And that was all?"

"She made some crack about how you'd be pleased that the engagement was off. And then she insisted that I shut up and drive her home."

"I see," Eleanor said thoughtfully.

"It strikes me that nothing is ever quite normal in this family," said Ken. "Have you noticed that? Usually it's the girl who screams for marriage and the guy who tries to wriggle off the hook."

"Can you be quite sure that you didn't give the impression of wriggling?"

"Look, it took me a minute or two to get used to the idea," said Ken. "I didn't instantly leap up shouting 'Goody!'

if that's what you mean. I'd already told you we weren't planning on having kids right away, so it was bound to come as a shock. But as soon as I caught my breath, I decided it wasn't so awful, really. Sure, it will mean a bit of a scramble this winter, but what the hell? Jessie can help with the typing, and if the kid screams too much when I'm trying to study for final exams, I can always send the two of them up to Laura for a couple of months. For the rest, I'd probably be better off having Jessie there than missing her. I don't feel trapped. This was all on the schedule, and if the schedule gets moved forward a little that's no great tragedy. That's how I spelled it out, and I don't see how it could have sounded like wriggling to anybody."

"Nor do I," said his mother. "Have you seen Jessie today?"

"I called her this morning and said I was coming over, and she asked me not to. Said she was thinking things out her own way, and didn't want me around confusing the issue."

"How did she sound?"

"Very determined. She is the captain of her fate, she is the mistress of her soul."

"It seems a bit confusing," said Eleanor. "Perhaps your father will be able to shed some light when he gets back."

"What's Dad up to?"

"He's seeing Laura on his way home from work. And you have to get over this idea that things are going on behind your back, Ken. We're all involved now, even more so than if you were getting married at a conventional tempo. Has it occurred to you that this baby inside Jessie is our grandchild?"

"No, it hadn't," he admitted. "It's a thought. But I don't know that it will carry much weight with Jessie."

2.

Offhand, George could not recall ever having entered the Tavern in broad daylight before. It was where one went for drinks after the movies, or a nightcap after an unsuccessful party; he could not imagine its daytime existence except as a hangout for people who drank too much, a refuge for those who found home uncongenial, or a rendezvous for clandestine lovers. Arriving there at a little before six on a glorious August evening seemed to argue a failure somewhere in one's life. George felt furtive, as if involved in some guilty or sordid undertaking.

The air conditioning, geared to the crowd that would arrive later, came as a shock. In his damp, feather-weight suit George shivered slightly as he peered the length of the plywood-paneled room given an implausible antiquity by copper warming pans hung here and there. One of the men seated at the bar looked around and said "Afternoon, George."

He smiled and nodded, not even pausing to identify the man (Hogan? Mercer? Green?), having seen that Laura was already awaiting him in a booth in the back. It was a wretchedly awkward moment, mitigated only somewhat by their lucky *rapprochement* at the Hendersons' party a few evenings before, and he wished she had chosen some other meeting place. She had simply taken it for granted that it would be best if they met away from their respective homes and children, and he had accepted the Tavern without thinking, stupidly. He should have foreseen that they were sure to be recognized, their meeting misinterpreted, chewed over, and served up as gossip. A trivial but exasperating consideration at such a time.

"My poor Laura!" he greeted her. "I'm more horrified than I can say."

"That seems excessive, George," she said drily. "What emotions would you have left if somebody was maimed or blinded?"

He slid onto the padded banquette across from her, relieved to see that she appeared perfectly calm: a little tired and pale, perhaps, but not at all wrought-up. "You're taking this wonderfully well," he told her. "You would, of course."

"Were you a bit afraid of finding me in hysterics?" Laura asked. "That's not my style."

"I couldn't blame anyone for being upset," he said. "I am, myself. And I'll say right off that I'm thoroughly disappointed in Ken."

"I don't see why," said Laura. "As nearly as I can make out he's behaved most properly. I should think you'd be pleased with him."

"Because he indicates that he's still willing to marry Jessie?" George demanded. "If he hadn't that much fundamental decency he'd be thrown out of the house."

"I'm somewhat surprised at you, George. This doesn't seem entirely in character."

"Well, I'm surprised at everybody else," he grumbled, and then fell silent at Laura's warning gesture: the barman had come lounging over to take their order. What kept bewildering George was this universal attitude that *of course* Ken and Jessie had been sleeping together; he couldn't make out whether the women really felt that way or were just refusing to be startled by anything their children did. He felt like a fool remembering how he had imagined them, only a few weeks ago, wrapped in a romantic haze of sublimated sensuality where the touch of fingertips meant ecstasy. The picture had been built on memories of his own circumscribed young manhood. Naturally he knew that young people were infinitely freer these days; he knew that Ken was no virgin (as George had been at that same age); yet he had continued to think that sexual exploration was one thing and love something else. He was the romantic, evidently. It had not occurred to him that his son would embark on a full-fledged, matter-of-fact affair with the girl he proposed to marry.

"Had you known this was going on?" he asked as soon as the barman had left.

"Not to take an oath on," said Laura. "They tend to shield us from knowledge of this sort. But I'd had my suspicions, of course."

"Since last summer, apparently!" said George.

"Does that make a difference? George, George, think of all the other things they might have been up to! They haven't been orgying, they haven't been fooling around with drugs. They've been enjoying a private, discreet, old-fashioned love affair."

"Perhaps I'm envious," he said gloomily. "Yes, that's probably all it is. I wasted so many of those years being shy and inhibited and terrified of something or other—getting my face slapped, I suppose. Well, never mind that. What went wrong? And where the devil do we go from here? I'm still disappointed in Ken's lack of responsibility."

"Yes, we tend to assume the young man is at fault," said Laura, "and I suppose that's generally the case. But if Jessie refuses to divide the blame, I don't know that we have the right to disagree. She insists it was her own stupidity."

"That kind of haggling doesn't get us any further, anyway," George said impatiently. "I gather that Jessie has come up with some cockeyed notion that she doesn't want to get married now."

"Mmmm. And we mustn't start with the idea that this is

just an impulsive reaction. She's had the time to think it out, and she seems to feel very strongly."

"She's an idiot!"

"Perhaps, but she's making quite a lot of sense, just the same," said Laura. "The trouble stems from the attitude you expressed just a moment ago: that if Ken hadn't shown the fundamental decency to want to go ahead with marrying Jessie, you'd have thrown him out of the house. But Jessie doesn't want to be married as an act of fundamental decency."

"Now, wait a moment!" George protested. "I put that badly."

"Indeed you did," Laura began as preamble to something else, but he cut her off.

"Let's be perfectly honest," he urged. "If Ken had got some miscellaneous girl pregnant I'd give him holy hell for negligence, but I wouldn't expect him to follow up one stupidity with another and foul up his life for misapplied notions of honor. Undoubtedly I'd do whatever I could to help him out of the mess. None of that applies here. Those kids were as good as engaged; in fact, if it hadn't been for their schooling they'd be married by now. Obviously they thought of themselves as already married. So for Ken to react in any other way than he did would have been unthinkable. That's all I meant."

"I know it was, but you don't seem to appreciate that everything has changed," Laura said. "I have some sympathy for Jessie's point of view. People plan to get married, but either one has the right to change his mind down to the last possible moment—as no one knows better than I. It may make for heartache at the time, but it's probably for the best in the long run. And the difficulty here is that Ken has lost the option of changing his mind."

"Perhaps so," said George, "but there's not the slightest reason to suppose that he wants to."

"Who can be entirely sure of that?" asked Laura. "Not even Ken himself, and that's just the point. He's been brought up in a certain way to a certain set of principles, and he *is* a thoroughly decent young man. I'm sure there's no question in his mind what his duty is; I don't doubt that he's eager to do it. But I'm also sure there's a feeling of obligation which didn't exist before, and I can see why Jessie is frightened of it."

"That might make sense in theory, but we're talking about two very specific kids," George said. "Ken has to be considered too, and I get the impression that he's really quite pleased to have an excuse to move the wedding forward."

"Let's be realistic as well as honest," Laura said. "Jessie and Ken are both very young, and we can't help being aware that the cards are heavily stacked against such a marriage even when circumstances are ideal. The circumstances are scarcely ideal any longer. There are always conflicts, clashes, moments of animosity when even the best marriage seems like a terrible mistake. Do you think Jessie is mature enough to keep from resenting the baby at such moments? Do you think Ken is so mature that he'll be able to refrain from reminding Jessie, when he's furious, that he'd been trapped into the situation?"

"You're an unnatural mother," said George.

"Am I?"

"It's all wrong! Your daughter has the best of all possible reasons for marrying my son, and you sit there dreaming up reasons why she shouldn't. Sometimes I get the feeling that my own household is peculiar, but I'm unfair to them: the rest of the world is just as crazy."

"I'm not unnatural at all," Laura began, and then had to break off as the barman arrived with the tom collinses they had ordered because it was the first long, cool drink either of them could think of. George glowered at his glass: the slivers of orange and lemon amid the froth, the cherry on top, made it seem too festive, too frivolous a concoction for such an occasion. "I've just been explaining the way Jessie's mind is running," Laura resumed, "and, as I said, I have some sympathy for her arguments. Still, personally, I'm hoping that when she's had time to think it through a bit further she'll decide that these fears are exaggerated, that she's being overfastidious, and that it would be better all around if she got married. I'm conventional enough to prefer the conventional solution. But I wouldn't badger her even if I thought it would do the least good, which it wouldn't. She's been brought up to use her own head."

"So was Ken," said George. "I've decided that was a mistake."

"But you can't, just because they think in a direction you don't approve of," Laura said seriously. "It's not been easy, bringing up a girl without a man in the house, but I've done my very best and now I have to respect the end product. To be consistent I have to stand behind Jessie, whatever decision she settles on."

"I suppose she's thinking of an abortion."

"That's one of the three possibilities she's considering, yes. And she takes the idea much more matter-of-factly than I would. George, have you any idea how one arranges such a thing?"

"Not offhand," he said. "I suppose you ask around. Somebody always knows somebody. Alan Briggs might be a good one to begin with: in his work he has to deal with lots of arty people, writers, bohemian types. I imagine they're well informed on such matters."

"Oh, she's not asking for help," Laura said. "I just wondered if I was especially naïve. Jessie claims to know of three girls right here who've had abortions in the past year, and in two cases the parents had no knowledge of it at all, she says. It isn't until something like this happens that we learn what really goes on in Bradley's Bluff."

"In any case, not an attractive picture," said George. "What are the other possibilities?"

"She could slip off discreetly, have the baby and give it up for adoption. That alternative hasn't much appeal for her. She says if she went through the bother of carrying the baby for nine months she'd undoubtedly hate to have it just vanish out of her life."

"And I should think Ken would have something to say about that."

"In her bolder moments," Laura went on, "she's inclined to feel that the conventions are a lot of old-fashioned nonsense, and why shouldn't she brazen it out? Simply go ahead and have the baby with every intention of keeping it herself."

"In theory that ought to be admirable," said George, after a moment's thought. "I like to think that we're civilized people, even though Eleanor keeps casting doubts on the subject. If we had a daughter, and she came home from college pregnant, saying she wouldn't have the man on a silver platter but intended to have the baby, I hope I'd respect her integrity and courage. Certainly I'd stand behind her, and knock down the first person who dared to snicker. I agree that the stigma of illegitimacy is so much rubbish. But there's a hitch in the case of Ken and Jessie. I don't think Jessie has been out with another young man for a couple of years. When the baby becomes apparent there won't be any doubts about who the father is. And if they aren't married, it will be taken for granted that Ken must have reneged. This is a friendly neighborhood: she'll get all the sympathy and my son will be a pariah! Is that fair?"

"Public opinion is frequently unfair," Laura said. "Should we change our principles out of fear of that unfairness?"

"Here the public wouldn't even be given a sporting chance

to be fair," George said. "We can't go around with signs saying Ken Davenport Did His Best But Jessie Sydrock Has Principles."

"These embarrassments don't last, one scandal is soon replaced by another," Laura said callously. "I think Jessie's feeling is that once the baby is *there,* the sense of pressure will be ended. She and Ken will be able to take a fresh look at one another, with all the options open again, and decide whether they still want to get married."

"It's a preposterous arrangement!"

"From our point of view. But we may find ourselves stuck with it."

"There's a fourth alternative," George said. "Let them get married now. For a wedding present I'll put enough money into escrow to pay for all the costs of a divorce. The understanding will be that as soon as it's convenient after the baby is born, Jessie goes out to Reno. Even if they are blissfully happy they *have* to get divorced. Afterwards they can take as many fresh looks at one another as they like, and decide whether they want to get remarried."

Laura looked at him admiringly. "That's a clever idea, George, and a very generous offer."

"If you ask me, it's the most asinine proposition I've ever heard of," he replied, "but it would save a lot of awkwardness and it ought to satisfy Jessie's principles."

"It very well might, one can't ever tell," said Laura. "I'll certainly urge it as strongly as I can. The only flaw I can see is that Jessie may feel it lets her off too lightly."

"I beg your pardon?"

"Well, I do get the impression that she's punishing herself."

"She's punishing all of us!"

"That's incidental. I know she feels that she behaved very foolishly, and she seems determined to suffer for it."

"I've wondered about that," George said. "It does sound as if she deliberately let herself get pregnant and then repented of what she'd done."

"Something of the sort," Laura agreed, "which would account for the intensity of her resolve to protect Ken now. But it's the one thing she won't talk about. I gather she finds it too shaming."

"With all respect to Jessie's pride, this is something we ought to know about," George said. "Until we do, we're really just struggling in the dark."

"I'll keep trying," Laura said. "This new suggestion of yours will give me an excuse for having another go at her—though I can't say I relish the idea of scratching away at her privacy."

"They haven't shown any great consideration for *our* sensibilities," said George. "Find out whatever you can as ruthlessly as you have to. Let me know—no, there's no need for that. We'll be seeing you tomorrow, I expect."

"Tomorrow?" said Laura, momentarily at a loss. "Oh, that wretched costume ball. Yes, I suppose we'll be there, keeping up appearances to the last."

3.

A man in the midst of a personal crisis should not have to go to a costume dance, regardless of whether it was given in the name of a worthy charity. This was the argument, simple and dignified, which Ken had tried to impress upon his parents. The argument had foundered on the demands of politeness. He was reminded that by a happy chance the annual ball coincided with Marie-Odile's birthday; this made for an economy of celebration, but it meant that Ken could not pass up the dance without shunning Marie-Odile's birthday party. This he could not, in decency, do. The French girl naturally had no idea of what was going on, would hardly credit a sudden excuse of ill health, and had done nothing to deserve such a brutal snub. He would have to go, and that was final.

But he hadn't long to brood about the capriciousness of a fate that obliged a man to dress up like a fool and be gay just when his life appeared to be coming apart at the seams: he discovered that Jessie would be there too. Over the telephone she was still multiplying reasons why she didn't want him hanging around the house arguing with her, but that morning she had added "Anyway, I'll be seeing you this evening, won't I?"

"Are you going to that thing?" he had asked incredulously.

"Sure, it'll be my last appearance as Diana, the virgin huntress. Or did you think I ought to hide myself away from respectable people?"

"But you shouldn't be dancing!"

"Ken, darling, don't be a blithering idiot. I explained the other day that it's barely started: usually I'm like clockwork, and when I was a couple of weeks overdue I decided it was better to know the worst than lie awake fretting. But I feel lovely, and I'll damn well play tennis if I feel like it. Besides, a miscarriage would solve all our problems, wouldn't it?"

"No, it would not!"

"Now, look," she had said, "I'm going to that party and I intend to enjoy myself. I want you to promise you won't drag me off into a corner to nag at me. I've had quite enough lecturing from Mummy."

"I happen to love you very, very much," he had said furiously. "Is that nagging?"

"It depends on the tone of voice. You know what I wish? I wish you'd just flirt with me gently, as if it were last month, without any hints about making an honest woman of me. I'd like that. I don't want to be serious this evening. After that, we'll see."

"Okay," he had said. "Just so I can remind you of how much you mean to me without it being held against me."

So it was in an altogether different frame of mind that he went up to the attic later in the day to rummage through the trunk which held his sleeping bag, skiing sweaters, stamp albums, memorabilia from his days at Courtney, and the costume—vaguely suggesting that of a Spanish grandee of no particular century—which served him on these occasions. With the aroma of mothballs came the memory that the cloak was torn, ripped during some horseplay of the year before, and neglected in the annual conviction that by next year he would be too old for such mummery.

He went to Martha appealing for help, and met with a flat refusal: "I'm too busy this afternoon, and that's a fact. Take it to your grandmother; she hasn't anything to do, and she sews better than I do, anyway. I'll manage to press it for you afterwards, though."

Recourse to his grandmother was just what Ken had been hoping to avoid. In a moment of filial weakness or exasperation his father had unburdened himself to Mrs. Davenport, and ever since then Ken had been doing his best to keep out of reach of the old lady's tongue. But with his mother and Marie-Odile off in the city for the shopping spree that was Marie-Odile's birthday present, Ken could see no alternative to going in search of punishment.

Mrs. Davenport greeted him with ominous benevolence, sent him to fetch her sewing box, and set to work repairing the tear without any remarks about the heartless way frail old ladies were imposed upon. "I envy you going off to this frolic this evening," she said instead, unexpectedly. "It's one time when I regret my age. I would dearly like to be there, if only to look in for a few minutes. Just to get a glimpse of my first great-grandchild."

"Your first . . . ?" said Ken, and then gulped.

"You have no idea what a happy woman you have made me," his grandmother went on sweetly. "I had feared the Davenport blood might be thinning out. Your grandfather only produced a single child and your father did no better. But now it seems possible to imagine the countryside littered with our descendants—under various names, of course, depending on whom the mothers may marry."

"If I have anything to say about it," said Ken, "my children will be named Davenport."

"That would be desirable, to be sure," said his grandmother, "but you've chosen an inefficient way of going about it. The only safe way of perpetuating your name is to marry the girl in advance. George was remiss in not calling your attention to this detail."

"Yes, but then you might find yourself stuck with a girl

who wasn't fertile," Ken said, resolved to go down fighting. "I was worried about that."

"I'm glad your mind is at rest," said Mrs. Davenport. "That makes you unique in two households. The rest of us are aware that there are still a few odds and ends to be tidied up."

"Technicalities," said Ken.

"What was an experiment in fertility to you, your ladylove seems to have regarded as the simplest way to obtain the companionship of a baby while avoiding the nuisance of a husband. A very natural attitude, when you stop to think of it, for the daughter of a widow."

"I don't believe Jessie really feels like that," Ken said. "When she's thought it over she'll realize that she's honor bound to marry me."

"We can hope she'll acknowledge the obligation," said Mrs. Davenport, "though she's a mettlesome girl and likely to chafe under constraint. You may well have been wrong in trying to compel her to the altar—but perhaps you doubted your ability to acquire a wife by more conventional methods of courtship."

"It wasn't that," said Ken. "I was scared she might meet a more attractive man this winter."

"A very understandable anxiety," said his grandmother, "and one that may continue to plague you, as your father's son, even after you've been married for fifteen years."

"I'd be happy to take my chances," he replied, "if I could just be sure I was getting married at all."

"Well, you've done your crude best to achieve that end, and now you can see that that approach doesn't necessarily succeed. Life teaches us these little lessons: they may be painful for the moment, but they add up to experience and wisdom. Next time you will know better, I'm sure."

"There isn't going to be a next time, this is it!" he burst

out, and then could have kicked himself for betraying his resolve not to let himself be goaded.

"There, there," said Mrs. Davenport consolingly. "You're young. The world doesn't stop short just because one girl turns you down. When you fall in love again you won't make the same mistakes. You'll know that there are more elegant and flattering ways to propose to a girl than getting her with child."

4.

Ostensibly the costume ball was intended for the younger set. "They do so love dressing up," would say the Chairman of the House Committee, whose capacity for hypocrisy was unlimited. "It's a pleasure to see them having such a good time." Then he would issue strict orders to the little band to confine itself to foxtrots and waltzes.

In reality, most of the youngsters showed only an impressionistic obedience to the requirement of fancy dress, letting an eyepatch suggest the pirate or a bandana the cowgirl. It was their parents who spared neither expense nor effort in turning themselves out as middle-aged matadors and matronly Marie Antoinettes, and who would still be drinking and dancing long after their children had slipped off in search of less formalized entertainment.

George, who danced no more than courtesy obliged him to, sat at their reserved table, puffing at the fat cigar that was part of his costume as an Abominable Tourist, and surveying the colorful throng with unwonted cynicism: wondering how many of the other people there were also keeping up a show of carefree gaiety while domestic calamity awaited them at home. A few he knew of by report. The Ferrises, dancing together although rumor insisted their marriage was in even worse straits than Alan's and Cathy's; Bob Applegate, who was clinging to office space while he looked around for another outfit that needed an incompetent executive in his early fifties. Was it snobbery, he wondered, or some more fundamental instinct that demanded the maintaining of appearances till the last possible moment? But then a glimpse of Ted Orchard across the room, a death's head in a monk's cowl, restored George to some sense of perspective. Ted was due to go into the hospital within a week or two, with very little chance of coming out again; in contrast to what *he* must be feeling, their anxieties were trivial, not anxieties at all, really, but cause for celebration. It was preposterous that a new life should be a source of embarrassment even for a moment—and he should have been delighted to see that the procreators of that new life showed not a trace of such embarrassment. Ken and Jessie were now dancing happily nearby, she leaning back in his embrace, chattering and laughing up at her lover, seemingly without a care in the world.

Marie-Odile, between partners, came and settled beside him: fetching in a Columbine costume rented in the city the day before. "They are such an adorable couple," she said, gesturing at Ken and Jessie. "And so much in love that it makes one envious, regarding them. It seems a great pity that they cannot get married right away."

"Funny you should say that," George said. "I was just thinking the same thing."

"But Ken's university is only for men, is it not?" said Marie-Odile, "and Jessie's only for women? That seems an unnatural arrangement, and unhappy for both of them."

"Perhaps we shouldn't let it be such a stumbling block," George said, as if puzzling the matter out loud. "After all, there *are* some married students at Ken's college, living off-campus, of course. Why not one more? It's just for a year."

"But what would Jessie do?"

"Do? What she'll do whenever they get married, I suppose: look after Ken."

"No, no," said Marie-Odile. "I mean her studies. She cannot finish them at Ken's university. And she has not yet her diploma, that I know."

"True," George conceded judiciously. "But from another point of view she already has as much of a diploma as she'll ever need."

"You are joking with me," said Marie-Odile. "Jessie could not leave without taking her diploma. Not just to get married, that would not be serious. They have to wait. Or is it that you do not believe that Jessie is very serious?"

"That depends," said George. "I don't think she'd be heart-broken if she wasn't graduated. However, she's a girl of very serious principles in other respects, although I hadn't realized that until recently."

Marie-Odile sighed. "There are still so many things about this country that I do not understand," she said.

"Sometimes I find it confusing, myself," George told her.

For a while he had assumed that Laura Sydrock would come to join him at the table. But when he finally caught her eye and beckoned, while she was dancing, she gave a slight shake of her head and looked away; presumably she felt it would be unwise for them to go into conference, as it were, where they could be seen by Ken and Jessie. So George waited till he was sure Laura had quitted the dance floor and then went in search of her: Petrarch's Laura in embroidered damask and black among the crowd of Cossacks and fairy godmothers, harlequins and hula-hula girls. He found her in the bar, part of an animated group, and gestured with his head towards the terrace; a moment later she joined him there. They drifted past the little tables to the far parapet, overlooking the swimming pool; a limpid green oblong of underwater lighting. From behind them, through windows on the far side of the Club, came the bare rhythmic thumping of the music, all melodic line lost along the way.

"How do we stand today?" George asked.

"I don't know," said Laura. "Jessie's been in an awkward mood."

"You're too indulgent with her moods," he said. "I won't say Jessie's a spoiled child, I've never seen much sign of that till now, but there's a streak of wilfulness that might have been curbed."

"She's suffered from the lack of a father, especially the past five or six years," Laura replied. "A mother's authority, by itself, invites rebellion from a girl; I've had to be sympathetic, often, when I would have preferred to be impatient."

"At times a little impatience is in order," said George. "This is one of them. Procrastination isn't going to help at all."

"Well, what would you have done? Yesterday she was grumbling about this dance, but this morning she woke up looking forward to it—she couldn't think of anything else. Several times I tried to talk to her, but she really wasn't paying attention. Finally she said: 'Let me alone today, Mummy, I'm going to have fun this evening, I'm going to dance and flirt and get tight; it's the last lap of my girlhood and tomorrow I promise I'll be a full-time woman.' What answer would *you* have made to that?"

George reached for a fresh cigar. "Then we're no further along than we were."

"Perhaps we are, I'm not sure," Laura said. "I did pick up one detail in passing. I chanced to speak of Eleanor—I know: I was wondering what costume she would wear after all these years—and Jessie blurted out something to the effect that none of this would have happened if Eleanor had stayed in France. It was almost a slip of the tongue. Jessie has been very careful about blaming nobody but herself, and she changed the subject when I asked what she'd meant. But there had been real bitterness in her voice, I'm sure of that. So I wondered whether Eleanor had been showing some opposition to their engagement, although Ken hasn't hinted at anything of the sort."

"Hmm," said George, groping for a reply that had some affinity to the truth, but not too much.

"Did she, George?"

"I know she felt they were both dangerously young to be thinking of marriage," he offered. "It doesn't seem like Eleanor to make an issue of an argument like that, but of course I'm off at the office all day. I wouldn't know about the conversations she might have had with Ken."

Laura looked dissatisfied with this offering, as well she might. "I really don't think Jessie would be embittered by anybody raising such a stale argument, do you?"

"Just at the moment I don't want to hazard any guesses about how Jessie's mind is working," he said unfairly. "I don't pretend to understand what's going on."

"But wouldn't it be worthwhile to raise the question with Eleanor?"

"Oh, I fully intend to do that," said George, whose intentions went further than Laura could imagine. In fact, a little later when he got back to their table at the edge of the dance floor, he was ready with some unusually cutting observations to make to Eleanor about the trouble she had caused. But for the moment she wasn't in sight. Ken was alone at the table, thirstily disposing of the birthday champagne.

For the time being George was vaguely ill at ease with his son, aware that he had been unjust to the boy. George did not feel entirely blameworthy: the teachings of a lifetime had tricked him into assuming that the man was responsible for "getting a girl into trouble." That a girl would accept the onus of her pregnancy singlehanded, so to speak, was a novelty for which he had been ill-prepared. He had blustered, and now the memory embarrassed him, yet he could not think how to frame an apology which would not seem to connive at a situation which he deplored. Any apology would feed Ken's manifest feeling of self-righteousness, and this seemed all wrong, even immoral. So George swallowed his guilt, endured his unease, and tried to act as though nothing had happened.

"Jessie seems wonderfully lighthearted this evening," he remarked.

"I don't know where she gets the nerve to call *me* insensitive," Ken said. "You'd think this bloody dance was being given in her honor."

"It's a shame the rest of us aren't permitted to celebrate with her," said George.

"She's too stubborn to be believed," said Ken. "I haven't seen her for two days, and all she'll talk about is the music and the costumes and do I like the way she's done her hair? That's no way to treat the father of her unborn child."

"Perhaps she's still annoyed at you," George began, but this promising moment of rapport was interrupted by the arrival of Cathy Briggs, leaning over their table, sparkling with some suppressed emotion.

"You're taking French, aren't you?" she asked Ken.

"Sure, but you'd do better going to Mother or Marie-Odile."

"You'll have to do," said Cathy. "What does *célibataire* mean? I could figure out *très riche et très charmant,* but what the hell is *célibataire?"*

"A bachelor," said Ken.

"That's what I thought, the bitch," Cathy said, turning to George. "Do you know what your wife did? A while ago I was standing chatting with Marie-Odile and Eleanor came sauntering over, told her there was someone she ought to meet, and then switched into French: a very rich and charming bachelor. And then took her over and introduced her to

Fred Palmer. And the two of them have been dancing together ever since!"

"It's the child's birthday," George said soothingly. "I expect Marie-Odile had run out of dancing partners."

"It's possible to dance with a man without knowing his financial and marital status," Cathy retorted. "I think I'll borrow Tom Updyke's battleaxe and decapitate me a sister."

She vanished back into the throng. George saw that his son was looking at him with quizzical amusement, waiting for him to make some comment. "Life doesn't necessarily get less complicated as one grows older," he said.

"That could be our family motto," said Ken. "I like to remember the time the local rag described us as pillars of the community." He, in turn, jumped up and went off, answering some unseen summons.

George caught the eye of a passing waitress and ordered a double whisky, feeling in the need of something more fortifying than champagne. The speed and ruthlessness with which Marie-Odile had been transferred to a new assignment took his breath away. Although he approved of the move, it added one more item to the account he had to settle with Eleanor.

He had ample time to organize his thoughts before he saw her approaching through the costumed crowd, looking utterly lovely, utterly innocent. Her hair was caught back in a filet, she wore a flowing robe of pale gold, cut to leave one shoulder bare. The effect was Grecian. Ken had whooped at the first sight of her, but forborne asking whom she might be impersonating.

"Well, I hear you've been meddling again, my dear," he greeted her, refilling her glass.

"I never meddle," she said serenely, sitting down. "Who has been telling fibs about me?"

"It's a bad habit you've brought back from France," George

said. "I don't remember your carrying on in this fashion in the old days."

"Has Cathy been complaining because I've extended Fred Palmer's horizons?" Eleanor asked. "As much as anything, that was done for your sake."

"Naturally," said George.

"You seem to have grown fond of having Marie-Odile around the house," explained Eleanor, "and I felt there should be an added inducement to bring her back next summer. I do hope she comes. Otherwise we may be a bit lonely rattling around in our place."

"Apparently the future has no uncertainties for you," said George. "Ken and Jessie will be happily married and off on their own someplace?"

"That's as it should be, don't you agree?" said Eleanor. "Parents and parents-in-law shouldn't be too much in evidence the first few years. And, in any case, there won't be time for a proper honeymoon this year."

"I refuse to worry about the honeymoon till I'm a little more certain of the wedding."

"Oh, that will straighten itself out," said Eleanor. "As a matter of fact, I was thinking that I ought to stop around and see Jessie tomorrow."

"Would it surprise you to discover that you weren't welcome?"

"Indeed it would."

"Then you may be in for a shock," George told her. "I'm afraid Jessie is on record as feeling that none of this would have happened if you hadn't returned home."

"I've accepted responsibility for a great many things," said Eleanor, "but I don't see how Jessie's pregnancy can be numbered among them."

"For a self-styled realist you have one remarkable delusion," said George, trying to give an affectionate tone to his indignation. He didn't want to sound harsh, but he felt Eleanor should appreciate the folly of what she had done. "You think you can meddle with other people's lives and the other people won't notice what you're doing. Which simply isn't so. If I was able to recognize your true reason for inviting Marie-Odile for a visit, then so was Jessie—she's not a stupid girl. But that possibility doesn't seem to have entered your head."

"No, it didn't," Eleanor admitted. "I never would have thought she was as insecure as that."

"It's not necessarily a sign of insecurity to be a bit terrified of you, my love. Occasionally I am myself. Jessie is quite sensitive enough to have noticed your lack of enthusiasm for her, and when you blandly planned to bring a rival into the house I can't entirely blame Jessie for panicking, trying to ensure her hold on Ken in any way she could. That she regrets it bitterly now, sees what she did as dishonorable, is exactly what I'd expect of Jessie: she's willful, but thoroughly decent at heart. But I think you ought to face up to what your meddling has brought about."

"Clearly I have to face up to a new picture of what's been going on," said Eleanor thoughtfully. "Now there can't be any question about my having to see Jessie tomorrow. Perhaps I ought to warn Laura that I'll be coming around."

"And perhaps you should let the rest of us see what we can accomplish," said George. "You might just make matters worse."

"That's always a risk. But I have to try to undo whatever damage I may have done. I can't sit idly by when other people are being punished for my sin."

"I admire your restraint in allotting yourself only a single sin," said George. "Which one did you have in mind?"

"I've always contended that for an honest person there *was* only one sin," replied Eleanor. "Good intentions."

George made no effort to pursue the relevance, if any, of

this ambiguous remark, being secretly relieved at Eleanor's decision to take a hand in untangling this muddle. Laura seemed reluctant to exert her authority and he doubted his own ability to deal with a young girl in an emotional state; but he had a boundless faith in Eleanor's talent for rearranging her world to suit herself. As long as she had opposed the marriage he had despaired of it, but now that circumstances had forced her to change her mind, and she was determined to act, he was disposed to see Ken and Jessie as already halfway to the altar.

5.

The front door opened even before Eleanor could touch the bell, making it evident that Laura had been watching for her from a window. "I was just going out," Laura said brusquely, and then canceled out any suggestion of coincidence by adding, "That seems smartest, don't you think?"

"Yes, probably," said Eleanor. "Did you tell Jessie I was coming?"

"I debated that with myself all morning," said Laura, "especially since the poor child seemed to be suffering from something remarkably like a hangover. And finally decided it was the only fair thing to do."

"How did she react?"

"She said we could take turns badgering her if we liked, but it wasn't going to make the slightest difference in the end."

"Quite proper," said Eleanor. "I find that Jessie improves on acquaintance—or is it just that impending motherhood brings out the best in her?"

For an instant Laura paused, clearly uncertain whether to construe this remark as a compliment to her daughter or a joke in poor taste. Then she said quietly, "Of course, I have no idea what Jessie did to earn your disapproval in the first place," and went on across the lawn to her car.

Eleanor entered the house, hesitated in the doorway to the living room. Jessie was curled on the sofa, smoking a cigarette, flipping through the pages of a magazine; she glanced up finally, but made no effort to rise.

"Hi," she said. "I gather Mummy's gone off, leaving you in possession of the lecture hall."

"I haven't come to lecture," said Eleanor. "It's the last thing I had in mind. But there does seem to be an area of misunderstanding between us, and I hope to clear that up."

"I don't know of any misunderstanding," Jessie said. Her attitude suggested that only politeness was preventing her from going back to her magazine.

"Then my first task will be to call it to your attention," said Eleanor, crossing to sit down in one of the armchairs. "You see, I've heard of your remark to the effect that none of this would have happened if I hadn't returned."

"I didn't mean to say that."

"But you meant it?"

"Sure I meant it!" said Jessie. "It's true."

"Then there can't be any doubt about the misunderstanding," said Eleanor, "and it's up to us to get it straightened out as quickly as possible. No doubt the fault is largely mine. But I have spent the greater part of my adult life suffering from an antagonistic mother-in-law, and I've always been determined to be on the best of terms with my own daughter-in-law when that time came. And so I shall, but it's important that we don't start out with any false ideas about one another, won't you agree?"

"I'm not your daughter-in-law," said Jessie.

"I have every hope that you're going to be."

"Do you?" Jessie asked ironically. "You didn't feel that way last week."

"To an extent that's perfectly true," admitted Eleanor.

"At least you're honest."

"Except when I think I have good reason not to be," said Eleanor, "and even then I'm frequently wrong. But I came resolved to be tiresomely honest with you this afternoon, as the only way to clear the air. Certainly I had reservations about you. Is that surprising, under the circumstances? I had been away for years—my own doing—and returned to find my son grown into a young man. Just when I should have been prepared to relinquish him gracefully, my instinct was to want to hold onto him just a little longer before he left. Wrong of me, but natural. I wanted to know him again, I wanted him to know me and hoped he would like me."

"You needn't have had any fears on the last score," Jessie said. "I've spent the whole summer hearing about what a remarkable woman you are."

"How very exasperating for you!" said Eleanor. "But you would know that my novelty would wear off in time. And you can see that I would have been bound to resent any girl who was threatening to whip Ken away before I'd had him to myself for a while. Yes, I found reasons for disapproving of you. But there's nothing remarkable in that. Lots of mothers find it impossible to believe that any girl is good enough for their sons. Mrs. Davenport was one. That's something no girl pays any attention to, once her mind is made up. I cannot believe that you were so shaken by my disapproval."

"It wasn't only the disapproval," said Jessie. "It was the fact that you could obviously wrap Ken around your little finger."

"I very much doubt that I could. In any case, why would I do anything so destructive to a young man's dignity?"

"What about his beard?" Jessie demanded hotly.

"Ken's beard?" said Eleanor in surprise. "My dear child, was I completely mistaken? Did you actually *like* that beard?"

"I hated it!" cried Jessie, sitting up and crushing out her cigarette with some violence. "So what? He had a right to a beard if he wanted one. And he was so proud of his defiance."

"All the same, it was a tawdry defiance and a shabby beard. You couldn't say anything, of course: your part is to defend his opinion of himself, not tear it down. But I wasn't bound by the same limitations; I could have a try at getting rid of the horrid thing, and whether I failed or succeeded you couldn't be critized. Frankly, I thought you'd be grateful to me for succeeding."

"It was the *way* you did it," said Jessie. "Persuading him that it took more courage to shave off a beard than to grow one! If you could do that you could persuade him of anything. And Ken's worshiping the ground you walk on, and your disapproval of me, if only because I wasn't French. And then your importing Marie-Odile the moment you heard we were thinking of getting engaged. . . ."

"So George was right," said Eleanor. "That was what made you panic. No wonder he's indignant with me. But what did you expect to accomplish by what you did?"

"I don't know!" Jessie stormed. "You don't expect anything when you panic. I stopped giving a damn about anything except holding on to Ken. Maybe I had some unconscious idea of trying to force the marriage through, though I must have known I couldn't go through with that. Maybe I felt that if I was going to lose Ken I still wanted a part of him. I don't know. There was a stretch there where I wasn't thinking, I was just reacting to a threat."

"I am very much to blame," said Eleanor, "but not for what you suspected. There was no threat."

"I thought we were going to be so honest—"

"Just a moment," Eleanor interrupted firmly. "You can think what you like about my character, but you're going to have to learn to have some respect for my intelligence, Jessie. I'm a realist. I came back to find my son in the middle of his first wholehearted love affair. He wasn't just sleeping with you, he was obviously madly in love with you. And anyone with a spark of realism knows that's the one time a young man cannot see any other girl on earth. I knew that. George's mother knew it when she said I could pack the Folies Bergère into the guest room and Ken wouldn't notice. And you would have known it, too, if your wits hadn't been addled by hearing so much about what a remarkable woman I am from a somewhat tactless lover."

Jessie muttered something under her breath and reached for another cigarette.

"That's one point, and there's another," Eleanor went on. "Even if I'd been innocent enough to think Ken could be distracted by another girl, would I have chosen such a girl as Marie-Odile? You've come to know her. She's an adorable child, or at least I think so, but above all she's *serious,* and especially about affairs of the heart. She could no more try to lure away another girl's man than she could fly. It's not in her nature. Isn't that evident?"

"It is now," Jessie said dully. "I guess I'd realized she wasn't much competition, but by then the damage had already been done. It was the *idea* of her coming that got stuck in my head, well before she got here. Oh, damn, damn, *damn!*" Jessie buried her face in her hands for a moment, then shook her head and looked up, forcing a small, rueful smile. "Have I really been such a complete idiot, Eleanor? All by myself?"

"Not necessarily," said Eleanor, "and that's why you're entitled to the rest of the story and the reasons why I blame myself. But this has to be between ourselves. I'd rather that even Ken doesn't hear of it."

"All right," Jessie said in an apologetic voice. "Can I get you a drink?"

"Not just yet, though I may be thirsty in a little while," Eleanor said. "I want to talk about me for a moment, I want you to try to imagine the awkwardness in the homecoming of a runaway wife. Nobody else has given a thought to that, certainly not George. He's a darling person, but he's not subtle. He walked into my living room in Cagnes-sur-Mer a few weeks after Pierre was killed, and said 'Don't you think it's time to come home, Eleanor?' and thought he'd handled the situation quite neatly. I could foresee more of the complications. But I quickly found that I was still extremely fond of George, and of course I was dying to see Ken, so I decided to give it a try. And I'm very glad that I did, even though you'd have preferred it if I'd remained in France."

"You're perfectly right to rub that in," said Jessie. "I deserve it."

"The awkwardnesses appeared exactly as I expected they would," Eleanor said. "As soon as I got home my position became ambiguous: was I a properly chastened wife or an impenitent hussy? George's intentions were of the best, he wanted to blot out the past, but the six years of my absence were bound to stick in his craw because he couldn't tell how I felt about them. Did I repent my adventure or regret that it had ended? Was I still secretly in mourning for Pierre, had I loved Pierre more than I could love him? Had I been happy there—and, if not, then why had I stayed so long? And George's nagging curiosity kept alive the injustice of my going unpunished for his sufferings. George is far too decent to *think* in terms of punishing me—he would deny the charge indignantly—yet he kept punishing me despite himself, with little barbed reminders of the past. He couldn't leave it alone."

"I don't understand," said Jessie. "George is crazy about you, even I can see that much. If he was all that curious, why didn't you just sit down and talk it all out with him?"

"Because that's the one thing you must never do with an infidelity until it's very ancient history."

"You're both thoroughly reasonable people," Jessie objected.

"Nobody is thoroughly reasonable," said Eleanor. "This won't mean much to you now, while you're looking forward to a one-love lifetime, but you can file the advice away for the day it's needed. An infidelity you never know about doesn't exist. An infidelity you know about in the abstract will be galling, if you care, but can be suffered. The unforgivable error is to fill in the details which the other person's imagination can feed upon—and there's never any telling which these details may be. A raw sexual fact may be passed over, while the knowledge that you and your lover read the Sunday papers in bed together will be the thing that festers. Since you don't know, you keep quiet. If I'd tried to talk it out with George, he'd have asked questions—and any given answer, coming from me, could easily have made things much worse. Yet they weren't improving as I'd hoped they would. I was really at a loss, till I thought of sending for Marie-Odile."

"Then Ken's talking to you about our engagement was just a coincidence?" Jessie asked skeptically.

"My dear child, you and Ken are very properly absorbed with one another, but there are other things going on in the world," Eleanor said gently. "My own life is more important to me even than Ken's marital plans. Something I said to him that day put me in mind of Marie-Odile—nothing whatever to do with you; it was about flower-arranging, I believe—but once I'd thought of her, that was the obvious solution. She's devoted to me, she'd never thought highly of her cousin, she'd spent last summer with us in Cagnes and knew that I wasn't entirely happy. And she's a clever girl; I knew she wouldn't need more than a hint to make her understand I was counting on her to exorcize George's curiosity."

"And that's truly the only reason you invited Marie-Odile?" Jessie asked.

"Apart from being very fond of her company, yes," said Eleanor. "But of course I didn't want George to know what I had in mind, or he would have distrusted anything Marie-Odile had to say. I had no idea how to account for the suddenness of my invitation, and then George himself provided an explanation. He's irritated by my Francophilia, and he suspects me of being much more devious than I am. He leapt to the idea I was bringing in Marie-Odile as your rival; he's absurdly romantic, and quite capable of believing that such a scheme would make sense. And I'm ashamed to say that I welcomed his inspiration and played right along with it, as the easy way to keep him diverted from the truth. Later I used a version of the same story to pry Mrs. Davenport out of her bedroom. All along, my intentions were good. I couldn't see any harm in what I was doing, never dreaming that you would arrive at the same conclusion. But now I have to face the possibility that some gesture or expression of George's, or some remark of his mother's, reinforced your notion that Marie-Odile was my private candidate to be Ken's wife."

"I honestly don't remember now," said Jessie. "I'd like to think so, but probably not; probably it was all my own paranoid little idea."

"Don't be so greedy with the guilt," said Eleanor. "I'd like my share of it."

"What difference does it make?" Jessie asked. "I don't see that this changes a damn thing—except to prove that I was even more of a fool than I'd realized."

"There is one slight change," said Eleanor. "I don't expect it will seem as of much consequence, but you've managed to eliminate the main reservations I had about the marriage."

"Good grief," said Jessie. "You mean I've stumbled on a new method for bringing a man's mother into line?"

"Perhaps," said Eleanor. "I don't know that it would always work. Getting yourself pregnant to catch a man is as old as the hills. But getting yourself pregnant and then refusing to marry the man, out of principle for his sake, is an effective way of disposing of any doubts about whether a man is loved as strongly as his mother wants to see him loved."

"Clever me," Jessie said bitterly. "I wish I could say I'd worked that one out."

"The other drawback that I saw," said Eleanor, "was that you'd both have been learning about marriage at the same time that Ken was learning his job. But if you get married now, the marriage will be well established by the time Ken takes up his post at Courtney, and the baby's demands on your attention will offset your demands on Ken's."

"You've worked it out very tidily—except for a couple of details," said Jessie. "I don't want to get married just because I *have* to get married. And Ken shouldn't have to get married just because I made a damn fool of myself."

"Let's take your point of view first," said Eleanor. "It strikes me as somewhat inconsistent. A few weeks ago you were looking forward to marriage although you and Ken were already better situated than most married couples are. You were seeing one another as much as you liked, more than I normally see George, for example. You were sleeping together whenever you wished—"

"That's an exaggeration."

"I'm sure there was no more inconvenience than acted as an aphrodisiac. Your romance was never interrupted by petty domestic considerations: Laura and I were attending to those. In practice, you would have found marriage a distinct step backwards, consisting of a great many distractions and disadvantages in exchange for the doubtful privilege of sharing the same bed all night. And that would have held true until the time came to make a home for a baby, which is the only real reason for marriage anyway. Yet now that you have the real reason, you've turned against the idea."

"Well, I don't suppose I have, actually," said Jessie. "Leave my feelings out of it. It's Ken who would be trapped by my stupidity, if I allowed him to be."

"More good intentions!" said Eleanor. "Haven't I just given you a vivid illustration of how much harm good intentions can do?"

"That was different," Jessie said.

"No, it's always the same, when you start thinking you

know what's best for another person," Eleanor insisted. "You can never be sure what damage you may be doing. How can you decide what's best for Ken? So far you haven't even let him come around to express his own opinions on the subject."

"Because I know precisely what he'd say!"

"And you've discounted his sincerity in advance?"

"What *can* he say?" Jessie demanded. "He knows what's expected of him. He's in a box with only one way out."

"Then you must think he's a weakling, more frightened of the conventions than you are," said Eleanor. "You don't think he has the courage to fly in the face of what's expected of him —he'd mess up his life instead. If you've lost all respect for him, then you're out of love with him and there's nothing more to be said."

"I begin to see what Ken means by your ability to turn things topsy-turvy."

"Why do you say that?" asked Eleanor. "If you know other girls who've had abortions then you know that other young men have found ways of backing out of these situations."

"But Ken wouldn't even try."

"Because he lacks the resolution or because he doesn't have the slightest wish to?"

"Because it's against his principles," Jessie said.

"You may be right, there," said Eleanor, "but men keep a wide range of principles on hand, and generally act on the ones they find expedient. It's an unimaginative man who can't find a set of principles to prevent him from doing whatever he doesn't want to do. No, you have to let people shoulder the responsibility for their own behavior. You've done your part by being perfectly honest and scrupulous. You've given Ken every opportunity to cut and run. If he chooses to stay, I think you should do him the credit of assuming he made that choice deliberately, for reasons that seemed good to him."

"And marry him?" Jessie wailed. "But I *can't*. Don't you see how humiliating it would be?"

"Have we arrived at the real stumbling block, then?" Eleanor asked. "Not a lot of ethical abstractions. Not simply concern for Ken's position. Your own pride."

"Perhaps it is. And you can't understand that?"

"Oh, all too well," said Eleanor. "Pride and I are old companions. It's one of the things that make it difficult for a runaway wife to come creeping home when she finds she's made a mistake. You and I have more in common than I'd realized, Jessie, and now I *know* we're going to be good friends. There's nothing like a shared vice for bringing people together."

6.

Occasionally George felt that Marie-Odile's tactfulness was more than human. She had sensed that his mother's jibes were becoming unendurable this particular afternoon, and had lured Mrs. Davenport away with an offer to teach her French varieties of solitaire. George and Ken were left alone, if not at peace. Ken, especially, was in a state of nerves, prowling the room in a manner suggestive of his Aunt Cathy, shifting stacks of magazines about for no reason at all, lighting cigarettes and putting them out, and glaring out the window as though impatience would bring his mother into sight.

"I can't imagine what's taking her so long," he remarked, not for the first time.

"Better a few extra well-spent minutes now than nine months of increasing embarrassment," George said.

"And I don't see why you're so confident she'll accomplish anything," Ken said fretfully. "Jessie doesn't trust her worth a damn."

"Then Eleanor will need some extra time."

"More than a single afternoon," said Ken. "Jessie's a stubborn little witch, and she's got it fixed in her head that Mother doesn't like her. *I* couldn't budge her."

"You will forgive me for pointing out that doesn't mean she can't be budged," said George, abandoning any pretence of looking through the *New Yorker*. "The next time you see Jessie, don't be surprised to learn that Eleanor is one of the few people on earth who really understand her. I've seen it happen too often. With men it can be almost instantaneous, but women succumb too, after a while."

"Anyway, it seems all wrong," said Ken. "As if I were clinging to her apron strings. I'm the one who ought to be over there, doing my own arguing."

"The situation has grown complex," said George, "and I don't see how you argue a girl into marrying you if she's disinclined. What arguments would you use? We can take it for granted that the appeals to reason have been exhausted by Laura. The emotional appeals don't work as effectively as they used to. 'I love you' is answered by 'I love you, too.' 'I want you' is answered by 'You've had me.' And 'Let's get married' is answered by 'Why bother?' That's the new way of doing things, evidently, and the thought of it makes me feel old."

"But if Mother isn't appealing to Jessie's reason," said Ken, "and she isn't appealing to Jessie's emotions, then just what the hell *is* she appealing to?"

"That's a good question," said George, "and the only truthful answer is that I don't really know. There's no point in pretending that your mother is a remarkable logician—she isn't. She calls herself a realist, but she's usually at right angles to any reality I'm familiar with. Yet I know for a fact that a lot of sensible people think she's cleverer than I am, and when it comes to dealing with people—getting them to do what she wants—she undoubtedly is. Don't ask me why or how."

"I think it's because nothing surprises her and nothing upsets her," said Ken. "That makes you feel she's really listening, and that she's on your side."

"If she's been converted to Jessie's side, we're done for," George said. "However, we shan't be in suspense much longer. She's just pulled up."

Ken spun around to see the car out front, and instantly his nervousness seemed to vanish. Instead of rushing to the door he collapsed bonelessly into an armchair and lit a new cigarette with a creditable appearance of indifference. Eleanor entered to find her men in a state of placid silence, as if they had run out of conversation in her absence.

"Hello there," said George, studying her for some clue to her success or failure and finding only a faint trace of weariness. "How did it go?"

"The car is all yours, Ken," Eleanor said, tossing him the keys. "The field is clear. Laura shouldn't be back for another hour or so."

"Is Jessie expecting me?" Ken asked languidly.

"I didn't threaten her with your arrival," said Eleanor, "but I don't think she'll be surprised when you turn up."

"Okay," said Ken, but his nonchalance didn't carry him as far as the doorway. He hesitated, then asked: "What sort of state of mind is she in, Mother?"

"She's wondering the same thing about you," said Eleanor. "If you want that girl, you'll have to convince her that you're a lot more eager to get married than she is. Are you?"

"It looks that way."

"Then don't be too proud to say so," Eleanor said. "You can't take too much reassurance to a woman who knows she's made an idiot of herself. It's wildly out of date to drop to one knee before proposing, but this is one case where the symbolism makes a certain amount of sense."

"I'm reading you," said Ken, and added, "Wish me luck!" just as he vanished out the door with a resolute stride.

George waited till the boy was out of earshot before asking "Is it going to be all right?"

"Possibly, probably. That will depend on how much eloquence Ken can muster." Eleanor slipped off her shoes and put her feet up on the sofa, leaning back against the cushions. "I'm worn out. Most of the morning trying to make Cathy see reason, and most of the afternoon with that stiff-necked child—

though I must admit I do like Jessie more all the time. Would you fix me a drink, George? A good strong martini."

"I made sure Martha left us a bucket of ice," George said, getting up. "Eloquence is all very well, but it only convinces someone who already wants to be convinced. I was counting on you to make her more susceptible to persuasion."

"Of course I did what I could," said Eleanor. "Jessie and I are the best of friends now."

"Naturally," said George.

"We disposed of several of her more trivial objections to getting married, and spent most of the time on the problem of her self-respect."

"If her version of self-respect catches on," said George, "damn few children are going to be born in wedlock."

"You never do anything foolish, George, so you haven't much sympathy for the difficulties of swallowing your pride. It has a horrid flavor, especially when one is young."

"On the contrary, I'm positively oozing with sympathy," declared George, "though it isn't for Jessie alone. I'll welcome her as a daughter-in-law with unqualified enthusiasm and a tactful regard for her self-respect. But I also have sympathy ready for the rest of us if she goes ahead with any of her other schemes: we'd *all* have some unpalatable medicine to swallow! Doesn't she think of that?"

"Of course not," said Eleanor, "and if that's the sort of argument you had in mind, it's just as well you weren't the one to see her. She couldn't care less about anybody's feelings but hers and Ken's, quite properly. If she can get out of this false position gracefully, she'll do it; otherwise she'll settle for a solution that satisfies her pride, and to the devil with the rest of us. That was what was wrong with your notion of offering them a divorce as a wedding present. Jessie would rather be the courageous heroine of her own drama than be bribed into submitting to our conventions. And I was inclined to sympathize."

"I hope to God you had something more constructive to offer than sympathy," said George.

"Not by pressing my own wishes," said Eleanor. "I did point out that she could feed her own pride only at the expense of Ken's, and this was selfish—that pride, like everything else between people in love, ought to be shared. To build a really fine marriage on such a shaky foundation would be the highest test of their maturity, something they could both be proud of, although the most delicate task would be hers. The argument was straightforward enough; the difficulty was in putting it so Jessie wouldn't notice it was much the same approach I'd used to Ken's beard."

"To *what?*" asked George, so startled that he overdid the vermouth and had to begin again.

"Never mind. In effect, I was challenging Jessie to rise to an occasion, and she's young enough to be intrigued by a dare. The rest has to be up to Ken."

"Life must have been a great deal simpler back in the days when parents arranged these matters among themselves," George said. "My courage fails at the thought of Ken as a diplomat. Suppose he muffs it?"

"I don't expect that he will, but that's why I spent the morning with Cathy trying to convince her of the advantages of adopting a baby," said Eleanor. "I don't know that I entirely succeeded, but I got far enough to offer Jessie an alternative that leaves the future wide open, with a minimum of embarrassment for anybody. If Jessie turns Ken down now, she and Cathy can spend the winter in my place in Cagnes, and the baby will be born there. Next summer Ken can go over; unless he muffs that opportunity too, he and Jessie can spend a few months honeymooning in Europe and then go straight to Courtney. If that doesn't work out, Cathy could reappear with a baby she'd adopted abroad, and Jessie could drift home later by way of Japan, having been on a trip around the world. Everything would stay fluid till the last moment. I was so eloquent about the delights of the Côte d'Azur that Jessie may feel it's an act of noble self-sacrifice to renounce all that by marrying Ken now and shivering all winter."

But George had momentarily lost interest in his son's marital prospects. His methodical stirring of the martinis slowed and stopped as he considered the more important implications of what Eleanor had just said. "You know," he observed cautiously, "that makes it sound as if you've finally given up any idea of using the house in Cagnes yourself."

"It does, doesn't it?" said Eleanor.

"Is that what you intended to say? I mean, was it something I was supposed to notice?"

"I don't throw out remarks like baited hooks," said Eleanor. "Generally I say whatever is going through my mind. But I'm flattered that you pay such sharp attention to my chattering; that's a rare virtue in husbands."

"I can't promise always to be so attentive," he said, "but this is something I've been listening for for a long time." He felt like bellowing in joy and triumph, but at the same time he felt that what he had been given was as delicate as it was precious: any violent outburst on his part might frighten it out of existence. But he pushed aside the light highball he had already made for himself, and added gin liberally to the pitcher of martinis. "I expect there must be a reason," he said. "Not that I care. Happiness shouldn't pause to ask for reasons. But I'm curious, I'll confess. From the way you mutter at the breakfast table about our foreign policy I can't believe you've formed any new admiration for your native land. And I haven't acted well enough over this mess of Ken's to hope that you've discovered a streak of nobility in me you'd never noticed before."

"Well, no," said Eleanor, smiling.

"Yet suddenly you're here to stay. . . ."

"It doesn't seem at all sudden to me," said Eleanor, "but I'm thinking of the long voyage and you're thinking of the moment of arrival."

"Just chance that it was this week rather than last?"

"Oh, I can find you a reason, if you really want one. I've always told you my only talent was for adaptability, but to exercise that talent you need something a little novel to adapt to. And now I have it. I'm going to be a grandmother, or at least I think I am. I've been working very hard to that end today, anyway."

"It's a prospect that not all beautiful women would find so appealing," said George.

"Has my beauty done anyone much good?" Eleanor asked. "I rather look forward to at least one creature on this earth who will be bored at hearing what a beauty I used to be, who will see me simply as an eccentric old lady with an interestingly wicked past and a lot of strange ideas. And I have hopes of a more successful career as grandmother than I've had as either wife or mother."

"Then may God protect your grandchildren," George said piously as he filled the two glasses. "I can feel deeply for them even in the moment of my happiness."

"But do I really make you so happy, George?" asked Eleanor curiously. "That is something I've never entirely understood. I don't see that I make you a comfortable wife even now."

"Happiness shouldn't pause to give out explanations, either," said George, taking one of the glasses to Eleanor. "My happiness is my own secret, and I'm going to keep it that way. As long as you don't understand it, you'll never be tempted to meddle with it. Happy days, my love."